AARON

INHERITED EXTINCTION
BOOK TWO

C M STOLWORTHY

Aaron

CHAPTER 1

$\mathcal{W}$alking across the grass, I shove my hands in my pockets. Should have put my coat on my main thought. Yeah, but then Mother would know he was missing my inner voice mocks. The full moon illuminates my path with its silvery light as my feet crunch the frost laden grass. The cold penetrating my house coat, not having time to dress properly as this disaster unfolded.

My brother is kneeling by the pond. I can see by the shake of his shoulders he is crying. What could be wrong that he was out here crying? In the middle of the night in near-freezing temperatures. I had long ago given up on the workings of my brother's mind.

Running forward, I sink to my knees and put my arm around his shoulders. Pulling him to me, his skin feels cold, and I wonder how long he has been out here.

'Adam, what are you doing?'

'It was cold and the pond it has frozen with the frog spawn in.' Adam turns his large blue eyes to me. His tear streaked; Snot covered face a picture of devastation.

'Adam, it will be fine. This is nature. Now come in before

Mother notices we are missing,' pulling Adam to his feet leading him back into the house. We are too late.

Mother is waiting at the door. Her foot taps against the floor, the only indication of her annoyance. Even in her night clothes she is perfect without a hair out of place. It's meant to intimidate but I find a certain comfort in it.

'Let me do all the talking,' I whisper in Adam's ear. He nods his head as his large watery eyes rest on me. His bottom lip quivers as his hand slips into mine. I curl my fingers around his and give a squeeze of reassurance.

'Where have you been?' Her arms crossed over her chest as her foot taps. Her narrowed gaze surveys us both with a frown.

'Just in the garden, Mother,' I smile, projecting as much innocence as I can. Adam stands behind me, his head bowed. I can hear his sniffles.

'At three in the morning?' Her raised brow is mocking me as I conjure up an argument.

'Is that the time I thought it later?' she looks between the two of us. I know she doesn't believe me. Her expression of disbelief is testament to that. I hold her gaze, making my eyes wide.

'Without coats? Look at you. You are both freezing. Get upstairs and I will get Milly to run you a bath,' Mother huffs as she surveys the both of us. Tugging on Adam's hand, I lead him upstairs.

'Sorry Aaron,' his voice quivers with his obvious distress.

'It's okay,' entering the room Millie is waiting for us.

'Hi Millie,' I say, my voice cheerful. Millie brushes her brown hair back where it has come loose from the steam. Her night dress is hitched up her thigh where she was bending, and I admire her legs.

'Master Aaron, you have upset Madame Emma,' she chastises me. I know she saw me looking.

'It would seem so,' I answer as I try to keep a straight face.

'You made her twitch,' Millie giggles, and I can't help my chuckle. Adam tugs on my hand, and I turn my attention back to him.

'I am sorry Aaron,' he holds my gaze, my mirror image except he is thinner, fragile. A shiver shakes his frame as my features soften to hide the anxiety.

'Adam, get out of your wet clothes.' I brush his hair out of his eyes. He nods his head and shuffles toward the connecting door. Turning back.

'Sorry Aaron.' his eyes were watery again.

'Don't worry about it mate,' I give him a big smile to show I am not annoyed. I am worried, though. This could make him ill. He isn't robust like me.

'Is my bath ready?' I say, keeping my voice cheerful.

'Yes, do you need help?' her voice is sultry and I smirk. Her fingers undo my pyjama top buttons. She pushes it off and goes to undo my trousers. Her hand is already on me, and her eyes betray her lust. With a swallow, I compose myself.

'No, Adam will be here in a moment.' I remove her hands, holding them in mine for a little longer than perhaps I should. Milly is a dreadful flirt, and honestly, I enjoy the banter.

'Shame,' she mutters under her breath.

'Millie, you will never pass your Mother exams if you interfere with your charge,' I raise a brow and a very attractive blush flushes her skin. She steps back and her arms drop to her side.

'You know it is only you,' she pouts.

'Help Adam, you know how distracted he gets.' I try to dismiss her. If they caught us, we are both in trouble, but she will face instant dismissal. That would be catastrophic for her little family that rely on her wages.

'He is such a child.' she whines. 'You are much more fun,'

'Milly,' my voice commanding.

'You aren't my charge,' her parting shot as Adam shuffles in.

Laid in bed as I read my adventure novel. Snug and cosy after my bath. A mug of hot chocolate on my side table courtesy of Milly. My door cracks open and Adam shuffles in. In his hand, his mug. Putting it down next to mine, I shuffle up as he scoots into my bed. We sit in silence sipping our chocolate. I read my book out loud until he settles to sleep. Curling around him, I turn out the light.

I wake sometime later, far too hot. In the silence, I can hear his sniffles.

'Adam, what's wrong?' Reaching over, I put the little lamp on.

'Aaron, I don't feel so good.' I can feel the heat from him.

'How long were you out there?' I turn over as I gaze at his face. Noticing the flush to his cheeks.

'I don't know. I was worried about the frog spawn,' he mumbles, snuggling down further into my bed. Mother bustles in tutting. She sticks a thermometer in his mouth. Reading it, she tuts again. Her satin house coat is rumpled, and she no longer has her slippers on. I smile at this observation, and she glares at me. Scooping Adam up, she bustles out the room. My door banging shut muffles the voices outside as footsteps hurry along the hallway.

That was the last time I saw him. He got very ill as influenza swept through the house with devastating consequences. Mother isolated me in my room. My door opening has me looking up as my Mother comes in, her face grave. I put away my cards as she sits on my bed.

'Where is Adam?' My first thought is always for him.

'He is very sick. Along with most of the boys. We need to move you to somewhere safe.' she takes my hand.

'No, please don't,' I beg.

'This is best. You have a match, and you need to be kept safe until you are twenty. A lot rides on this match. We can't have you getting sick.' she glides gracefully to her feet. 'already lost three boys. We can't afford to lose you,' she turns as she reaches the door. My question stopping her.

'What will happen to him?' Worry in my voice, Adam could die? Why hadn't this occurred to me before? Maybe because it had always been present in our lives. We had a sister, a rare triplet. She died as she disappeared when we were small. I remember her giggle but no longer her face. I guess she looked like us.

'They will find him a match in due course and his education will intensify, keep him distracted.' She bends and kisses my cheek. 'You sleep, busy day tomorrow,'

'He will need a friend,' I mumble, my voice quivers with worry.

'Emma has organised that already. Aaron, you need to stop worrying about him and concentrate on staying strong.'

It is still dark when the car arrives. I am bundled into blankets and hustled out. The home is deserted. Too early for the boys or Mothers to be awake yet. I glance back one last time before ducking into the car.

CHAPTER 2

I watch the girl through the window, her floppy hat conceals her face. Somehow, I think she is smiling as her fingers dig into the compost and she plants up the pots with summer colour. She places them around the terrace. As she stands, her eyes connect with mine and a smile graces her lips as she raises a hand and waves at me.

I wave back. I would like to garden. Mother would never let me. I can almost picture the look on her face as she contemplates compost and just dirt. No, she would not allow that. My eyes find the girl again. She is admiring her handy work. Reaching for a broom leant against the wall as she sweeps up. Glancing up, she waves again before collecting her things and skipping down the steps. She strolls across the lawn to the sheds.

Tiredness is all that paints my days. The exhaustion I have grown used to as I struggle against the contaminant. The contraceptive drug that was supposed to save humanity was our destroyer. Preventing male births and those like me are constantly ill if we survive at all. This is the second move since I left my brother. I have been ill the whole time I have been here. Mother says it is more contaminated here. They will move me again soon.

I watch a group of males tumble onto the patio. Their laughter and exuberance brings a smile to my lips as they chatter. They are "Adam's." They are the property of a company called *Gen-Corp*. Gen-Corp are specialists in genetics, human genetics, and they, like me, created in one of their laboratories.

I like them am an example of genetic and by extension physical perfection, blonde hair, blue eyes, in my case. Perfectly proportioned features. At just six feet and lightly muscled, they bred me to exact detail. I, though, am not an Adam but an Echo child. So, my body works a little differently. I am also rare. The product of a rogue scientist. I am far more sensitive to the contaminate than them. Which is why I get sick.

Even though they try their best to screen my food and water, it is not enough, and eventually my body must purge it. After I will be fit and fertile which is the reason, I am cosseted. I am a valuable commodity bred to breed.

Right now, I am laid in my bed as the shivers wrack my body. Closing my eyes, I try to rest. Waiting for the sickness to pass.

'He is sick again. Do we need to delay moving him?'

'No stick to the schedule,' my mother's voice as she paces the room, her heels making a tapping sound on the wooden floor. Of course, she isn't my mother. She is one of the numerous women who have cared for me. I don't remember my birth mother. Not that she was my mother, she was just the vessel used to create me.

This Mother is the third one I remember. The one before, Emma, stayed to care for my brother, Adam. This one is called Bethany and I quite like her. Turning, she smooths her dark hair although it is in its usual neat bob, not a stray hair out of place. The form fitting dress perfectly shows off her hourglass figure. Her face perfectly made up even without makeup. She is stunning. Her brown eyes rake over my shivering form. She isn't alone. Another Mother, Lisa, is in my room with her. Lisa is like her supervisor, I think.

This is the third move in as many years, and I am sick of it. Having to start again. I have a moment as I think about Adam how much I miss him. This all started after they separated us. Someone is after us that much. I know I hear things see the way my new Mother is always anxious. All this moving from home to home isn't normal. Most never move until they are matched at eighteen.

I wonder if Adam, my brother, even that isn't normal, is moved constantly. My life that much duller without him. I remember how he spent all his time exploring the grounds. Fascinated by the local wildlife, if indeed there were any. He would read books on adventure or looking at atlases of the world, telling me all the places we would go. How we would leave this place and travel having adventures of our own? How we would fall in love that would consume our souls. Yeah, he was always the romantic.

Personally, I was quite happy where I was. I had no intention of going into the wider world. A world that viewed me as a commodity to be bought and sold. Something to be used and thrown away. No, I am not interested in that.

I miss him just getting his sketchbook out and drawing while I slept, but always there. A tear slips down my face. My mother's voice is soothing as she brushes my hair, her familiar perfume drifting around me comforting.

'The next place will be better,' she coos in my ear.

I drift to sleep. Waking sometime later. Not sure what woke me. It is still dark, the only light from the dying embers of the fire. With a sigh I go back to sleep. The house is quiet. Someone is shaking my arm urgently.

'Let me sleep,' I grumble, trying to turn over.

'Aaron wake up come on,' the urgency in my Mother's voice jolts me awake. Glancing around the room as I sit up. My gaze settles on Mother. She is dressed down in jeans and a jumper, trainers on her feet, and she is holding her pistol. My eyes open wide in shock.

'What's going on?' Outside I can hear shouting and running feet.

'Get up sweetheart,' she says, obviously seeing my fear and using the endearment she always uses with me. Milly bustles in a pile of clothes in her arms. Without saying a word, she has me stripped and redressed in no time. No flirting or banter. Two guards burst in, startling me further.

'He needs to be moved now,' the first guard growls.

'Miss with me,' the second guard hustles Milly from the room. I push my feet into my boots and do the laces up when the whole building rocks from an explosion.

'Now,' the guard grabs my arm and hauls me up, pushing me forward.

'Do not touch him,' my Mothers barks, annoyed.

'If they catch him, they will do more than touch him,' the guard retaliates, clearly angry.

'Aaron,' my mother takes my hand and drags me down the back servant stairs.

'Wait,' the guard stops us as she looks around the partially open door. 'Now go,' she pulls the door open. Mother dashes across the drive, dragging me with her.

'Get to the stable,' she shouts above the noise of gun fire and screaming. She shoves me in the right direction as she pivots and fires her gun. I run as fast as I can. Pushing the door to the stable open.

Entering the stable, it surprised me to see a horse. Its tack on. I adjust the saddle as Mother rushes in. Boosting me up, she jumps up behind me and steers it out of the barn until we are flying across the countryside.

Ahead the pink dawn tinge the sky as our pace seems to slow. I can feel her weight against me, heavy. Looking down, her hands loose on the reins. Taking control, to keep going until a farmstead comes into view. It seems to have habitation. Well maintained with a tidy garden. The sign says Battlefield Hall. Two windows throw golden light onto a gravel drive. I veer off toward the stables, away from the house. People are trouble. We just need somewhere to overnight. The rendezvous pre-arranged. I know the drill for these circumstances.

'Mother, Bethany, speak to me,' my voice seems to rouse her as her eyes flicker open.

'Aaron I am sorry, I have failed you,' the wind almost swallows her whispered reply.

'No, you haven't. Hang on, this is a farm we are safe here. I will get help,' I steer the horse toward a barn. Slipping off, I only just catch her. The weight of her body knocks us both to the ground. Dragging her inside. I can see the blood and I know there is nothing I can do to save her.

'You are not safe here. Be brave. Find the others' she lifts her hand and strokes my cheek before it drops to her side. Tears run unchecked down my face as I hold her.

Voices pull me from my stupor. Clambering over bales, I conceal myself so I can see who comes in. Two women walk in looking around. They first see the horse and then my Mother. Kneeling they examine her, the bigger one shakes her head.

'She is dead. I will bury her later,'

'Do you think she was alone?' The much younger girl asks peering around the barn. I duck down.

'I don't know Janey, she looks like a Mother,'

'Oh well, I will sort the horse,' Standing they approach the horse. The slighter one of the two strokes his nose, talking to him quietly. Removing his tack, they lead him outside. I wait in my hiding place, watching as they come back with a blanket and place it over my Mother. When they leave, I turn and slide down, leaning against the bale. I collect a horse blanket and climb back up to my hiding spot. Curling up I let sleep claim me, too tired to formulate a plan.

'Boy,' her voice is timid as I watch her enter. In her hands are a plate and a mug. She looks around and then puts the plate and mug on a bale. Giving the barn another look, she backs away. Her hands in her pockets silhouetting her slight frame. I wait until I am sure she has gone and then dart out to where the food is.

On it is a small pie and a piece of bread. Eating it without a thought, as I am so hungry. I down the tea. Hearing foot-steps, I dash back to my hiding place. The girl enters carrying a pile of blankets. She looks around and puts the blankets down and picks up the now empty plate.

'Sleep tight, boy,' she says, gazing around. Taking the blankets, I build a nest among the bales safely concealed from prying eyes. Curling up, I wonder how she knows I am here. How does she know I am a boy? Sleep claims me just as quickly as ever.

'Janey, how do you know he is still here?'

'I don't know, I just do. Oh, Melissa, he must be so fright-ened, and he must have seen his mother die. How terrible is that?'

'Your heart will get you killed. You know that, don't you,' the older girl huffs? 'Now hurry, we have work to do in the field.' Melissa turns and leaves.

'Boy,' Janey calls a bowl in her hands. I watch her put it down. 'Boy, you can come out. I won't hurt you,' she coos. Pulling my hood up, I crawl out my eyes trained on her…....

'Hello,' she smiles as I approach caution in my steps. She

is very skinny with large brown eyes set in a pixie like face. Dark brown hair is cut short, curling just below her chin. Slim trousers accentuate her almost stick like legs while a loose shirt drapes hiding her body shape beneath.

'Here you go.' Picking up the bowl, she hands it to me with a wooden spoon. Her voice is soft and when she smiles, her eyes crinkle at the corners and two dimples appear in her cheeks. Her eyes travel over me as if committing every detail to memory. I wonder what she sees. A small scruffy boy with pale hair that is just slightly too long framing a face that is just too pretty to be called handsome.

'Thank you,' my voice is gravely. I dip the spoon in and taste it.

'My names Jane, my sister calls me Janey though,'

'Aaron,' I grunt, while shovelling the porridge into my mouth.

'Do you like tea?'

'Yes,' spooning more porridge in my mouth.

'Why don't you come to the house, and I will make you some,' she looks at me, her brown eyes so hopeful. Shaking my head as I pass the bowl back and back away.

'No, I will get my horse and be gone,' I answer as she nods.

'He is in the field. His tack is over there,'

'Thank you,'

'Where will you go?'

'To find the others, we had a meeting place,' I explain without giving too much away.

* * *

'I TELL YOU JANEY, he has gone. Look see this is the second day the food hasn't been touched,'

'No Melissa, he is still here, I am sure. The horse is still in the field. Help me look, please,'

'Alright if only to show you I am right,' Melissa huffs as she climbs the bales. While Janey scrambles over the lower hay ones.

'He is here,' her triumphant voice jolts me into a sort of awake state. 'Oh, my Melissa, he is sick,' she calls as her hands caress my face, feeling the heat of the fever.

'Help me get him to the house,' she begs Melissa as she scoops me up.

'Janey, he will die. Why don't you just leave him. It would be less complicated. You know they don't survive out here,' Melissa tuts but does as Janey requests.

The house smells of furniture polish and baking bread as Melissa carries me inside and up a flight of stairs. She smells of sweat and outside her muscular arms holding me. Kicking open a door, she places me on something soft that I assume is a bed. Instinctively, I curl up as the fever ravages my body.

'Where will you sleep if he is in your bed?' Melissa objects. 'You can't keep him, you know that.'

'Why can't I? Look at him? He is so delicate and pretty. I can't let him just die.'

'He is an Adam, and they don't belong out here. They aren't for the likes of us, you know that.' She gives an indulgent sigh. 'Janey he isn't robust like other Adams we have seen. His chances are slim.'

'Please Melissa, let me keep him,'

'If he survives, I will think about it.'

'Thank you,' Janey beams. If I wasn't so sick, I would worry about that last comment. As they discuss me as if they are acquiring a new pet.

I feel a cold soft cloth wipe the sweat from my body as my head is lifted and cool water runs down my throat. Careful hands lay me back down as a soft voice talks to me.

'Sorry Adam, please don't go...stay with me,' I mumble, delirious.

'Shh, you are safe,' soft hands soothe me.

'Mother where are you?' opening my eyes, I can't focus. The light hurts and I try to throw my arms over my face.

'Calm down, sleep,'

Waking, I am alone pushing up. I notice I have pyjamas on, certainly not mine. They are pink with big purple flowers. Reaching across, I pick up the glass of water and drink it in one go. I sit for a while listening to the quiet of the house. I drift back to sleep, waking as she climbs in next to me. She snuggles down, her arm going over my waist as she curls around me. I lay paralysed, unsure what to do. I have never slept with anyone other than my brother.

'Aaron, are you awake?' her quiet voice in the dark.

'Yes,'

'How are you?' concern fills the room.

'Fine I think,'

'Good Melissa thought you would die,'

'Melissa doesn't like me,' I state.

'She doesn't like people.' Her smile is against my lips. 'Well, if it makes you feel better, I like you!'

'I like you as well.' Relaxing into my pillows with a smile on my lips.

'Night Aaron,' I listen as her breathing settles as she sleeps.

I wake too hot and can't move. I look down. Wrapped around me is Janey, her head tucked into my chest, and her dark hair is tickling my chin; her lips are slightly open as she breathes, deeply asleep. I lay still, not sure what to do. I gaze at her face. It's quite a friendly face, straight delicate nose, high cheekbones, and that mouth with its slightly full bottom lip, so she looks like she is pouting.

I move my gaze back up to her hair, and notice she is

awake, watching me with her liquid dark eyes. She blushes and moves away from me.

'Sorry,' Janey climbs out of bed and walks to the bathroom she has a shapely figure, small high breasts, a narrow waist, and round hips that top long strong legs, oddly I have never seen a real girl naked, I close my eyes and groan. I lay there, truly uncomfortable, and watch her get dressed.

I am immediately hard, and I haven't given a sample for days and I kinda need to.

'What's the matter Aaron? Do you feel ill again?' she asks, her voice full of concern, and then her eyes widen?

'Is that you?' She smiles, walking over to the bed. Before I can stop her, her head disappears under the blanket.

'Oh, good lord,' she giggles; it's muffled where her head is under the blanket. I sit up, feeling uncomfortable.

'Yeah, thanks for that,' I mutter dryly.

'Does it hurt?' she asks, looking at me biting her lip.

'What, no,' I frown. 'I, um, haven't given a sample for a couple of days,' I mumble, blushing, not sure why I am embarrassed haven't ever been before.

'Let me help,' she pushes me back down and then I feel her mouth warm and wet on me. A groan of pleasure bubbles up my throat. It feels amazing. Closing my eyes, I just let the sensations overwhelm me as she holds my hips down as I feel the tightening in my belly before I explode into her mouth. She crawls up my body with a big smile.

'That was amazing,' she hops off the bed. 'Did you enjoy it?' she glances over her shoulder.

'Y...yes,' I stutter out. 'Where did you learn to do that?'

'Oh, I read it in the book Melissa has hidden in her room. Never thought I would put it into practice,' she answers as she skips from the room. I make my way downstairs. The house is old with flagstone floors and stone window frames. It is also very large. I try a couple of doors before I find the kitchen. Janey is kneading bread and smiles at me. I pull out a chair and sit and watch her.

'Tea,' she puts a cloth over the bread and places the bowl it is in, into the bottom of the oven. Lifting a large, doomed lid, she puts the metal kettle on the hot plate. 'You look better.' she sits next to me and takes my hand.

'I feel better,'

'Good. Melissa has contacted the authorities to let them know you are here.'

'What, why?'

'You are underage. It isn't safe out here for you,'

'Oh,' Janey gets up and makes the tea. The evening passes quietly. Janey takes my hand, and we drift back upstairs. I am still sleeping in Janey's bed, although from our exploring yesterday there are hundreds more. The rest of the house closed up. Her and Melissa only use a small part of the house.

'Why do you stay here?' I ask as I get my night clothes on.

'Where else would we go? This has been our family home for hundreds of years,' Janey snuggles down next to me. 'Melissa has dreams and plans for the house, but the disaster and all that followed put paid to that.' she turns to me, excitement shining in her eyes. 'Now you are here,'

'Yes, I am,' I answer sardonically.

I am almost dressed when Janey brings me a cup of tea.

'You are beautiful,' Janey breathes so quietly I almost don't hear her.

'Hmm,' I look up as I pull my jeans on. To see Janey gazing at me. Dressed in her usual blouse and flowing skirt, and looks lovely.

'My Mother thought I was too pretty,' I shrug.

'Yeah, I can see her point. I feel a little inadequate stood next to you mister beautiful,' Janey chuckles as I fumble with my shirt buttons.

'Here, let me help,' Janey does the buttons with deft

fingers. 'Your hair is a mess,' she bites her lip and runs her hands through my hair, ruffling it a bit. I gaze into her eyes as she does it, biting her lip in concentration. I can smell her, all sweet, sort of like outside after the rain. 'Aaron,'

'Hmm,' we are so close she is watching me with a strange expression on her face. Leaning forward, closing the gap, I kiss her. I don't know why I just do. I feel her arms drift around my neck, her fingers in my hair as I place my hands on her waist. She bites my lip, and I let her slip her tongue into my mouth. I have never done this before.

My hands move under her shirt, feeling the indentations of her ribcage, and I feel an urge, like I feel when I am going to give a sample. A little voice in my head tells me to stop that this is wrong, but it's nice and I don't want to stop, as if something inside me is driving me on against my better judgement.

'Aaron, I...' I hear Janey moan as she kisses my throat, moving down.

'What did Melissa mean when she said the likes of you?'

'We aren't special, just ordinary, but I am clean, able to breed and soon I will be of age. And it scares Melissa because they will take me to be matched.' Her mouth is back on mine, stopping any further talking.

I push her back, her skirt riding up. Her hands move down, and her mouth covers mine again and I can't help it when I groan as her hands slip to my jeans. With deft fingers undo them, releasing me. Wrapping her legs around my waist. The next few minutes are a frenetic motion of hands and lips and bodies. Gasps fill the room as we push clothing out the way. Yet again I explode inside her as she mumbles my name, holding me tight.

'Janey, what are you doing?' Melissa's voice hollers up the stairs. The moment shattered. I roll away from her and gather up my jeans, pulling them on. We should not have done that. I glance around.

'Janey,' my voice wobbles.

'That was amazing,' Janey giggles, pulling her clothing straight and I suspect she knew exactly what we were doing. She leans over and kisses me deeply. After that, our time together changed. Is this love? Is this what Adam dreamed of finding? I don't know. I enjoy being with Janey. Touching her, kissing her, sleeping with her, but do I love her? I can't say. I certainly care about her and enjoy all our activities.

We spend our days in the room with the books. Reading while laughing at stupid things. Melissa doesn't think it is safe for me to go outside. Despite that, I feel free for the first time. I know it won't last. Melissa has already contacted the authorities. I push that to the back of my mind.

'You can kiss me again.' she glances at me sideways. I nod and we spend a while practising kissing, which always leads to more. I feel content here, safe. We lay in a tangled heap from the kissing. Until Melissa shouts. With a laugh, we make our way downstairs. To be confronted by Gen-Corp security.

CHAPTER 3

a body rushes from behind them and wraps around me in a rib crushing hug.

'Aaron, we thought we had lost you,' Millie gushes as she stands back surveying me.

'I am fine. These two lovely ladies saved my life,' I explain, concerned that the security is pointing their guns at Melissa and Janey.

'We need to get you back. Find a new Mother for you,' Millie is trying to steer me to the door when a smart lady walks in. The guards immediately move lowering their weapons.

'Melissa, good to see you well.'

'Thelma always a pleasure,' Melissa answers, turning to Janey. 'Janey honey, make some tea, please. I believe I have some negotiating to do.' Turning to me. 'Sit down Aaron, this concerns you,' I sit as instructed.

'What do you want, Melissa? You cannot keep him.'

'I am aware. I want Janey removed from the breeding program. Any consequences from this I want to keep on the understanding you and you alone can have access to it.'

'The boy?' Thelma raises a brow.

'He is yours. He will not return here or have contact with us or any consequence,'

'And if there is no consequence?'

'Thelma, they are Echo's. She felt the pull the minute he entered our barn.' A calculating smile pulls at her features as she observes me. I look down at my hands in my lap. 'The fact he sits over there and does not move to sit next to Janey suggests there will be a consequence,' Melissa smiles as all eyes turn to me and I feel the heat of a blush climb my skin.

'Very well, I will leave the girl in your capable hands.' Thelma climbs to her feet and we all follow. 'Come Aaron, let's return you,' she holds out her hand and I hesitate before taking it. Glancing back at Janey, I see her whispering to Melissa, paying me no attention.

The next few days are a blur. They find me a new home and Mother, all supervised by Madam Thelma. This is the distraction I need as I try to forget Janey and our time together. Knowing I won't see Janey again is painful.

Now I am sitting on my bed in my new room watching my new Mother stalk back and forth.

'Aaron, you need to talk to me,' she stops and looks at me. I don't want to talk to her. Much less tell her what happened. It is mine away from here, away from control. I don't want them snooping through Melissa and Janey's life. So, I sit not talking.

I get ill. Shocker. It convinced mother it is stress and who am I to tell her otherwise? Maybe it is? The days pass in a blur and I half think my time at the farm with Janey was just a dream my imagination conjured up. A coping mechanism after the death of Bethany my Mother.

Millie bustles in, followed by my new Mother and another Mother I don't know. Not that I care. I miss Janey, truth be told. I miss reading the books and giggling. Most of all, I miss kissing.

'Thelma is here with her daughter. She wants him moved to a facility in Scotland.' My new Mother moves to the bed. She smiles as she takes my temperature.

'How are you doing, sweetie?' She murmurs, and I attempt to smile? Sitting on the bed, her skirt rides up her thigh slightly.

'Much better. Thank you,' I reply.

'You don't have to be so formal.' her concern for me is partly because I am her charge but mostly because I am a frighteningly valuable commodity. A male of breeding age. Kept hidden from society while nurtured to become a means by which they can procreate.

'Aaron, you and I we are safe here,' she takes my hand. 'I know you went through an awful trauma. But trust me, you are safe.'

'I know, I feel safe.' I squeeze her hand to show my sincerity.

'Good, should have you back to your lessens in no time.' she ruffles my hair. Snuggling down, I drift back to sleep. Two days later they move me. I hardly notice, as my grasp on consciousness is tentative.

My health has improved for the first time in months. Some places are more contaminated than others and Scotland is relatively clean. I like it here. The landscape is amazing. With its vast forests and mountains. The air is icy fresh. Adam would love it here. The wildlife is amazing. With wild cats, red squirrels and Pine martins that are so cool. I miss him so much. I miss Janey, but that is fading now as well. Melissa was right. Janey wasn't for me. We did not match, and my being there put them in danger. I understand that. Right now, I have other things to worry about.

Turning to the mirror, I pull the tie, making the knot, and

sliding it into place. My eyes cast a critical look over my appearance. The dark grey tailored suit hugs my body. Puberty finally put in an appearance, and I have filled out with muscle definition. The tie matches my crystal blue eyes as the dark grey compliments my almost white hair. At almost six feet, I am as tall as my Mother when she wears heels.

My Mother bustles in she surveys me with a smile. Reaching me, her hands immediately adjust my tie.

'Why do I have to go?' I frown.

'Because you are being introduced to your companion,' Mother reply's while removing imaginary lint from my jacket.

'Do I need a companion?'

'Yes, of course how else will you learn,' She answers with a smile bustling around the room tidying. Learn what? I want to ask but know better. So, I hold my council and follow her from the room.

Tania leads me to the meeting room. Taking my seat, I can't help wondering why I am required for this. Everyone else already present. My gaze travels to the lady talking. Light brown hair pulled away from her perfectly made-up face. Complimented by the fitted business suit in a navy blue that hugs her petite frame. Thelma Ramsbottom head of genetics division of the large corporation that now owns the world.

Taking over as governments crumbled as the male population died and civil unrest prevailed. They stepped in with a solution and brought order back. So, by default in charge of the Adam Program.

'As you know since the incident, we had with him we have renegotiated his sale and Match,'

'You did?' my Mother raises a brow.

'Yes, making that complete debacle not such a disaster. His value trebled.'

'I understand Tribe have bought him. Even though they dispute his ownership.'

'Yes, they realised it was the only way we would return him,'

'Tribe want him trained and educated. They are sending someone to help.' Thelma smiles at me again. 'They will match him,'

'He only has one more year here?'

'He will start immediately and of course his training will continue with my daughter as will hers. This is beneficial to us all,' Thelma's eyes sweep over me a satisfied smile on her face. She reminds me of a cat about to toy with its food. I am most definitely the food.

'His alliance will be advantageous to all,'

'Is he to breed with his companion?'

'That is not the aim but when they come of age, it would be a bonus,' the girl

stares at me and I raise a brow eliciting a shy smile.

'Now his fertility has been proven. It would be a pleasant bonus.' Thelma eyes me with a calculating smile. What does she mean? How has my fertility been proven? Do they know? I know Janey and I had sex and I know the consequence. I also know that was illegal. They would arrest if I got her pregnant, wouldn't they? That would be impossible. They did not match Janey to me. Janey wasn't an Echo like me, was she? No, I am being paranoid. After all, I haven't been arrested. I turn my attention to the girl. Deciding to analyse this conversation later in the privacy of my room.

Slumping in my chair I study her. The girl is Thelma's daughter, Gillian. She is quite pretty having the same pale brown hair as her mother. Her glasses make her look cute. I wonder why her eyes haven't been corrected. She gives a delicate shudder when they discuss the breeding. Rude I decide as I know I am far from unattractive. I tune back into the conversation.

'So, you want them to be companions when sixteen,' my Mother raises a brow.

'Yes, with his match confirmed they both need to be educated for their future lives,' Thelma looks me over and I pull myself upright. A blush creeps up my neck. I cast my gaze to the girl. I know exactly what they are insinuating. Reminding me how my life is one of control and obedience.

'When do they want him returned?'

'Oh, when he is twenty as normal,' Thelma smiles at me making my blush worse.

'After sixteen?' my mother enquires.

'He will stay with my daughter until eighteen then he will be moved to the research facility in France until twenty. I want some tests run before we hand him over.' She turns her attention to me. 'He is one of few surviving Echo boys we have, and he is healthy and fertile,' She smiles at me.

'His brother?'

'He is too delicate according to his Mother, Emma. Not as mentally or physically stable,' Her gaze sweeps over me again and it is all I can do not to squirm. 'You will get the program later today.' The meeting over my Mother escorts me from the room.

'Adam?' A voice calls making me stop. Turning I see the girl walking toward me.

'Aaron, my name is Aaron,'

'Yes, sorry I forgot,' she smiles holding out her hand. I take it and we shake. 'Gillian, but my friends call me Gilly,' she lets go of my hand.

'Am I a friend then?' I raise a brow as I tease her.

'If you want to be,' she blushes.

'Yes, I would... Gilly,' she beams at me as I flirt with her.

'You are much nicer than your brother,'

'You have met Adam? Is he alright?'

'Yeah, he is fine. Doesn't say much,' she shrugs. 'Showed me his moon moth caterpillars.' She gives a delicate shiver.

'No, he wasn't a brilliant talker,' I smile. 'Could have been worse he could have shown you his frog spawn or even his Axolotls,'

'Oh yuk,' she giggles. 'I heard what happened to you. You were very brave,' she looks at me through her lashes.

'Not really,' I counter back. 'The people that helped me were really nice,' I smile as I think about Janey wondering what she is doing.

'Yes, they were compensated well,'

'Compensated?' I frown.

'Yes, you are a precious commodity we are very grateful they took such good care of you before returning you to us. Especially now you have a confirmed match,' Wow that made me feel human.

'Gillian,' we both turn at her name.

'I must go. Nice meeting you,' Gillian turns and hurries away. I watch as her mother questions her. Gillian glances back at me before disappearing through the doors.

'Who is my match,' I walk next to my Mother my hands behind my back showing her respect.

'She is very important, and this match will be a great alliance for the company,' Mother answers her voice full of pride.

CHAPTER 4

*S*tanding in the corridor, I turn the map in my hand. I am lost biting my lip I try to keep it together. The threat of tears is burning my eyes as I want to give in to the frustration hating feeling helpless. This is my first day in the school building.

Pushing that all away, I glance at the map again while running a hand through my pale hair, biting my lip as I survey the doors along the corridor. Would it have been too much trouble to number them?

'You lost?' A boy with dark hair and pale eyes smiles at me as he saunters toward me.

'Yeah,'

'You the sick boy?' He peers at me and looks me up and down and yeah, I know I am small and delicate to look at. I certainly don't look the fifteen years I am supposed to be more like twelve.

'Yeah,' why deny it.

'George,' he holds his hand out for me to shake.

'Aaron,' I smile as he studies my timetable.

'Ah, looks like you are with me, English this way,'

'Thanks,' I follow him to class. Why we need to learn this stuff is beyond me. Adam used to say to keep us occupied while giving them a feeling of moral obligation. He was full of theories like that. I push thoughts and memories of him away. I miss him and wonder what he is doing? This probably.

English passes in its usual mind-numbing way. I sit at the front at an empty desk. Trying to ignore the curious looks aimed my way. I sigh at the thought of starting again, trying to make friends I don't need or want, but I need to fit in. I have a year here so might as well try. The end of the lesson a relief as I wait for the room to clear before leaving my seat.

'Aaron,' the teacher calls my name. Stopping at the door, I turn to her.

'Your Mother wanted you to read these,' she passes some books to me.

'Oh, thank you,' picking them up I can see they are old, and I suspect they are banned text. Why would Mother want me to read these? They are written by George Orwell and the Bronte sisters and set in a time long past. Is this the extra stuff they want me to learn?

Standing in the doorway I hesitate before entering the food hall. It is bustling with activity. I make my way to the lunch line.

'Hey, Aaron, you can sit with me,' George ambles up behind me.

'Oh, um thanks,' taking my tray, I wait for him and then follow him to a table. Two other boys join us. Edward and Oliver. I notice a raucous table and raise a brow.

'They are the popular boys,' Edward explains. This is new to me.

'Stay away from them they are trouble,' Oliver adds.

'Oh, um okay,' I glance over at them and quickly look away before they notice. One boy keeps his gaze on me for longer than I feel polite.

'Who is that' I ask George. He follows my line of sight.

'Oh, that's Heath,' George says. 'He is beautiful isn't he,' George's voice takes on a dreamy inflection.

'Yes,' I answer looking away as I stuff some potatoes into my mouth.

'Some think him an Echo,' Oliver says reverence in his voice. I raise a brow and surreptitiously glance at the boy Heath. He is delicate to look at like me.

'Possibly,' I reply finishing my lunch.

'What do you know about Echo's?' Oliver looks at me his expression expectant. I sigh.

'You can't tell anyone ...but I am an Echo,' I say gazing around.

'Really,' they blink at me then burst out laughing. They don't believe me so that's good I suppose.

Ambling along the corridor, I miss the group of boys hanging about. My focus on the timetable and map in my hand as I make my way to my afternoon class. I have kept to myself as much as possible can't see the point of making friends as I will be gone in the spring. I have stayed friends with George and his friends. Surprise isn't an emotion I show as they surround me, forcing me to stop.

'Well, what do we have here if it isn't the weakling?' A large boy with black hair steps forward. He would be handsome if his features weren't twisted in a sneer. 'I heard he is so pathetic they don't even milk him,' the group snigger as he pushes my shoulder, making me stagger back only to be pushed hard forward.

'Looks more like a girl to me,' another brown-haired boy remarks, knocking my books from my hands.

'Shall we check boys?' I shake my head and try to move away.

'Please don't.' I am pinned to the wall, and I can't see a way out.

'Oh, and how are you going to stop us?' The first boy raises a brow as he gets up close.

'Like this,' I pull him close, catching him by surprise as I bring my knee up. He immediately drops to the ground, groaning as I sweep my things from the floor and run. Darting around a corner in my desperation, I try the first door. As the pounding of footsteps closes in behind me. Out running them isn't an option as the door opens. I slip inside and lock it. Leaning against it closing my eyes as I get my breath back slumping as they run past.

'Watcha doin,' startling I open my eyes to see a boy lounging against the wall with his arms crossed. He doesn't look like an Adam, as he isn't wearing dark slacks and a blazer over a shirt. The uniform of sorts. He is wearing jeans and a shirt without a blazer. I notice it hung on the back of a chair.

He pushes away from the wall and walks toward me. Pushing his glasses up his nose as he pushes his pale gold hair off his face. I wonder briefly what he is doing in here until my gaze registers a laptop and files on one desk.

'I was being chased,'

'Why?' He steps closer, he is slight, with pale grey eyes that are surveying me intently. His golden hair swept back, exposing the delicate bone structure of his face. My eyes open wide as I realise, he is beautiful, not ordinary. He is an Echo certainly not one of the staff or an Adam, he is just too perfect. Well, almost as he is wearing glasses, but these just seem to add to his charm. Highlighting his pale grey eyes.

'I... because...,' giving up, I shrug. Walking further into

the room, I pull a chair out and sink onto it. 'They don't like me,' I mutter eventually.

'Why?'

'I don't know because I am different,' I reply, frustrated with his questions.

'Well, you are small, and you are quiet. I have noticed that about you,' he says, looking me over. 'You look like a girl as well that can't help,' My brows raise into my hairline. That was rude. I try to remember seeing him in class.

'Well, thanks,' I grumble, and he laughs. He has noticed me. Do I stand out that much?

'I like you,' he says. 'Tobias, but my friends call me Toby,' he holds his hand out to me.

Glancing at it, a moment, I grasp it. 'Aaron,' smiling, I shake his hand. 'You don't know me,' I emphasize.

'No, I don't ...yet' his smile softened the words.

'So why are you in here?' I choose to ignore his jibe.

'Oh, just finishing a report ... on you,' his lips still linger with a smile as he raises a brow. He is pushing me trying to get a reaction, and I realise Toby isn't as he seems. Will he be a friend or another enemy? I seem to collect them.

'Come on, I had better return you to your mother,' he takes my hand and unlocks the door, pulling me out behind him.

'Have you always been in this home?' I ask as we amble along the corridor.

'Oh, no arrived just before you,' Toby glances at me. 'Here you go,' he stops outside my door, and I wonder how he knows this is my room. Then I remember the report.

'Thanks, I... hockey later are you playing?' My hand on the door handle.

'Oh, no. I can watch though,' I glance up at him with a smile.

'See you later then,' pushing the door open I step inside. Looks like I might have a friend.

* * *

IT'S HOCKEY THIS EVENING, I like hockey; I am relatively good at it and some of the other boys enjoy having me on their team. Because of the rain, we are playing indoors. It's faster this way and I love it. The boys that attacked me are on the opposing team and I am sure this will not end well. Until now, I had avoided them mostly.

I stand waiting, anticipation grips my stomach as I bend slightly poised, ready with my stick. George has the ball and is running toward me, his control of the ball, precise, he glances up and catches my eye. I see a corner of his mouth twitch up ever so slightly. I smile and run as the opposition converges on him. Moving into place as he swiftly passes the ball. I hear and feel the thud as it connects with my stick. I control its momentum and run as George gets into position, as I pass it back and drop back as George passes it forward, our teammates knowing where they should be, moving as a smooth machine. So, absorbed in the game, I don't see the boy run into my side swiping his stick against my legs, the flare of pain the first clue as I am tripped up and sent sprawling to the floor. Too late to avoid the second boy and his stick as it connects with my head.

I wake in my bed with a bandage around my head. On seeing I am awake; my mother sits on the edge of my bed.

'What happened?'

'I tripped, it was an accident,' is all I mutter.

'You seem to have a lot of those,' she sighs. 'Aaron you are not to play anymore sport,'

'Okay,' no point in arguing. It will just lead to more questions and more trouble for me. She stands and gazes at me for a while before leaving the room.

Now I am alone, I let the tears flow. Wallow in my pity. I miss Janey she would have made me feel better. A friend would be nice, but that will not happen. Even George avoids me, and I know why. Afterward, I curl up on my bed and sleep the rest of the evening away. A pleasure taken by stupid, selfish boys.

'Aaron are you awake?' His quiet voice has me turning over.

'Yeah,' pushing up as he walks through the door backwards carrying a tray.

'I brought you something to eat,' he places the tray on my knees and removes the coving with a flourish. 'Sorry, it's just soup and a sandwich,' he chuckles.

'Thanks,' smiling I tuck in. 'How did you get up here?'

'The servants passage the house is riddled with them, found them by accident,' he grins.

'I saw what they did,' he looks at me, waiting for my answer. 'Why haven't you said?'

'What's the point?' I shrug.

'I can show you the passages,'

'Thank you,'

'Can't believe the boys haven't found them,' he breaks a bit off my bread roll and pops it into his mouth.

'My brother would have if he had been here,'

'You have a brother? That's rare.' he looks at me closer.

'Identical twins', I explain, putting the tray on my bedside table.

'Ah yes, of course.' he laughs.

'You know him?' My voice betrays my surprise.

'No, not really. I read your file. My mother wants us to be friends.' he looks away as he blushes.

'Oh, didn't know we could read each other's files,' I remark watching him.

'No, normally you can't,' he shrugs, eating more of my roll. Good job I am not hungry. 'But my Mother wants us to be friends, and she knows I am not so good at that,' He shrugs.

'Me neither,' I add and we both chuckle.

CHAPTER 5

*L*eaning against my locker I wait for Toby. My life improved exponentially with him as a friend. Of course, the secret passages helped a lot.

'Aaron, you waiting for Toby' George asks as he ambles up to me.

'Yeah,' I shut my locker tucking the book I wanted under my arm. As Toby saunters over.

'Geography next you are going to enjoy this,' Toby reveals with a smirk.

'Oh really, why?' I raise a brow. A boy stops by our little group he looks us over and then settles his gaze on me. I recognise him as the boy Heath.

'Leaver's bonfire at the weekend are you going,' he holds my gaze, and I will myself not to blush.

'Um, I would have to ask,' I mumble out. Could I be anymore pathetic?

'I look forward to seeing you there,' he smiles before melting into the crowd. I stand stunned.

'Why would he want you to go?' George looks at me with an expectant expression.

'I don't know I have never talked to him before,' my reply distracted as I try to decide what he wants and if I should go. What if it's a trap to get to me again?

With lessons over, I amble back to my rooms. Deciding to read up on all I have just learnt and have an early night as I am not allowed to do sport.

'Stella I am back,' I call out as Stella appears from the small kitchenette. Most of my meals are prepared here so my Mother can monitor how much of the contaminant I am being exposed too. Stella is my new Millie. Millie didn't come with us when I was moved here.

'So you are,' she smiles and bustles around me like a mother hen. Taking my bag, she ushers me toward the bathroom to wash my hands. The table already set for tea. Stella isn't like Millie. She doesn't flirt just tries to fatten me up. Clucking that I am too skinny. Stella of course is immaculately turned out. Her chestnut brown hair sleek and perfect. Her make up perfect. She is training to be a Mother.

'Have you made a sponge?' My voice full of hope.

'Of course I have, just for you,' She brings the cake out and sets it on the table with the delicate sandwiches. 'Your Mother wants you bathe after tea,' she informs me as she leans over and pours my tea. 'Would you like me to help you,' her voice all business no flirting. How I miss Milly.

'Erm, no not tonight I am tired,'

'Okay sweetheart, holler if you need me,'

'Thank you, Stella,' I smirk. Stella is very curvy. She is in her second year of training, and this is her placement. Year, then she has one more year of training to be a Mother. Her brown hair caught up in a bun as her hazel eyes twinkle at me. It showed her curvy figure to its best in the form fitting dress all Mothers wear. She bustles around me, getting ready for the evening milking. I don't do this often being an Echo.

Glancing up as my Mother bustles in and joins me for tea.

'May I have a sample after tea' she announces as she helps herself to a cup of tea and a sandwich?

'Of course,' placing my cup in its saucer. 'May I attend the bonfire party,' My voice has an inflection of nonchalance, so she doesn't know how important this is to me.

'You have been very healthy while here,' she muses. 'If your recovery is good and your sample healthy, then yes, I don't see why not.' she glances at me with an indulgent smile. 'You are making friends?'

'Yes, I have made friends,' my reply has her smiling.

'Good,'

'Thank you, Mother,' I push to my feet and make my way to my bedroom to prepare. In my head I do a fist pump as a small smile graces my features.

* * *

I SAUNTER down to the lake. I have a thick jumper on as Stella fussed over my outfit. Worried I would catch cold. It was best to humour her, or I was never getting out.

'You made it,' George beams at me handing me a bottle.

'Stella was more protective than normal,' I chuckle as they roll their eyes. Their Mothers don't have assistants so find mine funny.

Taking a sip, I am surprised that it is beer. The alcohol gives me a pleasant buzz as I survey my surroundings.

A large bonfire crackles and blazes surrounded by logs that groups of boys sit on chatting. Music drifts around us from a source I can't locate. Some boys are dancing. I notice Toby laughing and dancing with Oliver.

'Come on, Aaron dance with me,' George pulls me up. Laughing I don't resist.

I sneak away some time later with a bottle of beer in my hand as I slip my shoes and socks off. Letting the cold water of the lake swirl around my toes. My sweater back with the others it was too warm to wear with all the dancing. I rarely get a chance to paddle or have bare feet. So, this is really nice. I lose myself in thought as I wiggle my toes in the cool water. Sipping my beer, I can't remember being this relaxed.

'Can I join you?' I startle at the voice.

'Oh, um yeah sure,'

'Heath,'

'Yeah, I know, Aaron,'

'Hello Aaron,' I think he is mocking me.

'So why are you over here on your own?'

'Oh, um I just wanted to feel the earth against my toes and the air on my skin,' he takes his shoes off and joins me. 'And paddle. I'm rarely allowed outside, so I thought I would make the most of this opportunity,'

'Ah yes, you are the proper Echo,' He smiles.

'And you are the imposter,'

'Yep,' he chuckles. 'So, you have a match I presume,'

'How do you know all this?' I narrow my eyes he is very well informed. He looks around exaggeratedly. Leaning toward me he cups his hand around his mouth as he whispers in my ear.

'Not such an imposter,' My eyes widen as I step back to look at him.

'Yeah, I have a match. Leave next month. As, will you?'

'Yep, best make the most of it then,' I turn to him to find he is close.

'I guess,' our eyes lock and it is as if we are the only ones here as the sound of the party fades. He leans in and I don't move. Unsure of his intentions as something seems to pull us closer. Then his lips are on mine, my eyes open in surprise. They are soft and hard all at once. His hands move to cup my face and I kiss him back.

He nibbles my lip and I gasp allowing his tongue access as

he deepens the kiss. I can feel his excitement and mine. He pulls away and looks at me with lust filled eyes and that is all it takes for me to realise what I have done. Scooping up my shoes I run.

I can hear him shouting my name as I dash across the lawn and up the stone steps that lead to the staff entrance. Making it to my room I shut the door and lean against it. My chest heaving and it isn't from just the run. I close my eyes as I try to regain some control. What have I done?

'Aaron,' he is outside my door. Scooting out of bed I open it. 'Your sweater,' he hands it to me. In my haste I left it behind. He smells of bonfire and outside. A blush stains my cheeks.

'Thanks,' he smiles at me, and this couldn't be more awkward. His eyes sweep my body, lingering on my bare chest.

'See you around Aaron,' he turns and walks back along the corridor. Closing the door, I lean against the wall.

It had been two days since the incident, as I now referred to it. Yesterday was Sunday, so I kept to myself. I have English first. As I walk along the hall, I can see my friends by my locker. I dread seeing him. What would I say?

'Hey Aaron, you okay?' George looks me over.

'Yeah, outside isn't always good for me,' I smile as I open my locker retrieving my books.

'Oh, poor little Echo,' Oliver teases as Toby drifts over.

'English next,' I manage a nod finally finding my book.

Glad when the lesson finishes. Somehow, I just couldn't concentrate. Trailing out last after the other boys. A yelp bubbles out of me as hands grab me from behind and drags me into one of the hidden passages. They push me against the wall as the dark envelopes me and I feel lips on mine. Soft and urgent, I let out a small groan. The kiss is amazing. I can feel their excitement press against my belly, and I know I should pull away, but I just can't as my hands grab their hips. Eliciting a moan from them. Finally, I pull away.

'Heath, you scared me,' I complain.

'How did you know it was me?'

'Well, who else would have the audacity to kiss me?' I raise a brow as he flicks a light on. His smirking face appearing with the light.

'You ran,' he accuses.

'Yeah, sorry you sort of took me by surprise,' my explanation is inadequate.

'So, you aren't avoiding me,'

'Maybe a little,' I confess as a blush heats my skin.

'That's okay. I like your honesty,'

'If we get caught…' my voice trails off.

'We won't,' he kisses me again. Pulling away he takes my hand. 'Come on, we will be late.' The corridor is clear as we run to class. Toby raises a brow as I slide into my seat. He makes no comment at my dishevelled state.

'Aaron, you got human biology next?' George asks as he ambles up to me. I am swapping out books for the afternoon.

'Yeah, just waiting for Toby,' I shut my locker tucking the book I wanted under my arm. 'Then we have politics,'

'I hear you are leaving,'

'Oh yeah, I am Sixteen and I move at the end of the month to start my training for my match,' I reveal with a smile.

'Do you know who she is?'

'No,'

'I can't wait to start my training. I heard sex is so much better than milking,'

'Yeah, and who told you that?' Toby chuckles as he saunters over.

'Just rumours,' George defended a blush on his cheeks.

'You know it is illegal until they match you at twenty,' Heath answers grabbing me around the waist.

'Well, yeah, but we still have to learn how to do it.' George turns his gaze to us. 'Is that what they teach you in Human Biology?' His question full of hope.

'Yes … well, sort of the mechanics. To be honest, the whole thing looks gross,' I remark and give a shudder. Hoping my lie goes undetected. Sex is amazing, and it is times like this I think about Janey.

'Really! Well, that's disappointing,' George answers doubt in his voice. 'See you both for lunch,' he waves as he saunters off swallowed by the crowd.

'How many boys are leaving?' Toby asks as we take our seats.

'A dozen I think all have confirmed matches,' I answer as the lesson starts with a banana?

'Aaron don't get caught,' I snap my attention to him.

'What do you mean?'

'Don't get caught. If you do, they will ship him out to be modified, you know that don't you?' he locks his gaze with mine and can clearly see I have no idea what he is talking about. He huffs, annoyed.

'You are Echo's. So, you are drawn to each other,'

'What do you mean drawn to each other?' I frown confused.

'Echo's give off a pheromone, it alerts another Echo. It works in your brain, so you bond and mate with your chosen. A fail-safe to ensure the continuation of the species,'

'Wow made that sound so romantic,' I drawl as he sniggers. 'So, what's the problem?' I frown.

'Look, our sole purpose is to make babies. They do not encourage your behaviour. If you or him can't fulfil that obligation…. Then you are of little use.'

'They would euthanise?'

'Yes, if you or him can't conform. They would remove you to a facility, milk you until twenty and then euthanise,' the colour drains from my face.

'It's just a bit of fun,' I whisper my heart is shattering as I worry for Heath.

'For you maybe, for him,' Toby shrugs. 'Look Aaron you are an Echo, that alone protects you to a degree and of course your match and Gilly,' He takes my hand and looks up at me his expression serious. 'You are also proven, so that protects you even more. Heath is not nor does he have powerful allies,'

'What do you mean proven?' This is the second time I have heard this when referring to me.

'Last year when they lost you,' he raises a brow and I blush.

'Janey,' I whisper.

'Was that her name?' I nod.

'She is safe, isn't she?' This blurts out a little loud and I glance around to make sure no one is listening. I am worried now. I thought she was safe with Melissa.

'Yes, she is safe,' I relax as relief washes through me.

'What do you mean, proven?' Toby leans in and lowers his voice.

'They don't want you to know, but she had a baby a male baby. A healthy male baby,' All the colour drains from my face and I scramble to my feet running from the room. Reaching the rest room. I throw up. Sinking to the floor my head on my drawn-up knees.

'Aaron,' I don't look up when I hear my name and the door opens.

'Will I be punished? Will she be punished?' all these worries crash in my head.

'What no, do you have any idea how valuable that makes you. They couldn't have asked for a better outcome. They even renegotiated your match,' Toby pulls me up and leads me back to our common room. He sits me down and fetches me a glass of water.

'Heath is an Echo without a confirmed match. This is a dangerous time for him. If they can't match him,' Toby shrugs. 'You know milking is a waste with Echo's,' I nod stunned with understanding.

'They will match him?' I bite my lip.

'Probably but if his behaviour prevents him from a successful mating, they will euthanise,'

'It is just a bit of fun,' I murmur.

'For you maybe, for him it will have serious consequences if they catch you,' Toby remarks as he pushes the door open to the dining hall. I, however, am grabbed from behind and manhandled into a closet. Damn, I hate being small. My train of thought cut off by lips crashing against mine, the smell of citrus invades my senses.

'Heath I will miss lunch,' I moan.

'We only have tomorrow, and you will be gone,' he grumbles seeking my mouth again.

'Heath, we shouldn't,'

'Aaron,' he moans and kisses me again I feel he is mocking me again.

'Heath, if we get caught, they could kill you,' I blurt. He steps back and studies me.

'What did Toby say,'

'That, it is wrong that you could die,'

'Aaron, it will be fine. I have a match. I know my duty,' he sighs and takes my hand. 'Come on,' pulling me from the cupboard.

The smell of sausages and onion gravy drifts around me and my tummy grumbles as we take our seats. Heath sat next to me looking perfect while I look rumpled as usual. Toby rolls his eyes at my dishevelment and shakes his head.

The Mothers stand as we are about to leave. A hush descends on the hall. I glance at Toby. We are being moved early. They do this to reduce the chance of us being stolen. Heath takes my hand his expression devastated.

'Numbers 304011 to 306011 please stand and follow me,' Toby and I both glance at the number tattooed on our wrists and then get up with the dozen other boys. Heath pulls at my hand a lone tear tracks down his cheek as he lets my hand go. This is over I will never see him again. I bite my lip as I try to keep it together.

My attention captured by two company guards entering the hall, they converse with a Mother and then march over to two boys hauling them to their feet. They stop by the Mothers and a brief exchange takes place. One Mother looks at the boy and slaps his face. Then the boys are removed.

'Aaron,' Toby takes my hand.

'This way please,' they usher us out of the room. I hear the buzz of conversation start up as the doors swing closed behind me.

'Aaron, you need to control yourself. If they had caught you, he would have been taken,' Toby locks his gaze with mine.

'I know, but I love him,'

'I know Aaron, but you have to focus on this to keep him safe,' I nod as we jog to catch up with the group.

They lead us along the corridor to the hall. Stepping through the door, Girls greet us. I blink as Gilly saunters over to me.

'Missed me,' she smirks as she wraps her arms around me and gives me a hug.

'Always,' I reply to be rewarded with her laughter.

'Ah, Aaron has your little heart broken,' she mocks as I nod. She was the only person I told in our emails to each other. 'They knew I had to step in to protect your little friend.' I blink and swallow. They knew, crashes in my head. 'He is matched. It is up to him now,'

'Did you match him?' I turn wide eyes to her.

'Yes, I took a personal interest,'

'He is safe?'

'You are such a fragile thing. I had to protect you. If he conforms and does as he has been trained, yes,'

'I loved him Gilly,' my whispered response.

'Of course, you did,' she reaches up and kisses me. 'You must forget him,'

'I... yes,' I hang my head. 'How,' I look up at her.

'Well, you have me now and I will teach you to protect that fragile heart of yours,' she smiles and kisses my cheek.

CHAPTER 6

*I*nsects buzz around my head as Gillian tickles my chin with a daisy. We have been together for two years now. They moved me to what was France. It possibly is still France, but a lot of countries lost their identity and their men. They house us in a facility run by Gen-Corp. Gillian lives here with me. When I am in the medical wing, she is learning to run a global business. At eighteen, I am not so runty. I am still small, not quite six feet. Gillian is … well, perfect. My best friend and partner.

We are in the walled garden around us, the remains of our picnic. I am laid on my back, my eyes closed as I soak up the sun. Gilly is laid on her front next to me, her feet in the air as she annoys me with her daisy. A rare day to ourselves.

'Aaron, can I kiss you?' My eyes shoot open to peer into her face which is currently only inches from mine. She has been making advances toward me for a while now. This is the first time she has been so direct.

'Why?'

'To compare,' she answers with as much innocence as she can muster.

'You kissed Adam,' pushing up I glare at her.

'He is so stroppy, and it is so hot,' she shrugs.

'Gilly,' I moan.

'What, he is nothing like you. Running away and hooking up with the United Human Federation. Then meets this girl only she isn't any girl. No, she is a princess of Tribe,' Gillian huffs clearly annoyed as I burst out laughing. She slaps me lightly on the chest.

'Aaron it isn't funny, he is looking for you the idiot,'

'Gilly, what did you tell him?' Her hair is in her face from all the gesticulating. Reaching up, I smooth it and tuck it behind her ears.

'To stop looking for you,'

'What else?'

'I made a deal with him,' she huffs. 'It isn't fair. Tribe will get you both now, and I am stuck with horrid Thom. He hates me, Aaron.' she looks at me all forlorn. Even though I want to be cross, I just can't.

'Gillian,' I cajole. 'What deal did you make?'

She huffs. 'He is at some dumb settlement embracing the rural life. I mean what a waste of all that education,' I roll my eyes at her outburst.

'What, why can't he be like you?' she pouts, so I lean forward and kiss her. I enjoy kissing her.

'Gilly leave him alone, yeah,' she pouts at me again.

'Only if I can have you.' she kisses me again, her hand at the waistband of my shorts. I pull it up and feel her smile against my lips.

'I need him though,' she grumbles pulling back a pout on her lips.

'So, what was the deal?'

'I told him I would protect him and that girl until he is twenty and then he has to come and work for me.' She shrugs and leans in to kiss me again. I let her.

'Do you think he will do that?'

'Oh yeah, he is all noble, and he has had some brushes with death and such already. He told me he loves her,' Gilly pouts again.

'Maybe he does is that such a bad thing?' She looks at me like I am stupid.

'Did you love that boy?' She asks. We never spoke about Heath after. 'Or that girl when we lost you?'

'Yes,' I consider my words. 'I was lonely and frightened. You know about my future and the match. He was exciting and forbidden. You all forget we are still teenage boys with hormones.' I sit up. 'Do you have pictures?' my voice hopeful.

'Of course,' she fishes out her phone and passes it to me. I slide my finger across and tap on recent photos. There he is giggling into the camera between Janey and Melissa. He has my eyes but his mother's colouring. He is sturdy. A happy, healthy three-year-old. A smile dances over my lips as I look through the latest pictures of my son Edward. I give back the phone.

'Want to have sex,' She pushes me down I don't resist.

'What if we bond?' I raise a brow.

'Your brother doesn't care about that,' Gilly moans while making puppy dog eyes at me. 'Besides, what about those hormones?' she fixes me with her intense gaze? 'Mum would be thrilled if we did. She spends more time with Edward than me.' She pouts, and it is all I can do not to laugh.

'How long are you staying?' Sitting up I reach for my water. Ignoring her outburst about my brother's private life. Frankly I find it gross thinking about him like that. The last time I saw him he was still a child.

'Just tonight you are scheduled to the medical centre tomorrow and I have to fly to London,' I groan at that, and she giggles. 'You start your training for your match. Mum wants you to have political training,'

'Oh, why? That sounds really dull,'

'They matched you to a princess of Tribe,'

'A princess? How many are there?'

'Oh, um four that are eligible to be matched even the heir. Oh, only three now your brother has one,' she pulls a sour face and I chuckle until she slaps my shoulder and pushes me down.

'Have you met them?'

'Yes, once, they are all right,'

'Going to elaborate on that?'

'Only if I can kiss you,' she giggles, and I chuckle back.

'Sure,' Grabbing her I pull her down beneath me and kiss her soundly.

* * *

TODAY I AM IN GEN-CORPS' main medical centre. It is part of the building I spend most of my time in. I have been in here about six weeks while they run their tests. I am eighteen next week and being moved to start my political training. A Château and I am quite excited about that. The Château not the training.

I am currently laid on my back on a bed in a hospital type room. I am not alone two doctors are stood in the room watching me and talking. Apparently, they're my personal doctors. The tall, skinny one is Patricia. She is a beaky looking woman in her forties. Her grey, brown hair is always up in a bun and there is nothing friendly about her. She is cold and clinical. Her colleague is a mousey looking woman called Deborah who rarely speaks and views me as an inconvenient problem that often annoys and doesn't give the results she requires and right now I am being annoying.

'How are the results, girls?' I smile cheekily and they both blush?

'Well, if we can stabilise your antibodies, we may be able to culture a vaccine that we could use, but that is proving difficult,' Patricia frowns and studies her notes.

I am special apparently, as I am immune to the contaminant. They are currently giving it to me and then taking blood samples in the hope they can culture a vaccine and eventually a cure. That is fine! I don't mind that, if I can help cure this world, why not? The downside is every time they do; it makes me sick, and I don't know how long I can cope with it all.

'So, still not allowed to test my brother or son,' I smirk as I throw my tennis ball at the wall and catch it, I know it annoys them, but I don't care.

'That information is classified, and you know it,' Deborah rebukes me and I stop throwing my ball for a second to scowl at her.

'Can this be my last day, girls,' I ask this every day and I already know the answer, but I still ask.

'No, we want to run a few more tests,' Deborah informs me in her clinical way. They always have a few more tests.

'Look at these results, his weight has plummeted, and he isn't eating, if this keeps up, I want him moved so that he can be force fed,' Patricia tuts and I hear the rustle of paper as she examines my notes, as I scowl at her, I don't like that idea.

'Hmm, perhaps,' the rattle of the trolley and the door swishing open indicates the girl that brings my meals has arrived.

'You could just let me be, you know give me a day off,' I retort and stop throwing my ball, I turn over and get comfortable. I am so tired; I don't know what they are giving me, but I am always exhausted.

'Hi, Aaron, ready for lunch, you must be you didn't eat your breakfast,' she sits on my bed, she always does, and, in a minute, she will touch me, I usually growl at her but today I can't be bothered.

'That was breakfast? I thought you were getting me a pet, and that was its dinner.' I grin and then go back to ignoring her, throwing my ball against the wall.

'Yeah, yeah, hilarious. I see you are your normal happy self.'

'Always,' is my answer with a smirk pulling at my lips, obviously looking her over.

Her white coat is open revealing her shirt and jeans; she rarely dresses in anything that isn't casual. The look suits her, with her slim figure and short hair it accentuates her cheeky look. Her mouth is turned up in a cheery smile and her eyes dart over me taking in every detail. Despite her ditsy appearance she is highly intelligent and shouldn't be under-estimated. She pats my shoulder like a naughty child and turns her attention to the doctors.

'Hello doctors, going to stick more needles in him?' She raises a perfectly shaped brow that gives her a slight pixie look. I think I would like her if circumstances were different.

'No, Naomi, we are not, we want to know why he isn't eating,' Patricia answers her tone annoyed and sulky at the same time. I can't help myself and smile.

'Oh, that's easy, he's depressed,' Naomi answers in her happy, cheerful voice. Stroking my face with her fingers, I bat her hand away and scowl at her.

'Yeah, I am so depressed, can I have some happy pills,' I drawl and Naomi scowls at me this time, so I smile sweetly back.

'Ah, yes prescribe him some tablets,' Patricia answers in her dead flat voice, she doesn't view me as a person, just her latest project. I let out an audible sigh and go back to throwing my ball.

'What? No,' Naomi glares at them and me. 'I thought you were clever,' she huffs, a frown wrinkling her perfect brows.

'Well, I am, but I can't answer for you girls,' I remark flippantly causing the doctors to glare at me.

'We are clever, how else do we make him better if we can't give him medication,' the tall scientist frowns, marring her perfect features. She looks at me and a look of annoyance settles on her face.

'Give him back his freedom, show him the garden, let him go outside,' Naomi glares at the two doctors. Oh, way to go Naomi.

'We can't do that, the risks are too great,' Deborah answers as she studies me. I sigh, run away. I don't have the energy to walk away, let alone run. What risks this place has so many guards it is ridiculous.

'What risks?' I frown looking between the three of them what aren't they telling.

'You could just give him his own bodyguard,' I perk up at this, it sounds like they might let me outside again.

'Please let me out, I promise to eat my lunch,' I beg, hey I'm not proud. I stop throwing my ball and sit up straight looking at them all.

'She has a point,' Patricia runs her finger along her bottom lip as she gazes at me dispassionately, totally ignoring my pleas.

'Yes, the last batch failed. We are missing something important. Maybe we should see if he can do it naturally, as we can't do it artificially. As soon as we take his sample, it degrades at an alarming rate. I believe we can only use him if he inseminates naturally.' She looks at me, her finger tapping her chin, a sour expression on her face, which is directed at me.

'We should get the girl back he likes her. See if they can

do it naturally a baby would be marvellous,' Patricia almost smiles. I raise both my brows at her statement.

'Doctor Echo's notes are so incomplete, until we get a live result I can't compare,' the two scientists turn and leave the room talking about their failed experiments; I shudder as I know what they are referring too. I go back to throwing my ball against the wall.

'Aaron, honey, eat?' Naomi puts her hand on my shoulder, and I flinch. She frowns and takes my wrist and takes my pulse, making me drop my ball. She picks it up and hands it to me, peering at me with her brown eyes as she does so. I feel bad about being horrible to her, as she tries her hardest to make it all bearable and sometimes, I get the impression she doesn't approve of this.

'What, yeah whatever,' shuffle up the bed getting comfortable so I can throw my ball again, effectively dismissing her. She ignores my blatant rudeness.

'Toby is right you are a right moody git,' she smooths her coat and pulls her shirt down about to flounce out.

'Wait, how do you know Toby?' I sit up and narrow my eyes at her as she turns to look at me.

'Of course, I know Toby. You didn't honestly think he would let you be in here without someone watching you, making sure they don't terminate you, by accident,'

'Gillian wouldn't allow them to harm me,' I snap back. 'Wait, Toby who is he?' I frown.

'He was your watcher as per the agreement with The Human Federation,'

'Hang on what agreement?'

'Aaron you are special and matched to someone important as well as partnered to Thelma's daughter. Let's not forget you are proven. Lots of protocols had to be put in place to keep you safe,'

She glares at me and then moves to the door, stopping

she looks back at me. 'You need to eat again, Aaron.' I settle back against my pillows and think about what she said.

'Well tell them to stop the drug it makes me sick,' I glare at her and feel satisfaction when she flinches slightly.

'They are. This trial is over,' she steps nearer. 'Thom has found him.' I can only describe her smile as triumphant, and I think I hate her that bit more.

'Who has Thom found,' I say this slowly and clearly so there can be no mistake.

'Your brother,' she puts her hand up pressing against my chest, stopping me leaping out of bed.

'He wasn't lost,' I raise a brow at her look of surprise. Pushing her hand off me as I lean up.

'He escaped, ran away, looking for you apparently,' she sounds annoyed and amazed at the same time. I for my part can't help the chuckle that escapes my lips.

'Yeah, I know Gillian told me,'

'What did she tell you?'

'Oh, that he was farming or some such,'

'Farming,' Naomi snorts. 'He fixed a solar farm, got it running a village and surrounding farms. He project managed the renovation of the dairy and worked out how to make cheese,' Naomi chuckled.

'Wow, didn't completely waste his education then,'

'No, that boy is far too clever for his own good. Word travels you know,'

'So where is he now?'

'Not entirely sure,' I can't help it and laugh. Who would have thought my quiet little brother could cause so much chaos. 'There was some sort of military thing he got caught up in,' she shrugs as I raise a brow. 'I think the Federation people have him again,' I can't help but laugh at the chaos he is causing.

'It isn't funny,' she is indignant now and I find that even more amusing. 'It attracts unwanted attention,'

'Well, maybe he doesn't want to go with you a lot.' I roll my eyes and hope Adam is far away from these people.

'So, what's the plan what do you need me for?' I gaze at her with an intensity that makes her blush and elicits a smile from me. 'He is in trouble, isn't he?' I raise a brow as her blush deepens.

'Well Thom has an intelligence report that indicates this particular group have been looking for Echo children. Looking for him.'

'So, what do you need me for?'

'Thom wants to use you as a distraction,' raising my brows in surprise at this suggestion. 'Give him and Gilly time to locate your brother and keep him safe,'

'Um, how?'

'Thom is going to leak information to them. Reveal an echo child is here and hopefully they will attack this facility.'

'That's crazy. What if you get hurt? What if I get hurt?'

'Oh, you care,' she ruffles my hair in a very annoying fashion, and I push her away.

'It will be fine your new bodyguard will look out for you and then take you to the next safe place to meet your match.'

'What does Gillian think?'

'Thom hasn't told her!' Naomi looks away, so she doesn't see the incredulous look on my face.

'Bloody hell,' I mutter.

'So, eat your dinner and I will get permission for you to go outside, you need to be strong Aaron, if this idiot plan is to work.'

Naomi is true to her word, and I am allowed back in the garden. I am slightly unnerved by the guard that follows me a few paces behind. Naomi assures me that the guard is sworn to protect me and will make everything authentic. I still think Thom's plan is nuts.

I find a bench and settle myself. We are near the sea. I have never seen the sea until I came here. I gaze at it for a while and breathe in the salty air. I would love to stand in it, but today I don't have the energy to walk down the cliff path, never mind back up it. So, I content myself by just looking at it.

Remembering the summers Gilly and I enjoyed. Forgetting how our lives were so controlled as we played in the sunshine. A smile spreads across my face. I really miss her if I am honest, and I don't relish meeting the new person I must be with. Expected to breed. This fills me with apprehension.

According to the app on my laptop, I am in what was once Europe. To be fair, it still is Europe but now it is divided differently. I am in what was once France, southern France, so the climate is quite pleasant. All of this now belongs to Gen-Corp along with what was once Spain and Italy and parts of Portugal. Germany and Russia are no-man's-land and are sparsely populated. Scandinavia is unknown, the app says closed. I think this is a glitch. You can't close a group of countries, can you?

Gillian gave me my laptop. I slide my finger across the screen and enter the password. She sends me reports to read and asks my opinion.

I find a report on the Adam program and its failure, settling to read it. I wonder why Gillian is letting me read this. I am so engrossed I don't hear Naomi walk over and sit next to me.

'Aaron, I have your lunch,' I look up seeing her smile as her eyes land on me before she plops down on the bench next to me, passing a plastic box of sandwiches.

'Oh thanks,' I take the lid off and pick up a sandwich my stomach growls and I realise how hungry I am.

'You need to come in, it's getting cold out here,' she takes my hand and rubs it. 'I am going to the village tomorrow I will get you a hat and gloves, if you are going to spend all your time out here,' she smiles at me, and I want to like her but there is something about her.

'Oh, um, yeah,' I eat the last sandwich and then pack my things away before climbing to my feet, following Naomi. My guard follows behind me. I glance at the building before climbing the set of stone stairs that flank either side of the plain doors that lead you into this amazing building. Well chateau as this is France, it fascinates me with its gothic architecture. I found its original plans in the library. Gillian laughed at me, but I didn't care, as I spent a couple of afternoons studying them.

I lay on my bed Naomi insists I have a nap in the afternoons. I am not tired but go along with it.

'Aaron are you asleep,' Gillian's voice is urgent as she bursts into my room. I pull my house coat on. 'We were too late. They shot him,' she blurts as tears spill over.

'Slow down who did they shoot?' I pull her to me. My arms around her.

'Adam, they shot Adam,' she snuffles as I let her step back.

'Is he dead?' my voice a whisper.

'No, he is in theatre they are removing the bullet,'

'I thought he was farming. Making cheese and stuff,' I exclaim as I follow her along the corridor. She gives a humourless laugh.

'This is your brother he never does *just*,'

The room is quiet. Antiseptic mingled with every breath I take. I abandon my book in my lap as I watch the occupant of the bed. My younger brother well admittedly only by five minutes. I shut my eyes, remembering Gillian's pale face as she barged into my room to tell me there had been an accident. Resulting in my brother being shot. Shot, how the hell did that happen? He was supposed to be safe with Emma, our childhood Mother. It turned out he ran. That was what almost two years ago. Gillian isn't sure where he has been, but he surfaced in a village living with a girl. When he first ran, he hooked up with The United Human federation, but they lost him.

I sigh and run a hand through my hair. 'Come on Adam wake up,' I mutter.

'Aaron?' I surge to my feet at his hoarse voice.

'Hey, how are you,' Moving to his bedside I pass him the glass of water with the straw. He takes a few sips and lays back down.

'They told me you died,' his eyes close.

'No, not yet' I whisper. 'So joined the resistance?' he gives a chuckle and winces.

'No, ran away and ran straight into them,'

'Was that before or after you decided to farm?' He chuckles again.

'Met this girl. Several actually. Girls bonkers, the lot of them,'

'Yeah, tell me about it.'

'Aaron, missed you,' his voice drifts.

'Yeah, the same. You sleep,' I return to my seat, watching him sleep.

'Aaron,' Naomi's quiet voice alerts me to the door opening. 'Come on sweetie bedtime,' she pulls me up into a hug. 'He is being returned to his home.'

'Oh, right?' I shuffle to the bed and bend to kiss him. 'Where does he live?' I frown as I turn to her.

'He belongs to a farming community. They have a few Adams and families,'

'Is he safe there?'

'Yes, Gillian and Tribe monitor it.' She takes my hand and leads me from the room. I pull free and stride to the bed.

'Get well mate,' I kiss his head.

'AARON, YOU ASLEEP?' Gillian enters the room, quietly closing the door. I hear her pad about the room. The clatter as she kicks off her shoes and the rustle as she removes her clothes. I wonder what she is up to. Why she is in my room? Although she often sleeps with me.

'No.'

'We may have sex?' Is all she says as she kisses me. Crawling on the bed in just the scrapes of material she calls underwear.

'Yeah, they want me to get you pregnant.' I gaze at her to gauge her reaction.

'Hmm, it might be fun. I have been learning about it,' she giggles.

'Have you really?' I chuckle at her answer. Raising a brow.

'So shall we,' she smirks in what I think is a suggestive gesture. I try not to laugh. 'Please Aaron, you won't be mine soon. You will have to be with your Match,' Gilly pouts.

'Thanks for reminding me,' I groan at the thought of just being given to a complete stranger.

'It's just sex, Aaron,' she is straddling my thighs, having pushed the duvet out the way. Her fingers fiddle with the waistband of my pyjama bottoms. It is then I realise she was asking out of politeness, nothing more. I don't really have a choice. It's an illusion to make me feel comfortable.

'Wow, thanks,' I mutter. She snorts as she rubs against me. I place my hands on her hips.

'You have done it before. Successfully, I might add,' she raises a brow.

'Gilly, I don't want them to have our baby.' I gaze up at her, my lip caught in my teeth, worry etched into my features.

'That won't happen,' she reassures me. Her fingers run along my lip, easing it free.

'Oh, did you have the lesson with the banana?' I ask.

She giggles. 'No, I did not,'

'Lucky you,' my answer dry.

'I miss you when I am away,' she kisses me.

'Cause you do,' pulling her beneath me, eliciting groans of pleasure.

* * *

I roll out of bed and grab my house coat from its hook. Pulling it on, I ambled down the hall to the stairs. Gilly never stays, just takes what she wants and leaves. This is fine by me. She has embraced this sex thing and I find it exhausting. It is dark and quiet as I make my way to the kitchen to get a drink of milk. The nearer I get, I can hear voices and laughter. I stop unsure and then shrugging my shoulders, I continued toward the kitchen.

I pushed the door open to find a group of the staff sat around the table, glasses in front of them and several bottles on the table. They all stop and turn to look at me as I hover in the doorway, unsure and a little self-conscious. Now every face in the room is looking in my direction. Andrea is the first to react and pushes Naomi off her lap and climbing to her feet, she advances toward me.

'Andrea will teach boy to drink like a Russian,' she laughs and slaps my back leading me to a vacant seat she pushes me down into it and selecting a glass and bottle she pours me a drink.

'What is this?' I ask cautiously, looking to Naomi, who is swaying slightly as she stands next to Andrea.

'It is Vodka boy, make you a man,' Andrea announces and

putting her glass to her lips she empty's the glass in one go, she then indicates I should do the same, which I do, with a lot of coughing and watery eyes, followed by raucous laughter from the occupants of the room. That seemed to be the ice breaker, as the conversations started up again, as did the drinking. I slump down on the table, my head on my arms. I have no idea of the time or how much I have drunk.

'Boy, needs his bed,' Andrea announces and scoops me up.

'I don't feel so good Andrea?' I mumble into her enormous chest as she carries me from the kitchen back up the stairs to my room. Naomi follows, swaying as she goes and giggling a lot. Andrea kicks the door open and strides to the bed. She puts me down and I just lay their unable to move. 'Andrea,' I announce, all serious, an enormous grin on my face.

'Yes Aaron,' Andrea slurs.

'Thank you,' I manage and then I run to the bathroom to throw up the entire contents of my stomach and pass out. I hear Andrea chuckle as she wipes my face and then picks me up and places me in bed.

'We had better stay with him, in case he is sick again,' Naomi suggests and giggles again, I crack one eye open to see them making out and I am grateful when the darkness takes me again. I don't want to see that, and I am never drinking again.

Two days Naomi kept me in my room and Andrea told me Naomi was very cross, but Andrea kissed her out of her bad mood over me. I laughed at that and wanted to know how long they had been together. Andrea's voice always softened when she talks about Naomi, and I had noticed how Andrea's eyes followed Naomi if she was in the room.

Today I am going to sit on the beach, I like it down here and I am stronger now the doctors have left me alone. I amble down the path and find a spot out of the wind where the sun can warm me up. I watch Andrea, for a bit as she walks around the beach. Going to each end looking for other ways off the beach. I like Andrea, she is Russian and although she says very little, I think she likes me. Gilly and I used to spend our summers down here.

Her small form stalks around the beach looking for any sign of intruders, her short dark brown hair blows in the breeze from the sea. She doesn't look how I imagined a bodyguard should look. Her sharp brown eyes miss very little, and I know she is strong from when she got me drunk and carried me to bed that time.

I return my attention to my laptop and the latest report Gilly has sent me; I am understanding now how something that should have been our saviour caused our downfall.

I look up as Andrea stiffens and moves to the start of the path that leads back up to the house. I can hear popping noises and wonder what they are as I go back to the report I am reading on the Adam program. She sends me all this stuff to read; she emails as well, flirting in between the serious stuff. That girl thinks about nothing else but what she has planned for me next time she is here. I enjoy her company. She is witty and very sharp, and I enjoy the challenge of her.

'Aaron,' Andrea calls and I look up again.

'Yeah.'

'Just stay here a minute, no matter what you hear don't follow me, understood,' I nod my head, and a shiver runs down my spine.

'Um, yeah, okay,' I manage and watch as she disappears up the cliff path. I get up and move off the beach. I sit near one of the sand dunes that will conceal me from the path if anyone other than Andrea comes down. I don't know why I do this; it just seems sensible.

I do not know how long I wait as I go back to my laptop. I only look up when I hear Andrea call my name. I don't get up as she has drummed into me not to for security. I shout from my place.

'Yeah, Andrea,' I stay sitting as she has taught me.

'I need you to come here,' she whispers. I climb to my feet, shutting down my laptop and pushing it into my bag. I see Andrea hurry over to me. She takes my arm and pulls me along the beach away from the path, I find this odd.

'What's going on?' I manage as we run.

'We are under attack and Madam Ramsbottom entrusted you into my care,' she answers tersely as she pulls me behind an outcrop of rock, she pushes me down and takes her pistol from its holster. I sit quietly as she peers over the rock watching the beach. It isn't long before we hear voices.

'Helena said to search the beach, she said he is here somewhere, and we are not leaving without him.'

'What the hell, what's so special about this one? Ever since we raided Glasgow, she has been hunting Blond, blue-eyed boys.'

'Yeah, well, I heard there is special, an Echo child, and he is worth a small fortune.'

'Maybe if we find him, we should keep him, sell him to the highest bidder, after we have had the pleasure, obviously,' I shudder at this and look at Andrea, my eyes wide with fear. If that is true what is stopping Andrea from doing the same. She must have seen my expression and smiles at me in reassurance.

'I am sworn to protect you,' she whispers, and I relax slightly. The women on the beach are getting closer and the tide is coming in there is no escape I realise. I look at Andrea, poised, ready to protect me, and I know someone else is going to die because of me.

Andrea's gun going off shocks the life out of me, so when it goes off the second time, I shudder as she grabs hold of me.

'Aaron there are too many of them. You are going to be

taken. Don't fight them. I will find you okay,' my eyes widen at what she is suggesting. 'Aaron, do you understand?' Her voice is urgent as her eyes dart around the beach and then land on me.

'Ye...yes I understand,'

'Good boy,' Andrea gazes around and then steps out from our hiding spot. Her hands in the air, her gun hanging from her left hand. I step out behind her and raise my hands. Watching as they circle us.

'We surrender please don't damage him,' Andrea addresses them slowly reaching for me. She moves me toward them. One of them pulls me forward. I automatically bow my head and place my hands behind my back.

'Well, well, look at you a true Echo, perfect for our little Echo girl,' she smirks at me as she runs her hands over me. I stand still, too frightened to move in case they shoot me. I am pulled around and my hands are bound behind my back.

'Move,' a hand shoves me hard and I stumble before regaining my balance.

CHAPTER 7

A pair of arms wrap around me and haul me to my feet, and I am vaguely aware of being dragged up a path, the smell of damp earth and the sea filling my nostrils.

I blink as I emerge into sunlight and notice the temperature is slightly warmer now. We are in the open. The acrid smell of burning assaults my senses but I don't have the energy to turn my head to see where it is coming from, although I have smelt that before, when I ran with my Mother.

When I was fourteen. The home I was in was attacked and raised to the ground. The staff and any Mothers were murdered. They took the boys to be playthings. My Mother got me away but died later in my arms. Lucky for me, a girl found me and kept me safe until Gen-Corp troopers came.

For this reason, the homes the boys are kept in are heavily guarded. Their locations kept secret. You wouldn't find my home on any map. I know the dangers out here. I had no interest in being free and struggle to understand why Adam would run away. Especially as I am now confronted with the biggest threat to my well-being.

I am lifted on to a horse. 'Don't try anything stupid,' her breath fans over my neck and ear as her arm snakes around me holding me tight.

The light is fading as the night draws around us. I am numb from the cold now just running on automatic pilot. Out of the gloom a building seems to rise its broken walls like fingers reaching upward. Behind it stands a house. Smoke curls leisurely from its chimney shimmering against the dusk.

I am lifted down and guided inside. The warmth from the fire makes my cheeks heat as I stand next to my captor. I see a few eyes on me, and I shiver again, ducking my head as my stomach clenches with nerves. I am far from safe here. Two women stand at the bar drinking wine, and they are blatantly looking me over.

'Oh look, isn't he cute,' one woman says, glancing at me?

'Some of them are just adorable, I heard they breed the aggression out of them,' another woman replies sipping her wine.

'Excuse me,' the first woman attracts my captors' attention. She narrows her eyes and glares at them.

'How much to have him for the night?' I blink at her question and await the answer.

'He is not available sorry,' She does what I think is a smile but honestly it makes her look menacing.

'Well, that is a shame as I would have made it worth your while,' Red wine woman answers. Looking me over one more time she turns back to her companion. Resuming their conversation.

'I heard you can go to that spa and be inseminated naturally. They buy up the retired ones.' red wine woman reveals her expression bland as if she is talking about the weather.

'Oh, really, is intercourse trendy again? Can't say I fancy it, doesn't sound very sanitary.' white wine woman grimaces.

'Shame he is very cute,' red wine says, her voice wistful.

'Must be special for that amount of protection,' the two women smile at me when they catch my eye before I am led away.

'In you go,' I am shoved into a dark room. I stand still for a moment while my eyes adjust to the gloom. I am not alone.

The first thing I do is get my hands in front of me by manoeuvring and wriggling my body. The whole time I am sure I am being watched that I am not alone in here. Where they are, I don't know.

With my hands free I drag a chair and jam it under the door handle so no one can barge in when I am asleep. Walking around the room I check the door opposite the bed to find a bathroom.

I have a much-needed shower and then lay on the bed feeling exhausted. The room is basic, but clean and warm. I need some sort of plan. They want to breed me. That much is obvious. That isn't happening. Curling up, I decide to sleep. I won't be able to protect myself if I am tired.

The bed dipping is the first indication they have come out of hiding. I was sure they were in the wardrobe, and I made a point of not looking in it.

'Hi,' they freeze at the sound of my voice. I can feel them trembling. 'I won't hurt you if you don't hurt me,' I say keeping my voice soft. Slowly I sit up. Before me is a small girl. Her long pale hair is a mess, and her clothes are crumpled. Large blue eyes much like mine blink at me. I smile and I am rewarded by a brief smile from her.

'Hello, I am Aaron,' I smile again and wait for her answer.

'Rita, my name is Rita,' her voice was so quiet I had to strain to hear it.

'Rita lovely,'

'You aren't scared?'

'Well, yes I am but I am certain they won't hurt me as they want me to breed with a girl they have,'

'Don't you want to escape?'

'In an ideal world I would but this isn't ideal. I don't know where I am, and I know people will hunt them down to get me back. So, I figured my job was to stay alive,' I shrug.

'People will search for me as well,' she frowns. 'It makes no sense why they would put themselves in so much danger?'

'I am extremely valuable. They said they had a girl like me. If that is the case the reward is worth the risk,'

'You aren't an Adam?'

'No, I am an Echo,'

'Oh, that is bad so, so bad,' her lip wobbles and her eyes tear up. I am not sure why that bit of information is so bad.

'Hey, it's okay,' I reassure. 'Look, why don't you have a shower and then you can sleep here with me. No one will hurt you. I promise. Then in the morning when we are both well rested, we can form a plan. Yeah,' I smile again as she nods her head and climbs off the bed. I listen as the shower runs. I am almost asleep when she comes out rubbing her hair dry. Taking a band from her wrist she quickly braids it securing it with the tie. I feel the bed dip as she climbs in. Before snuggling in to me. I wrap my arms around her.

'Thank you,'

'You are welcome,'

Banging on the door wakes me. This is followed by shouting. Clambering out of bed I pull my jeans on and amble to the door. Removing the chair, I open it to be confronted by three cross women.

'Morning girls,' my greeting cocky as I smile brightly. Casting my gaze over the three of them. They are dressed in black leather and normally they would intimidate me, but last night I reconsidered and decided to play them at their own game. Now yes, this could get me killed, but frankly, we are past that point.

'You locked the door,' the accusation has me smiling wider.

'Well, yeah, even I don't relish being raped.' I cross my arms over my chest and lean against the door frame. My entire posture is casual. They all blink at me with a stupefied expression. 'Okay girls, here's the deal,' I say as the silence continues. 'What time are we leaving, and could I possibly have some breakfast first? You know I am just a monster without my morning tea.' I raise a brow as they continue to stare at me. As another woman marches up to them.

'Here, we leave in ten be ready,' she shoves a tray into my hands and turning stalks off the others follow her as I step back into the room and shut the door. Leaning against it I take in a shaky breath.

'You were amazing,' the girl, Rita is now dressed, and her hair is in a tidy ponytail.

'Yeah, they are bloody terrifying,' I answer putting the tray down I pull on my shirt and jumper. Finding my boots and my socks I pull those on while the girl explores the tray.

CHAPTER 8

'Ready?' I survey Rita. She is wrapped in a deep red cloak with gold piping and a crest of some sort on one side over a pocket. She nods and I hold my hand out to her. As I feel her fingers wrap around mine, I push open the door. Two women wait. They walk toward the stairs, and I dutifully follow.

The place is deserted this morning. In the daylight it looks even worse than it did last night. The tables grimy and probably sticky with alcohol. The air still has a smoky smell mingled with alcohol and unwashed bodies. The bar covered in unwashed glasses and empty bottles. Rita's hand tightens around mine as I lead her outside.

The weak sunshine gives a soft glow to everything bathed in a tinge of gold. I take in the six women stood waiting, each holding a horse. They are all dressed the same, in black leathers. All have their hair tied back with bandannas and it just makes them look even more menacing if that is possible. I feel Rita stiffen beside me. I also notice the amount of visible weapons. My mind counting them while working out how many are concealed.

'She rides with me,' I state boldly. Yeah, the weapons thing, totally disregarded it.

'Can you ride boy?' A few sniggers follow that question, and it is all I can do not to roll my eyes. Because frankly that was beyond childish.

'Yes,' my answer immediate.

'Can we trust you?' one stands in front of me. If she is trying to intimidate me well, she has succeeded. I hold my ground though determined not to show weakness.

'Look, as mad as this seems out here, I am safer with you than without you.' I raise a brow. One woman walks over to me, leading a horse. She hands me the reins.

'Try anything, anything at all and you will be sorry,' she stands, so she is looking directly into my eyes. I hold eye contact with her. Taking a sigh, as if this is an everyday occurrence.

'Like I said I am safer with you than without,' I cock my head to one side and smirk. She steps closer. Lowering her voice she looks directly at me.

'They warned me you were clever. Make no mistake if you try anything I will shoot you. Maybe not to kill but I will hurt you just the same,' She steps away and one of the other women hands her the reins to a horse. I lift Rita up and then bounce up myself, getting comfortable with Rita in front of me.

'Aaron what are you planning,' she whispers at me.

'Nothing until I know where we are. We really are safer with them,' I brush her hair from her ear as I lean forward. 'We need to bide our time give Andrea chance,'

'Who is Andrea?'

'My body guard. She will be hunting us,' the horses and riders move out the courtyard and I follow. I am manoeuvred into the middle of them. I never wanted to be free. I can't comprehend what Adam was even thinking. How was this better? If one of these imbeciles doesn't kill me by accident some moron trying to take me from them might. Then there is the sickness. Out here I can't screen it out and eventually I will get sick. Life threateningly sick. Yeah, I read all the reports Gilly sent. I know exactly how my body works. Frankly none of that appeals. So, I am going to have to come up with some sort of plan. With a sigh I glance at Rita she is Echo. I can feel the pull building already I want to take her. Damn my stupid genetics that right now are another thing trying to kill me.

'Aaron you alright?' Her timid voice pulls me from my morbid thoughts.

'Yeah, outstanding,' I mutter and feel the giggle that makes her slight frame tremble. 'I will get sick out here,' I grumble to myself.

'We both will,' she sighs.

'What, but you are a girl?' I stutter.

'I still get sick; I am like you. It is me they want you to have sex with. They know we won't be able to help it, eventually. Why do you think they put you in that room with me?' She draws in a breath. 'You weren't the first. They have been dragging me all over trying to find a boy. The right boy,' She slumps down, defeated. 'I just want to go home.' her voice quivers.

'Do you know where we are now? Which part of France?'

'Why? What difference does it make?'

'Some bits are more contaminated than others,' With a shrug I go back to driving the horse.

'What you two talking about?' one woman moves close to us.

'I am Echo I will get sick,' I look at her watching for her reaction. She makes a derisive laugh.

'Getting sick is the least of your problems when the bond cements you to her,'

'Are you mad that could kill us both? Someone must monitor it,' I bark back. I can be reckless with my life, but no one else has that right. 'You know if we die you have nothing.' I raise a brow, letting arrogance paint my features.

'You won't die. There has already been a successful Echo mating. So don't think me stupid, little boy.' She takes the reins of my horse and leads us into a village. It is mostly derelict, with just a few houses still standing. A shiver makes my body flush cold.

'Aaron?'

'It's okay,' I murmur as I look round. This seems to be my go-to phrase. Because honestly, nothing about this place is okay. I pull her tight to me and inhale her scent. She lets out a small moan and I pull back, fighting the bond. The woman smirks at me as she casts a glance at me. No, I can't succumb to the bond. It will be the death of us both.

The house is large, built of stone, with two imposing chimneys at either end. As our group enters, a number of what I assume are guards watch our procession. All are heavily armed. I shiver and pull Rita closer to me.

Climbing down I lift her down and pull her into my side. The horses are led away, and we are ushered inside. The group split as three women herd us up some stairs. I gaze around at the neglected drab surroundings. A damp chill through out. I feel Rita shiver. We stop outside a solid wooden door. One-woman steps forward and unlocks it the solid clunk does nothing to calm my nerves.

Pushing it open. 'In you go,' a shove on my back has me stumble into the room. 'See you in a week. I believe that's how long it takes,' she laughs as she closes the door and the lock thumps into place.

'Aaron!'

'Still here,' I say unsure who I am trying to convince. I run my hand over the wall until my fingers graze the light switch.

Pressing it the bulb stutters and then starts to glow shedding a soft yellow light. A large four poster bed sits in the centre. That isn't what catches my attention. Sat on it is a boy and five girls all curled around him and they all look like Rita and me.

'Oh, Aaron they are collecting Echo's. This is really bad,' Rita whisper gasps as she clings to my arm. I step forward and plaster a smile on my face.

'Hello,' I greet, and I feel Rita suppress a giggle. 'What?' I frown at her. She shrugs but I can see she finds me funny. 'Politeness costs nothing,' I grumble back and Rita squeaks. I can feel her slight frame shaking so I know she is laughing.

'Aaron?' The boy extricates himself from the girls and stands up. He is decidedly grubby his clothes crumpled. His hair slightly too long. Contributing to his general air of neglect.

'Heath?' I squint as I try to reconcile this figure with the boy I loved. He rushes to me and wraps me in a hug.

'Heath, who are they?' A girl shuffles over to us and Rita sucks in a breath when she sees her belly.

'It's alright Suzy love, this is Aaron my friend from school,' Heath wraps his arm around the girl. Suzy squints her eyes as she looks at Rita.

'Princess Rita is that you?' Her voice hesitant.

'Yes,' Rita answers as the other girls crowd around.

'Will we be rescued now?' Another girl asks her round hazel eyes on Rita. 'I just want to go home,' a small sob escapes her. Suzy gathers her into her embrace.

'Hey Molly, it will be fine,'

'No, it won't you will die when that baby comes. We will all die. We are Echo's,' she turns away her anger gone as she sits on the bed and sobs.

'Are you a bonded pair?' Another girl asks.

'Yes,' I answer as they shrink back.

'Alfie you can come out,' Another girl with hair so black it seems to swallow the light around her kneels by the bed her hand disappearing beneath it. A small scruffy boy scrambles out from under the bed. He is malnourished. His clothes hang from his frame. He shivers as the girl wraps around him.

'Hush Alfie you are safe,' she comforts him.

'Hello Alfie,' I rummage in my pocket and produce a packet of biscuits that I stole from the pub. 'Here you go,' I hand him the biscuits as Rita hands him her unopened water.

'Thank you,' the girl says as she sits with him.

'What happened to him?'

'His bonded she didn't survive. To break the bond like that... well it often ends badly losing them both,' The girl answers as she wraps around him.

'Bloody hell,' I mutter running my hands through my hair.

CHAPTER 9

$\mathcal{A}$s the girls sob and comfort, one another on the bed, I stand and stare out of the window in frustration. I watch as the patrols slowly make there way along the perimeter of the fence that surrounds manor house. I try without much success to time them. Acknowledging I am tired and in the dim light it is a futile exercise.

It is getting late and the low sun in the sky is casting long shadows across the grass from the forest. As they continue their patrol, they pause and turn towards the forest. Confused, at this behaviour I look towards the forest as well. It is hard to make out in the gloom, but I could swear I saw something moving between the trees in the shadow. The patrol draw their weapons as they approach the forest. For a moment they stand still, staring into the gloom. Suddenly, they cry out and stagger backwards before turning so that I can see a long spear sticking from their chest before they stagger forward a few more steps and fall to the ground.

I cry out in shock as silhouetted figures start pouring from the forest towards the manor house.

'What is it?' Rita asks, her voice trembling. As her arm snakes around my waist I have noticed how she needs to touch me more often.

'I think we are under attack.' I pull her close. 'Something is happening, and we need to get out of here.' I say as I stride across the room and start slamming my hands on the locked door. 'Hey! Hey!' I yell as loud as I can, still banging on the door. 'Help us! Help us!' I continue yelling before someone replies from the other side.

'What's happening in there?'

'Help you have to help, there is something wrong with Rita.' I lie hoping it will be convincing.

'Alright step back. I am opening the door.' The voice responds. I hear the key turning in the lock and the door opens. Two vigilantes walk in, weapons raised. 'What's happening in here? Who is in trouble?' The leader asks scanning the room.

I back away from them eyeing their weapons cautiously as Heath and the others huddle behind me.

'There is nothing wrong with any of you.' The leader accuses angrily. 'Stop messing around and wasting our time or we'll make you regret it.' They snarl and lash out at me with the butt of their gun.

I stagger back, only catching a glancing blow as the vigilantes back out of the room again, weapons trained on us. As they approach the door, however, they are startled by a loud crash and the sound of gunfire.

'Now what is happening?' One of them exclaims as they turn towards the door and the sound of commotion.

'Heath now!' I shout as I lunge forward towards one of the two vigilantes. Heath following my lead leaps upon the other attempting to wrestle them to the ground and get their guns off of them.

The vigilantes struggle but with their backs originally

turned and taken by surprise they are no match for my strength. I force them to the ground trapping their rifle beneath them. They struggle and squirm as I straddle them pinning them down and rain my fists down upon their heads in a savage assault. For a few more moments they struggle before their squirming attempts to escape stop and they relinquish their grip on their weapon.

Beside me Heath is having less luck, his quarry is still standing, and they are both gripping the rifle between them. In a snarl of rage and exertion Heath pushes the woman back against the wall slamming her against it hard. The breath is knocked from her lungs and momentarily startled she lashes out with her fist smacking Heath in the face and causing him to stagger backwards letting go of the weapon. The Vigilante turns it and fires two shots into Heaths stomach. He stumbles backwards in pain and shock.

Stunned into action by the sound of the gun shots I quickly raise the first Vigilantes discarded weapon and fire multiple shots into the other. Killed instantly she falls against the door and to the floor out of the room. I rush to where Heath is now lying on the bed desperately clutching at the blood gushing from his stomach wound.

'Heath', Suzy has his head in her lap.

'Get the girls safe,' he whispers as his eyes drift shut and his body goes limp. Suzy looks up at me tears stream down her face.

Rita is by the door, a gun in her hand. 'Aaron, get over here.' She says, beckoning me over. I creep toward her. 'We need to go' I say as we peer down the hallway towards the entry hall. Throughout the house I can hear the chattering of guns going off and the shouting of the women who captured us accompanied by roars and bestial cries. We have been forgotten in the chaos.

'Aaron, Mumbles,' Rita whispers and I can hear the fear in her voice.

'We need to get out of here,' Turning I walk to the bed. 'Suzy, he has gone we can't stay here,'

'I know,' her lip quivers. 'Bella get Alfie,' Suzy instructs. I turn to see the boy Alfie a quivering mess in the corner. I stride over and scoop him into my arms.

'No one gets left behind,' I announce and walk purposely to the door Bella and Rita follow. Shuffling off the bed the other girls follow. Suzy drapes a sheet over Heaths prone form and turns to follow as we creep from the room. The house seems deserted as we get to the first-floor landing and proceed down the stairs.

I can see out to the entryway and the main driveway to the house. Out on the gravel, five of the vigilantes are crouched weapons raised and firing into a horde of people streaming towards the house. Their clothes are tatters and rags, and their hair is matted and unclean, their faces caked with blood and dirt. They scream incoherently as they rush towards the vigilantes. Each one that falls quickly replaced by more.

'Rita we can't go that way. There must be a side door or back entrance. We need to get into the trees,' I whisper while pushing her back. I back away before turning and following Rita and the girls across the hall and deeper into the house. We pass through the kitchen and reach the back door. Stopping at the door I peer out. It seems clear the gun fire coming from the front of the house.

'See those trees,' I point across the lawn. 'You all run to them. No matter what you hear you don't stop until you are in the trees. Understand?' I look at all their frightened faces as they nod confirmation. 'Go,' I command. I watch them for a moment and with a final look back I dash after the girls.

Alfie is limp in my arms I hope he has passed out. He really doesn't need to see this.

As I am halfway across the grass, I hear a shout of alarm and the crack of gunfire. I shift Alfie over my shoulder, so my hands are free. Turning, I fire wildly behind me back towards the house. My bullets, unsurprisingly, hit nothing. I glimpse a woman stood in the kitchen firing through the window towards us. She takes aim at me as I run, and I can sense my luck about to run out. I drop to the ground and fire, causing her shots to whizz over my head and her to flinch out of sight and into cover.

I stay lying prone when I see figures rounding the side of the house. At the same time, there is shouting and gunfire from the kitchen of the house where our assailant was hiding. I see figures through the window and know that the Mumbles have mobbed her. I get back to my feet, scooping up Alfie, and sprint to the woods. 'Rita!' I yell as I reach the tree line.

'Aaron,' she calls back and I follow her voice over a small hillock and down to where the girls are stood on the bank of a shallow river.

'Aaron the river,' Rita pants and pulls the girls in a different direction. I stumble as I feel the impact and pain flares in my shoulder. Rita shoves me hard; I tumble down the bank and splash into the water. I can't swim as I am engulfed in pain. Rita grabs me and pushes me across. The bedraggled girls already scrambling out. Bella has Alfie, dragging him to the bank.

The water pulls at us; I go under coming up coughing and gasping for breath. My shoulder is hampering me as the pain from it overwhelms me. Rita's eyes widen as she notices the blood-stained water. Grabbing me she pushes me to the far bank. I try to scramble into the reeds; she lets go of me and scrambles out. Turning she reaches for my hand just as the current tugs on my body. My fingers brush hers but with the injury I can't grip. I let go of the weeds to grasp Rita's hand as the current tugs me back. My head slips under again and I surface coughing. I hear Rita scream my name before I am pulled under again. The current sweeps me away.

CHAPTER 10

'*M*arcy, where are you?' A girl's voice I don't recognise. Pain arks across my shoulder when I try to move. Panting in breaths. I try to move further into the reeds where I have become entangled.

'Over here, I found something,' Her loud voice makes my head throb. I hear feet stomping through the reeds. I can see a pair of skinny legs and tatty boots. They squat down and observe me reaching out a tentative hand. I realise she is a child. A young child. Large eyes in a slim face blink at me with a tangle of light brown hair.

'Never mind that, did you hear all the shooting? It isn't safe here?'

'It's a boy,' the child announces.

'What do you mean it's a boy?'

'I found a boy. I think he's dead though. Which is a shame as he is beautiful,'

'Roll him over,' I feel fingers at my throat and then hands on my body.

'Is he alive?' I groan and try to open my eyes.

'Yes,'

'Come on, it isn't safe here,' Strong arms scoop me up I cry out in pain.

'Told you it was foolish coming this close to the big house,'

'I hate it when you're right,' She sniggers, and I would have smiled if things had been different. Sensations are all I feel. Numbing pain, the smell of blood. I am laid flat on something hard.

'Rita, have to find her,' I try to sit up as hands push me down, I am too weak to resist.

'Nessie, he is awake again,'

'Okay let's do this,' another voice answers. I want to move, but I can't as fear fills me. Strong hands lift my shoulders. 'Drink,' the command comes as they pushed a cup to my mouth and fire slides down my throat. I cough and some dribbles down my chin. 'Well done.' I am lowered down as something hard is placed in my mouth.

'What are you going to do?' I struggle to move.

'Help you and I am sorry this will hurt,' a face swims into my view. Dark chaotic hair, large brown eyes with a kind smile.

'Hold him down Marcy so we can get this bullet out,' The sound of ripping fills the room and I feel cold on my chest. Crying out when my shoulder seems to be bathed in liquid fire. Panting to get my breath. Before my screams fill the room and I pass out to the sound of metal hitting metal.

'Marcy, Nessie where are you,' the loud voice wakes me. Someone stalks over to where I lay. 'What is he doing here?' She whirls around to glare at the other girls.

'We found him down by the river. Thought he was dead turned out he isn't,' Marcy answers as she skips to where I lie. She is small and I guess about five, seven at most. Messy brown hair wisps around her face. Her face still in its baby-like shape. 'Isn't he pretty' she sits on the edge of the bed and takes my hand?

'Nessie,' the girl hisses. 'There are strangers. Looking for him. You will bring danger to our door,' She glares at me with open hostility.

'Who is looking for him?' The girl Nessie moves to my bed with a bowl in her hands. Steam rises and the smell of deliciousness has my tummy growling. Nessie sets the bowl down and then reaches to lift my shoulders. I hiss in discomfort. She gently brushes my hair from my eyes as she leans me back against freshly plumped pillows.

'Sorry,' she murmurs. Her plump lips turn up in a smile. Eyes like liquid chocolate appraise me. She is beautiful. High cheek bones long thick lashes frame those eyes accentuated by her dark hair bouncing in corkscrew curls. Her elegant long fingers hold the spoon gently bringing it to my lips. She is Echo, I can feel her, sort of. She is my exact opposite in a stunning contrast.

'You are like me,' I hold her gaze. 'Please I have to go. I need to find Rita,'

'Whoa you aren't going anywhere,' she puts the spoon to my lips.

'Please, I have to find her. She is fragile. She can't be out there on her own,' my voice rough. I don't know how long I have been here.

'You aren't going anywhere,' she raises a brow.

'Rita, find her. She will die,' I whisper between each spoonful of soup.

'Who is Rita?'

'She was held with me. They took us. Please look for her,' I turn my attention to the other girl.

'You need to give him back,' She glares down at me.

'No please,' I struggle to get out of bed.

'Who do we give him too, The mumbles or the vigilantes that stole him in the first place?'

'I saw Guard in the woods. Looking for him,'

'You can't be sure of that?'

'Well they ain't looking for us love,'

'No need to be rude,'

'How long has he been here?'

'A couple of days,'

'A couple of days too long,' the girl snaps.

'Yeah, alright Sandy,' Nessie snaps back. I close my eyes to exhausted to cope with their bickering. 'How do you suggest we do that when the village is full of mumbles and vigilantes?' Nessie snaps.

'I need to leave, find Rita,' I sigh out laying back.

'You will, but it isn't safe,' Nessie tucks me in. 'Marcy, tomorrow you need to find the Guard. Leave before dawn.' She turns to me. 'Do you have a name we can give?'

'Aaron,' I whisper out too weak to do much else.

'At last sense,' Sandy huffs.

'Look we keep him safe he will get sick you know that and when the vigilantly group leave, we get a message out to one of the Guard patrols that we have an unclaimed Echo,' Nessie glares at the other girl as she puts the bowl by the sink and banks the fire while Marcy draws the curtains. There hissing voices are angry.

'We can't be mice forever hiding away,'

'Better to be mice than dead,' Sandy storms across the room and disappears through another door. A banging on the door has them all freeze. Sandy rushes back in.

'Hide him,' Sandy hisses out grabbing a shot gun from a cupboard by the door.

'Who is looking for him?' The girl Nessie moves to my bed scooping me up I whimper with pain.

'Everyone,' Marcy moves a rug to reveal a square door in

the floor she pulls it open, and Nessie carries me down some wooden steps to what I assume is the cellar. It is cold as the dark envelopes us in its velvet embrace hiding us. Nessie lays me down on something soft I groan with pain and her hand smothers my mouth. Above muffled voices and booted feet walk about. It goes quiet before a shaft of light pierces the dark as the door is opened.

CHAPTER 11

*A*ndrea stands at the top of the stairs by her side Rita. Rita flies down the stairs to me I wince as she wraps around me.

'I thought I lost you,' she peppers kisses over my face.

'Not that easy to lose,' I mumble. 'The girls are they safe?' I search Rita's face.

'Yes, they are all safe thanks to you, Naomi is treating Alfie you saved him, and Suzy and the baby are fine,'

'I lost Heath,'

'I am so sorry Aaron. I know you loved him. Heath will have a son. I am so sorry Aaron,' Rita wraps around me her head tucked under my chin. She tangles her legs with mine. 'You sleep,' she whispers lifting her head to kiss me.

'Aaron, you need to eat,' Andrea wakes me her face a picture of concern. I push up noticing I have pyjamas on. Her hand brushes my hair from my face. 'You are sick?'

'I got shot,' my sarcastic answer. She hands me a bowl of pasta. It is delicious, or I am so hungry it seems that way. 'I am fine. Stop worrying,' I add, placing the bowl on the side table. 'Are we safe here?'

'You are safe they have been taken care of,' Andrea smiles and it is sort of scary. 'You sleep, my lamb,' she tucks me in, and her expression softens.

'How is he, is he getting better?' Andrea asks her voice full of worry. I must trust Andrea. Rita snuggles into me, and I feel better.

'He's Echo and his whole immune system is over-whelmed; he needs to be in a hospital. I know that is difficult considering who he is. There is a private facility close to here. I suggest you get him there.' Nessie takes my pulse again and shakes her head.

'He is severely dehydrated and is developing pneumonia if we don't get him to a hospital soon and get some antibi-otics and fluids in him, we are going to lose him,' she states her voice flat.

'No, I contact madam Ramsbottom, they compromised his security,' Andrea argues as I hear her pacing the room. 'Those vigilantes are still out there,'

'Andrea he is an Echo you know that. You know how he works. Why he was created, and you know how his body reacts to the contaminate. Why we protect him?' Nessie speaks to Andrea like a small child. I just snuggle into Rita.

'I know all that, but my job is to keep him safe and right now someone else knows about them and they will kill us to get to them. So, I must contemplate our next move or none of us will survive this, including him,' Andrea growls back. 'We have already lost one boy,' Andrea grumbles.

'Andrea, sorry,'

'Save the apologies we have trouble,' Sandy marches in a gun in her hand. Andrea immediately has her weapon in her hand and moves to the window. Carefully she looks out.

'Vigilantes,' Banging on the door startles Rita. I place my finger to her lips. Wincing as I sit up. With one hand, I try to pull my boots on and then pull a sweater over my head. Rita moves to help to tie my laces.

'Aaron, they will take us?' her voice quivers.

'Not this time they won't,' I glance over to Andrea, confident she will protect me. Sandy signals to Nessie. With a curt nod, she walks to the door and opens it.

'Can I help you?' she addresses two burly looking women stood in the porch.

'We have lost two of our group. They are young and very vulnerable. It is important we find them. May we come in and check?' She pulls her gun free, so it is easily visible. Making her intention clear.

'Of course, but I can assure you no one has been here,' Nessie steps back from the door and allows them in. Shutting the door Andrea and Sandy step up behind them.

'Drop your weapons and raise your hands slowly,' Sandy says clearly as Andrea walks so they can see she is guard.

The woman smiles as she places her gun on the floor. 'So, he is here, come to retrieve your property,' she smirks.

'My job is to keep him alive something you aren't so good at,' Andrea has a look of disgust on her face as I shuffle into the room.

'Still alive then boy,'

'You idiots shot me so yeah no thanks to you,' I raise a brow as I sit down with a hiss of pain.

'Here drink this,' Nessie hands me a cup of her disgusting bitter tea.

'Thanks,' I grimace as I take a sip.

'Aaron you should be in bed,' Rita bustles in. Her earlier fright forgotten as she worries about my health.

'Well, well bonded have they,' the woman's eyes light up and I want to roll my eyes.

'That isn't your concern,' Andrea snaps as she forces the woman out the door.

'Killing me won't stop them. More will come. The prize too much of a temptation,' her voice cut off by Andrea kicking the door shut.

'Come on up you get back to bed,' Rita hauls me to my feet. As two muffled shots sound through the house. Rita startles next to me.

'You have got to stop dragging me to your bed,' I quip to be rewarded with a snort. Distracting her from the drama outside.

'In your dreams tuber,' she mutters making me chuckle and groan in equal parts.

CHAPTER 12

*A*ndrea is setting a fast pace. She seems agitated and tense, saying we have lost too much time. I watch her as she urges the horses on, constantly scanning the countryside. Her entire posture seems very on edge. Andrea stops and Rita guides our horse next to her. My arm preventing me from riding my horse.

'What's the matter?' Rita asks as I gaze between them Andreas' face looks strained.

'I can hear hooves. I think we need to get off the road,' she jumps down from her horse and leads it over to a small copse of trees. Rita jumps down, she helps me down. The jolt makes me wince with pain.

'Sorry,' she leads our horse off the road and commands him to move deep into the undergrowth. He obeys and soon disappears with Andreas horse.

'What's the matter, what's going on?' I ask Rita as I follow her.

Rita takes my hand and leads me to some scrub and bushes she pulls me down. I wiggle a bit so as not to aggravate my shoulder. She gets down beside me slinging her arm around my shoulders preventing me from moving. She puts her finger to my lips in a shushing gesture as I am about to ask her what we are doing.

It's then I hear the thunder of approaching hooves I follow Rita's gaze to the road as six horse and riders thunder past mere metres from where we lay. My eyes widen as I recognise them as vigilantes, and I suspect they are hunting us. We lay there a few minutes more and then Rita helps me up.

'What do you suggest we do now?' Rita gazes at Andrea as she brushes her cloak removing the dead leaves that cling to it.

'I think we have no choice now but to head for your grandmothers and the chateau. We lie low there and build Aaron up and then make a dash for the coast and the ship. Hopefully, by then they will have lost interest.' Andrea runs her hands through her hair and sighs, and I can see she is tired. She slept little last night on guard with Sandy. It is getting late and none of us has eaten properly for quite some time and that is taking a toll.

'So, what do you suggest in the meantime the chateau is still a couple of hours ride away?' Rita points out, concern on her face, as she can clearly see how tired Andrea is.

'We split up, I take the road lead them away and you go across country,' Rita nods as she holds my hand tight, she is worried her posture is tense. Andrea pulls a map out of her bag and opens it. She shows it to Rita pointing to a place on it. 'We meet up here on the other side of the river and then make our way to the chateau no stopping, the horses should cope.'

Rita reaches up and kisses Andreas cheek. 'Be careful no heroics.' Andrea wraps Rita in a hug.

'Same to you,' she climbs on to her horse urging it forward she is soon galloping away. Rita whistles and the horse trots toward us, as Rita turns to me. 'Aaron, I want you Infront so I can hold you tight,' I nod.

'Are they looking for us?' I am so frightened I can't even hide my fear.

'Yes, I think they are,'

'Rita,' I breathe, and I kiss her.

'I will try to keep us safe, but we are going to do a brief detour, we are nearly there, and we may have to go off-road,' I swallow, with a curt nod I turn to the horse.

'Aaron, I will keep you safe,' Rita gazes into my eyes. 'Do you trust me?'

'Yeah, but who will keep you safe,' I mutter and kiss her, she kisses me back, we finally pull apart.

'I don't want you to die, I can't lose you,' I run my fingers through her hair and down her face as I gaze into her eyes.

'It will be fine Aaron, I don't intend to die just yet,' Rita kisses me once more.

She kicks the horse into a walk one arm around my waist as I use my free hand to hold the horses mane. Rita urges the horse into a trot as she leaves the road and goes across the fields.

Despite Rita's best efforts we soon pick up a tail she pushes the horse on across fields at a fast pace, but they have the advantage as they only have one rider per horse and their horses are fresher.

'Hang on Aaron we are nearly there,' Rita shouts as the horse gears up, and it feels like we are flying as Rita jumps some hedges and I cling on, but they are catching us up I hazard a glance behind and they are so close, it is then I see more coming toward us. Gritting my teeth against the pain.

'Rita give me up we can't outrun them,' I plead holding on as tight as I can.

'No, I will not,' Rita pants as she turns the horse so abruptly, I nearly fall off as I cling to it. We leap a hedge and

Rita seems to head toward the river she slows down slightly.

'Aaron, take the reins,' she shouts. I obey and she takes a phone from her pocket.

'Andrea the river,' is all she says and then takes the reins from me and urges the horse on again. We are parallel to the river at the last minute she turns him slowing him some more.

'Aaron I am sorry,' she shouts, and I stupidly let go of the reins to turn to her and she pushes me off the horse, I yelp in surprise.

I hit the water at such speed it drives all the air out my lungs as I submerge under the water. It feels as if I am being stabbed by hundreds of little needles as the water touches my skin it almost burns it is so cold.

My instinct is to surface as I inhale the water burning my lungs, but I can't, my brain can't send any instructions to my body it is so shocked from the cold water, I panic with the realisation I can't move. The shock of the freezing cold water has rendered my brain into a kind of stupor.

I feel powerful hands haul me from the water. Wrapping a blanket round me as I am pulled on to a horse. Coughing up the water I can't speak. I don't know what happened to Rita. I feel an arm wrap around me, and it hurts where my skin is so cold.

'Gotcha lamb,' Andrea says, and I feel relief run through me as I cough up more water.

'Ri...Rita,' I shiver.

'Don't worry about her, let's get you somewhere warm.' Andrea urges the horse into a gallop. I can feel my body going into shock from the cold as I shiver in the soaking wet clothes under the blanket.

'Hang on, lamb, not far and I can warm you up,' Andrea's voice sounds out of breath and urgent. The pain and cold to much as I pass out. I come to, to the smell of wood smoke and feel heat as someone rubs me vigorously.

'Come on wake up,' Andrea sounds desperate, her voice is laced with urgency.

'Andrea you can stop now he is awake,'

'What, oh right, damn it Rita, you nearly killed him, I thought I told you no heroics.' Andrea complains as she moves away from me.

'It was the only way I was going to get away, it worked didn't it,' Rita shoots back.

'You tried to drown me...again,' I mumble sitting up and glaring at Rita, as I take in my surroundings and cough. It is dark but I can see a small fire burning, behind me is a tent and I am in a sleeping bag in clean dry clothes. I frown as I realise, I ruined my clothes when I was pushed into the river. I wonder where Andrea got the clothes from, but she is very resourceful, so I don't dwell on it too long.

'Here drink this and stop moaning I was saving your life,' Rita passes me a streaming mug of tea. 'Or do you want to be used as a baby making machine,' She glares at me.

'If it's with you I might not object,' she huffs but I see the blush creep onto her cheeks. I wrap my hands around the mug and gingerly sip it. Trying to work out how throwing me in a frozen river was saving my life.

I feel awful but the hot tea helps. I drink it not looking at Rita she is angry with me, and I don't understand why. I notice Andrea watching me and I duck my head sipping my tea.

'So, care to explain the reason you tried to drown me,' I enquire raising a brow as I sip the hot sweet tea. It is warming my insides. I have never been as cold as I was when I fell into the river, and I am still shaking but I think that is more shock than cold.

'I wasn't trying to drown you,' Rita grumbles.

'So, it was a serious attempt on my life,'

'No, I wasn't trying to kill you alright,' Rita answers sulkily she walks over and sits next to me. I can't hold it in any longer and let out a chuckle.

'Aaron,'

'Rita!' I reach over and kiss her.

'Well, you know we were being chased. I knew we couldn't outrun them well, not all of them, so Andrea got across the river. I found a narrow bit and pushed you off into the water the vigilantes carried on following me and Andrea took you. I had led them on a wild goose chase while you were safe with Andrea,' she shrugs. 'It worked, didn't it?'

'So glad you're on my side, hate for you to really try to kill me,' sarcasm laces my voice.

'Oh, shut up and move over,' I do as Rita commands, and she wriggles into my sleeping bag wrapping around me. 'Go to sleep Aaron early start if we are going to get that boat,' she reaches over and kisses me.

'Why are we going on a boat' I am sort of excited, I have never been on a boat?' I thought we were going to the Château,' I frown turning my head to glance at Rita.

'We were, but we have run out of time.'

'To many vigilantes about, best if we get to the boat.'

'Why do we need a boat where are we going?' I ask looking at both of them.

'We are going to Tribe, and you will be safe there.' Andrea replies, pulling her phone from her pocket and frowning at it again. 'You two are so valuable that it is worth any risk to obtain you. I have to weigh up the safest route, and I don't think we can get to the Château because that's what they expect us to do.'

I snuggle into Rita to get warm. 'I love you,' she whispers so only I can hear, and I kiss her. Wow, she loves me. How do I feel about that? I don't know, I like Rita a lot.

'Aaron you are very hot are you okay?'

'I feel fine a bit tired but I'm always tired and hungry,' I shrug.

'Can't argue with that, after all you are a monster before your coffee,' she giggles.

'You love me, though,' I whisper back. I never realised how much I want that. Even with Heath and Janey, which was more the excitement of it. I wanted to belong. I want to belong to Rita.

'Yeah s'pose' Rita concedes with a chuckle.

'I love you as well,' I close my eyes I still have lots of questions, but I am tired and achy. I snuggle into Rita and drift to sleep.

CHAPTER 13

I lean against Rita we have been traveling for hours and I ache everywhere, my chest feels like it is being squeezed in a vice. My shoulder is throbbing and very sore. I don't want to tell Rita. I shiver and close my eyes.

'Aaron you okay,' Rita murmurs in my ear. Her breath in my hair.

'Yeah, hungry' I murmur back. That is sort of true and I know it will satisfy Rita as far as answers go. If I eat, I will probably feel loads better, that's what I need food and a good sleep. In a bed, not a sleeping bag. Although I enjoyed having Rita curled up with me. The bond is strengthening and soon I won't be able to resist it.

'We will stop soon, there is a pub that is loyal to Tribe we will eat there,' I feel relief as we enter the village. This village is intact, well cared for and I can't describe how happy that makes me feel. Rita stops outside the pub. She helps me down and I wobble leaning into her as I regain my composure.

'Aaron are you okay,' she looks me over and I plaster a smile onto my face.

'Yes, sorry, been sitting on the horse too long.' reaching for Rita's hand, she leads me inside. Andrea and I sit in a booth tucked way enough but so Andrea can see the door. Rita goes to order the food and drinks. The lady behind the bar seems to know Rita and I watch as she chats to her. It is the most animated I have seen, Rita. She isn't the scared little mouse I first met in that room. I look away and cough, clutching my chest that really hurts.

'Aaron you okay, when did you start coughing?' Andrea peers at me with narrowed eyes.

'Just a cough, I'm fine,' I mumble looking away from Andrea's scrutinising gaze.

'You two seem close have you bonded?' My eyes widen at this. 'You can tell me it is important,' Andrea cajoles, smiling at me.

I sigh and rub the edge of the table with my fingers. 'I can feel it. I haven't acted on it. They knew the people that had us and I knew it could get us killed.' I shrug and gaze up at Andrea. 'I don't know how much longer I can resist it,'

'You both seemed very comfortable together.'

'Yes, if I give in it will seriously hamper our escape,'

'Aaron let me worry about that,'

'I know what will happen Andrea,'

'So, you understand its consequences?' I blush even more.

'Yeah, I understand. We will want each other constantly until I get Rita pregnant. That alone will make her frightening valuable,' I confess and gaze at the ground, the consequences are so serious. I look up at Andrea. 'It just isn't safe to do while we are out here,'

'Aaron you won't be able to resist.'

'I know okay, but I have too. Please Andrea,' I want this conversation over.

'I will keep you safe,'

'I know you will. I trust you with my life,' I hold her gaze glad when she smiles.

'No one will harm you I promise. Gillian suggested they allow you to mature a bit. Have some fun.'

'I think that point has past,'

Rita walks over with our drinks. I cough and wheeze my chest really hurts. I don't want to tell Rita because we are already behind.

I feel better once I have eaten my soup and warmed up in the pub. I am reluctant to leave but Andrea wants to find somewhere to make camp for the night. I wish we were going to a house I would rather sleep in a bed than on the ground again. Maybe that's why I ache so much? Sleeping on the floor can't be good for you.

We make good time and soon get to the place Andrea had picked as our campsite. Andrea and Rita have the tent up and the horses sorted in record time. I gratefully crawl into my sleeping bag and fall asleep immediately. I don't even wake when Rita crawls in next to me.

Rita wakes me and I groan everything hurts from my throat to my chest and I feel hot and shaky.

'Aaron you okay,' Rita peers at me and I shake my head she touches my forehead and my face, I am burning up. I cough a dry hacking cough and groan again as pain flares in my chest and throat.

'Andrea he's sick,' Rita bites her lip as Andrea crouches down next to me.

'What's up lamb?'

'My shoulder,' I mumble. Andrea rolls me over and I groan. She gently pulls my shirt away to see it is red and swollen.

'Damn it is infected. Rita boil some water so I can clean it,' Andrea gets her knife out and I try to move away as I know exactly what she is about to do.

'Andrea?' I look up at her with concern.

'Going to have to clean it out. Sorry, this will hurt,'

'Wait, no, hang on,' I stutter out before pain explodes in my shoulder and I scream the last thing I hear is Rita's voice.

'Aaron I am so sorry,' Rita brushes my hair from my face as I come too.

'Don't... don't do that again,' my voice a whisper as I am still drowning in pain. I shut my eyes and drift to sleep or pass out.

I wake to Rita rubbing my arm. 'Aaron how you feeling we have to go,' I can hear Andrea on her phone she is talking in rapid Russian. Her native tongue she switches to this when she is agitated.

'He is sick, yeah, what, infection, yes right okay we will get him there you get the doctor there yes we are moving him now yes I understand,' Andrea shoves her phone in her pocket and looks at Rita. 'We have new instructions there is a village and a safe house a cottage not far from here a few miles if we go there a doctor will look at him.'

'I'm sorry Andrea this is my fault for pushing him in the river,' Rita's voice wobbles. I shiver but I am so hot, and my chest feels really tight making breathing painful I want to sleep but I can't as I struggle to breath.

'We had little choice if we were going to get you both away,' Andrea's tone softens.

'What's the plan,' Rita seems to pull herself together a bit and strokes my hair feeling the heat coming off my body.

'You get on the horse, and I will pass him up to you, this is where we are going,' Andrea pulls out a map from her back pocket and unfolds it showing Rita. 'It's about a ten-minute ride from here I will meet you there when I have packed the camp away alright.' Rita nods with a bounce she is in the saddle. Andrea walks over to me and scoops me up in my sleeping bag. 'You'll be alright lamb, gonna get you some help,' I nod as I take in another wheezing breath. Andrea passes me up to Rita. She wraps her arm around me as she urges the horse forward, I lean my head against her and close my eyes.

I don't remember the journey or arriving or being put to bed. In fact, I don't remember anything just hazy conversations and people whispering. I just try to breath try to persuade my lungs to behave like lungs again as I try to ignore the burning pain in my shoulder.

'How is he, is he getting better,' Rita asks her voice full of worry as I cough again and I can taste blood, damn that isn't good I sink back. I have to trust Andrea and Rita.

'He's sick, very sick he needs to be in a hospital, I know that is difficult considering who he is, there is a private facility not far from here I suggest we get him there.' The doctor takes my pulse again and shakes her head. 'If we don't get him to a hospital soon and get some antibiotics and fluids in him, we are going to lose him,' the doctor states her voice flat.

'Okay that's good Madame Ramsbottom will be alerted as to which facility we are in. We are going to need more protection,' Andrea paces the floor as she tries to think.

'If we don't get him proper medical treatment neither side will have him, do you understand, he will die,' the doctor states firmly and Andrea stops pacing.

I drift again. Waking I gaze around, the whole room is white and sterile a light is on above my bed casting a muted light around the room. I feel scared I don't know where Andrea is. I have never been in a hospital the boys homes I lived in before always had their own medical facility.

'When can I take him home, he has been here two days now?' Rita demands her voice full of authority. She is outside the room I feel relief as I sink into the bed relishing being warm and not in the tent. I have lost two days, no wonder I feel so rubbish.

'He is very ill, we could still easily lose him your highness' the doctor says in an even voice, but I can tell by her tone of voice she is using all her training in bedside manner and has a dislike for Rita.

I am curled up in bed as a nurse brings my breakfast, I don't want it, I just want to sleep.

'Aaron, you need to eat,' the nurse coaxes, I shake my head and shut my eyes. Just the thought of food makes my stomach roll. Rita isn't here either. I wonder where she is.

I am on a private ward on my own, they don't get many boys. I feel a little better but still have the oxygen and a cannula in my hand. The Doctor walks in and smiles at me she sits on my bed. She is older with a kind smile that makes her eyes crinkle at the edges. She isn't the same doctor I saw at the house.

'Hello Aaron, how do you feel?' She sticks a thermometer in my mouth, so I have no chance of speaking. She takes it out and frowns. 'You are one sick boy,' she gazes at me I have no answer. 'Well, you sleep, and we will see how you are in the morning give those antibiotics chance to work. At least your body isn't rejecting them at the moment. We will have to monitor that,' she smiles at me and gets up to leave as Rita enters the room.

'Doctor, how is he?' Rita smiles and moves over to where I lay and kisses my forehead.

'He is very ill and needs complete bed rest. He is under weight, dehydrated and is starting to develop pneumonia. Where has he been, why is he in this state, I thought the Adams were well looked after.' The doctor glares at Rita and the animosity in her voice is plain to hear. Her gaze takes in Rita and her features soften. 'You don't look so good yourself,'

'We were taken, and he looked after me, but he got shot and they were still after us... and I tried to keep him safe really I did,' Rita's voice wobbles. The strain of the last few weeks taking its toll on her.

'Hey, come on you are safe now,' the doctor pulls Rita into a hug. 'Please help us,' Rita tucks my hand under the blanket even though I am only half awake I listen to them talking.

'You are Echo's,' The doctor exclaims gazing at me as I drift while trying to grasp what they are saying. Rita sighs she sounds so tired, and I sort of know it is my fault for being sick.

'Yes,'

'Never thought I would see an Echo boy. Never mind a bonded pair,' she looks over Rita again before her attention moves back to me. 'I would really like to study him,' she muses. 'He is quite beautiful, like an angel' the doctor mutters. 'You get some rest as well young lady I will post security outside the door,' Turning she strolls out. Rita kicks her boots off and climbs onto the bed. Snuggling up to me I pull her close.

CHAPTER 14

I can feel people touching me and I moan I hate being touched by strangers. I feel the sharp pain as the cannula is replaced and the oxygen mask is put on my face. I must have fallen asleep as I come too, and the room is quiet. Someone is stroking my hair and they are holding my hand. I feel the covers being pulled back and something cold on my chest, and then the covers are pulled back and tucked around me.

'How is he?' Gillian is in my room.

'Fragile, and very sick,' I don't recognise the voice it has an accent, and her speech is careful like English isn't her first language.

'Oh, Florence he was never meant for you?' Gillian sneers. 'Does Rita know how you feel about her match.' Gillian laughs and I hear a growl.

'Shut up Gillian now where is Thomas; Mother is livid with you taking Thom like that.'

'Oh, you and Thomas are so annoying, and he is always in the way, why did you call him in any way, he is a complication I can do without,' Gillian grumbles.

'Because the other one has bonded to my baby sister and that is your fault,'

'What no I told Sophie not to. Why did your mother send her anyway always to feral that one,' Gillian huffs.

'Yeah, well she feels threatened and you know what she does when threatened,'

'Oh, dear Florence what will mummy say,' Gillian giggles.

'Yes, well she wants Thom to stop that from happening,'

'No, I have already sorted it he is quite safe. You and Thom will not interfere,'

'He belongs to us,' The room goes quiet, and I drift.

'That he does, have you talked to Sophie yet?'

'No, she is being stubborn,' the other girl growls. I really must lend Gilly my how to win friends and influence people book.

'What a surprise,' Gillian smirks.

'Stop interfering, he is ours, he belongs to us,'

'I know he does, and he will give Sophie what she wants as long as you all leave him alone,'

'Why should we,'

'Because Florence if you do this one thing for me, I can guarantee his return when he is twenty. Or Sophie will take him and hide again and neither of us want that,'

'Alright Gillian just this once I will trust you,'

'Oh, and Florence, if they don't bond, he is mine,'

'No Gillian he will be the consort,'

'Tut, tut Florence showing your true colours,'

'No Gillian I am doing my duty. What is expected of me,' the girl snaps back angry again.

* * *

THE DOOR OPENING rouses me from my light sleep. I just lay still my eyes shut. I know I am not alone, but I just don't want to interact with anyone. Where is Rita, she was here last night, I think? I can't keep track of the days never mind the nights.

'Naomi, will he get better?' It's the girl Gilly was taunting. Yeah, taunting is correct. What was her name... Florence that's it. Florence sighs and I feel the bed dip as she sits down and takes my hand stroking it gently. 'He is very beautiful, Rita adores him,' her voice wistful.

'She will recover. Just give her time they went through a traumatic experience,'

'He is yours if we can't get Rita to come round,'

'Do you really know if he can create boys?'

'Yes, of course I do, I have been researching all the old files ever since Thelma gave him to Gillian. He is amazing do you know he is really intelligent. They manipulated every aspect of his DNA and genetics, and I am sure his body holds the key. Besides we lost him for a time when he was fourteen and that little episode produced the most delightful child, Edward.'

'Gillian is too attached to him. It clouds her judgement,'

'Your jealousy clouds yours,'

'And him, what clouds his judgement,'

'Florence what do you want me to say. He adores Gillian they have been together since they were fifteen. Gillian has taught him every aspect of physical pleasure,' I can hear the smirk in her voice, and I know she only said that to rile the other girl up.

'If that's the case, why haven't they bonded fully?' the other girl, Florence huffs and ignores Naomi's dig.

'I don't know maybe it was circumstance. He is very intelligent not some dumb animal and you would do well to remember that. Let's not make the same mistakes we made with his brother' Naomi answers and I had never heard her so animated.

'Sophie was never going to conform and now she has the boy' Florence's voice betrays her annoyance.

'You just concentrate on this one and Rita. Or Gillian will take him back.'

'They belong to us though, she knows that'.

'I know that, but we couldn't get them to you safely and now the other one is with your sister. So, this one should return to Gillian,' Naomi crosses her arms across her chest with a smug smile on her lips.

'No that isn't going to happen,' Florence stands up and gazes at Naomi.

'Florence, you need to be gentle with her.'

'I am trying,', she sighs. 'How could this happen? She isn't like us she is sensitive and now...she is broken,'

'I will try my best with her,' Naomi answers and I can hear the sincerity in her voice.

'Thank you, Naomi,'

When they finally leave, I give a small groan and shut my eyes and go back to sleep. I wake to someone talking to me. I rouse myself enough to work out what they are saying.

'Aaron, are you asleep? Of course, you are I almost killed you. Don't mind if I hide in here for a bit, do you? Florence, my sister, is hounding me.' the bed dips and I feel her small body curl around me. Turning, I pull her close.

'I forgive you,' I whisper. Sinking back to sleep having her near is soothing. The bond strengthening. Almost complete, I don't have the energy to wake up, never mind initiate the final step.

For a moment there is silence. I can hear Rita crying. I could open my eyes, but I don't want to. I am so comfy, not fully awake, but not asleep either. I am alone in bed. When did she leave? Why is she crying? What did I miss?

Hearing a chair creak as she moves. Turning my head and open my eyes. Her face inches from mine. My mouth is so dry I can't make any sort of coherent sound, but it would seem that is proving difficult and not part of my current skill set. She is tiny curled in the chair, a curtain of long pale hair half coving her face. She looks over at me while using the back of her hands to wipe the tears from her face.

'Rita, what are you doing over there?' my voice croaks. Rita rushes over and picks up a glass of water with a straw.

'Aaron, sorry...here. Is that better,' she gives a mirthless laugh? 'It's all my fault you are like this in the first place. Mother is livid that I put you in so much danger. Didn't apologise that I got taken in the first place. No, they are all skimming over that detail. Still shouldn't complain, should I? After all it isn't me lying in bed half dead. To top it all you are my actual match. How about that for a coincidence if you believe in those,' Rita drags herself off the bed and I watch her leave, her shoulders are slumped as she shuffles out the room. So, she is my match, wow this should be interesting.

I have no concept of time passing, have I been here long? I hear the door and then a deep sigh of exasperation. A chair creaks across the room and I hear someone slump into it.

'Hey Aaron, I know I am supposed to let you sleep but being near you calms me. Good grief this place is boring. Can you imagine how much it sucks to be stuck here in hillbilly hell? I am a bloody princess for goodness's sake,' I hear the chair as Rita shifts getting comfortable.

After a brief pause Rita speaks up again. 'It's actually quite nice talking to you...probably because you don't talk back. They say not to disturb you and that you're sick. I have to say I agree, I'm no doctor but you look bloody awful, old chap. Naomi says I'm not to sleep in your bed anymore,' I hear the door and it sounds like someone jumps to their feet as the clatter of the chair toppling echoes around the room.

'There you are honey. What are you doing in here?' I hear footsteps and a faint gasp.

'It is nice in here. I didn't wake him promise,' Rita's voice is suddenly defensive and reserved.

'Why don't you come and help us, I know how good you are with horses,' Naomi cajoles, her voice soft.

'Maybe, I dunno, yeah, yeah I will.'

'Thanks,' I hear footfalls on the carpet and the door open and close. Silence shrouds the room and I drift off again. I wake and I am not alone. She is curled around me on the bed asleep. I carefully sit up with a bit of wriggling I get her under the quilt pulling it over her. I study her face for a bit. She looks much younger asleep the worry lines gone. Her pale hair frames her heart-shaped face. She reminds me of an elf with her small delicate features. Snuggling down, I pull her to me and wrap my arm around her. I feel protective of her, she sort of reminds me of Adam.

Someone is watching me. It feels like... when a cat sits on you and watches you. The home had one and it used to get in my room and freak me out. It's not a cat though, it's Rita.

'Hello,' she smiles her head propped on her hand. She is laid next to me. I have one leg over hers. It's very intimate and a little possessive. I try to think how to remove it causing the least amount of embarrassment.

'Hi,' I mumble out and she smiles at me even more.

'You know you talk in your sleep. I am so sorry about Heath. Who are Janey and Edward?'

A blush stains my cheeks. 'It wasn't your fault.' She wriggles away from me and sits up. She stretches like a cat her arms above her head arching her back.

'Best sleep I have had in ages,' she looks back at me over her shoulder.

'You're welcome,' I quip, and she laughs.

'Oh, was that an invitation,' I blush some more, and she giggles.

'Well, you're game is off as I still seem to be dressed,' she raises a brow and purses her lips. The door opening and Naomi bustles in distracting us.

'Rita, I knew I would find you in here, he needs to sleep.' Naomi frowns. She fusses around me, adjusting the oxygen and giving me my medicine.

'Yeah, I know, but I like it in here away from you, and everyone really.' Rita huffs and glares at Naomi. 'Why shouldn't I be in here. He is my match, and I thought he was dead, to be fair he doesn't look that alive, but he was the only thing that made our situation bearable. You know I used to dream about finding my match. All romantic and stuff, you know. He was so brave when we were held'.

'That's me rushing in to save the damsel. Not my bag at all. I am the practical one. You need Adam for romance.' I waggle my brows and she giggles. Talking is taxing and I close my eyes getting my breathing under control.

'What is the other one like?' Rita asks, sitting on my bed. I feel it dip under her weight. She reaches across and brushes my hair off my face. Her fingers cool and gentle as they whisper across my skin.

'Oh Adam,' she chuckles. 'He is a moody, obstreperous little git. With far too much intelligence for his own good. Been driving everyone to distraction,' Naomi kneels on the floor in front of Rita taking her hands. 'He is pretty like Aaron. All innocent blue eyes and blonde hair. Looks like an angel. Behaves like the devil,' Naomi smiles her expression wistful.

'You like him!' Rita smirks.

'Yes, I do. He gives no care about what anyone thinks. Knows what he wants and doesn't compromise. He will drive Gillian to distraction with his stubborn streak,'

'Should get along with Sophie perfectly then,'

'Yeah, she thinks he hangs the moon, bless her,'

'Make nice babies then?' Rita's head is bowed, and I can't see her face, but I suspect she is crying.

'Why don't you tell me, I want to understand, I want to help you?'

Rita sighs and wipes her eyes with her hand. 'Naomi, you don't need it in your head.'

'If you share it might ease the pain a little. I love you Rita, you can tell me anything and I will understand,' Naomi cajoles her.

She sighs again and I hear the chair creak as she shifts in it, trying to decide, I don't envy her I know how persuasive Naomi can be when she wants you to tell her something you would rather not.

'They hurt me when they found out I was a princess of Tribe. Played with me, talked about finding him and hurting him. Made me into nothing just an object,' she snarls, angry, and I wish I hadn't heard. She sounds so broken.

'What happened to the other girls?'

'They...they had a boy. Heath he was Aaron's friend, and they shot him in front of us. They had him a while forced him to bond with the girls. That would have been my fate if Aaron hadn't helped us escape,' Rita looks up at Naomi. 'Aaron didn't stop he kept going until we were safe. He didn't get time to mourn his friend. He saved Alfie's life even when Alfie had given up,'

'Yes, we recovered his body. The girls told us where the house was. Alfie is getting better he has bonded to Bella so that will help his recovery. What happened to him?'

'He bonded to a girl before they caught me, she died giving birth. To neglected and malnourished. Underage, I suspect. Too young to be bonding,'

'He must have suffered so much. I have never been so afraid, and I didn't know how to cope. We aren't prepared for that. I felt degraded and humiliated. He must have been so frightened,' She pauses. I didn't know what had happened before I was caught. 'When he was caught, he was so brave, and he made demands. Like being their prisoner meant nothing,

'We will bring those who hurt you to justice.'

'I know. How can I be matched to someone so pure and beautiful when I am so broken?'

I hear her sniffle, and I guess she is crying. I wonder what happened. What the circumstances were that she was in that position. 'They held me captive hunting for a suitable match. Hunting him. So, they could breed us. Like farm animals,' she lifts her head. 'I don't want him to be hurt because of me,' her single sob seems loud in the room's quiet.

'Oh sweetheart, come here,' I can hear Rita crying, proper crying. 'I won't let anything like that ever happen to you again I promise. Come on Aaron needs his sleep. Let's have breakfast?' Naomi answers gently, she sighs.

'They—they didn't defile me if that's what you are worried about. They just kept saying stuff, you know...about how they would breed us when they found him,'

'I know Rita,'

'How can you know you weren't there?' Rita hisses.

'I know how they operate...there have been other instances and not all have had a good outcome,' Naomi growls. 'Taking you, that was audacious and not their usual modus operandi,'

'I'm glad he has Andrea looking out for him and you and Thomas.' She sniffs. 'Will Thom protect the other one. Keep Sophie safe.'

'Yes, he knows where he is. Gillian won't allow anyone to hurt him,'

'Good, Naomi I don't know if...if I can be what everyone wants, what Tribe need. Florence would be so much better than me.'

'No Rita, Florence she lacks your compassion. She does it for duty she doesn't feel. You take all the time you need, and I will help you.' Naomi leans up and gently kisses her before taking Rita's hand and leading her across the room to the door.

'Will he pull through,' Rita glances at me. 'I talked to him earlier. He is amusing made me laugh,'

'Yes, he is making good progress, he is a fighter and a charmer.'

'Good, you like him. Don't you? I mean like, like him,'

'Yes, I like, like him, does that matter?'

'Nah, it's okay,'

'Well, he is your responsibility now. Do you think you can care for him? Show him the affection he needs,'

'I don't know…he is so fragile, and it is my fault he is here. I almost killed him,'

'Yes, he is fragile. We have to take care of him. As if he is one of your sisters,' Oh, Naomi she is good. Do I need a big sister? A little bit weird when they want us to bond and breed, frankly. I watch them over the top of my oxygen mask. Rita nods.

I drift back to the nothingness it's not sleep. It is more complete than that, I think they are drugging me to give me a chance to heal.

'Hi, it's me again, you know I like it in your room. It's peaceful. That is a stupid thing to say, I hate it here, do you hate it here is that why you won't wake up, I wouldn't if I were you. I am rambling sorry,' I hear her sit-down fidgeting to get comfortable. 'Do you mind if I sit here for a bit? It won't be long they will all be looking for me soon?' I hear a sigh and it is so sad.

'Rita, come here,' I pull the covers back, and she immediately scoots into bed with me.

'Thanks,' she leans over and kisses me.

'No seducing me young lady,' she giggles.

'How do you feel?'

'Sore, getting shot sucks,' I pull her into me needing her near.

'I bet,' she leans over me and kisses me on the cheek. 'You need to rest,'

I must have drifted off again. When I awake, I am alone the room empty. Hearing the door and the familiar creak of someone sitting in a chair.

'Hi how you doing, I am hiding in your room again, sorry I didn't visit yesterday, they wouldn't let me. The place is overrun with Adams they have shut another boy's home and the boys, and their Mothers are here, its chaos. Still, they aren't staying they will be gone tomorrow so I thought I would hide in here till they are gone, I am staying with you. Thom doesn't think I am fit to travel yet. I like Thom he is nice. I asked if I could stay with you. Naomi thinks I should help protect you like a big sister. Personally, I think that weird as we are matched and we will be expected to do, well you know what I mean, I'm rambling sorry,' I feel the bed move she must be resting on it.

'Can I get in?' I pull back the covers and she shuffles in. 'Thanks, Alfie and Bella are staying as well,'

I wake feeling…good, I blink the sleep out my eyes and nurse walks over and smiles at me.

'Hello young man feeling better,' she picks up my wrist and looks at her watch smiling.

'Yes, really hungry,' I mutter trying to sit up.

'Well maybe a lightly boiled egg and toast, how does that sound,' I nod, and she smiles leaving the room. I look around I didn't really register it when I was first brought in here, it is an elegant room with antique furniture and lots of chintz in greens and golds with thick flowery woollen rugs. The curtains cover large windows and I see the fire lit in the ornate marble fireplace, the drapes around the bed match the curtains.

My gaze falls on an overstuffed chair and I smile that must be Rita's chair, I wonder where she is. I can just see light through the curtains. What time of day is it? I have no idea of time or even what day it is, and I certainly don't know how long I have been here, not even sure where here is.

I look up as the door opens and Naomi walks in, she has a white coat on and a stethoscope around her neck. She smiles at me as she walks across the room to the bed. Putting a tray on the little table next to the bed.

'Aaron, may I listen to your chest,' she asks her voice is soft and her smile reaches her eyes, so I nod and watch as she rubs the end of her stethoscope on her hand she notices and smiles. 'Just warm it up for you,' she places it on my chest. 'Breathe in,' she asks. 'And out,' I obey she pushes my pyjama top up and puts it on my back. 'And again,' she instructs. 'Thank you, your chest sounds much better,' she pulls my pyjama top down and smiles.

'How long,' Naomi pulls me forward as she plumps my pillows easing me back, so I am sat up.

'Three days thought I was going to lose you,' she places the tray on my knees.

'Why did I get so sick,' I attack the boiled egg with gusto and Naomi laughs ruffling my hair.

'Geroff,' I grumble, and she leans in and kisses my cheek.

'You were run down from the experiments combine that with the cold water and the stress of being shot. You couldn't cope,' She opens the curtains, and I can see an ornate formal garden. The window isn't a window but glass doors that lead out to a paved seating area.

Rita comes into view in her arms trays of bright flowers. She has a floppy hat on concealing her face. It reminds me of a time past. I know the girl isn't Gilly and a pang of regret fills me. She turns in my direction and waves at me. I smile and wave back. I would like to join her, but I doubt Naomi will let me out of bed. Cradling the mug of tea, I watch her. Two people walk toward her and I recognise them as Alfie and Bella.

'Some ones better?' Naomi bustles back in and takes the tray. I watch them planting the flowers. Ruby takes charge and I smile watching them chatting and laughing before I snuggle down to sleep.

I hear the door, and someone walks in swearing softly I smile and open my eyes it is Rita. She is the highlight of my day she is so funny. She mimics everyone she is really good and so funny in her depressed way. I am so pleased she is here.

'Sorry spilt some of your soup,' she mutters as she wanders over setting the tray down on a side table while I shuffle up the bed. Once I'm comfortable she settles it on my legs.

'You should move onto solid food it would be a lot easier. I brought mine thought we could eat together,'

'Doctor Naomi won't let me yet, and she is a bit scary,' I see her face crumple and wonder what's wrong.

'Oh, am I supposed to feed you, sorry, I didn't think of that earlier and then I saw you looking a bit pathetic, oh sorry I have been rude, oh gosh rambling again sorry,' I laugh I can't help it I wince as pain flares in my chest, and I put my hand up and rub it, she grins and sits down.

'I...can manage...soup,' I finally manage. Why is talking so hard? She has a sandwich of some sort and a cartoon of juice. We sit in silence for a bit just enjoying each other's company.

'I BET you have loads of questions, don't talk just nod,' she smiles I nod. I would chuckle but that is well out of my skill set now. I hold the oxygen mask to my face and breathe as deeply as I can, it really hurts.

'We are in a château lots of Adams come here to be assessed and then they are moved on to different communities, apparently, they can't just go free they have to be assessed. She pauses, 'do you know Gillian allows this, she disapproves of the Adam program how weird is that' she pauses again then puts her hand to her mouth as if to tell me a secret. Maybe she is? 'They think I am a bit mental…you know' she glances around as if someone might hear her confession.

'You… don't seem mental… to me,'

'Thanks,' she beams. 'Is Gillian really your friend?' I nod. 'Naomi said you help her with her work. That you are the reason Gillian doesn't like the Adam program,' she raises a brow while waiting for my answer her expression expectant.

'Oh yeah, she is. I wrote loads of reports for her about its failings. Gilly is very clever and has lots of research about the disaster,' I whisper.

'I find her intimidating if I am honest and I will be expected to work with her,' she pauses. 'If they let me work you know after all this,' her lip wobbles and her eyes are bright. Please don't cry my first thought.

'Why won't they let you work?'

'They haven't said I am mental to my face, but I'm not stupid,' she looks down and her hair swings in front of her face. I think this is a sort of coping mechanism.

'I have above average intelligence and I have been well educated. Not that I need it to make babies, I don't even like babies; I hate it here, sorry rambling again,' she runs her hands through her hair. A big grin crosses her face as she looks at me. Oh no I can guess what she is thinking. 'With you,' she bursts out laughing. How is that funny?

She gazes at me with her wide blue eyes she is of course

beautiful. Not pretty like me, but properly beautiful, all perfect symmetrical features slightly pouty lips and hound dog eyes, even more so with her melancholy. Yeah, I find her attractive. Of course, it could be the Echo bond thingy. That I fought so hard to resist when we were in captivity.

'I'm not crazy, well I don't think I am. I am so glad you're here,' she looks away. 'I thought I would never find you and then I learn you are with Gillian,' she bites her lip. 'Do you love her? I mean sorry that was rude. I mean you have been with her for ages and Naomi said… well that she taught you stuff. It's alright if you love her, I don't mind…' she looks away a flush creeps up her cheeks.

'What, no, I don't love her. I do enjoy her company, but I can assure you there is no love involved,'

'She likes you though,'

'Yes, we have been friends for a long time,' I explain a smile on my lips.

'Do you love me?' She bites her lip. 'You said you did but you were very sick at the time,' she looks away as her clasped hands in her lap.

'I think so. I thought it was the bond thing but then I realised it was more than that,'

'You did? I love you too,'

'Well, yes I guessed that from the kissing,' She pushes my arm in indignation, and I laugh pulling her into me and kissing her.

'Aaron,' she whines when I let her go.

'I'm not well enough for more than kissing,' I smirk.

'Getting ahead of yourself,' she shoots back. 'But you are right you need sleep,'

She picks up our lunch things and shuffles out the room. I sigh and settle down for a nap. At some point she snuggles into my bed with me.

CHAPTER 15

I have been out of bed for two days, and I am exploring the château today, it is awesome I never thought I would get to look around it. I say real sort of loosely, as it is one of those mock stately homes built as a castle by someone with lots of money and a large ego. I am in the back wing wandering down a corridor admiring the paintings, I love art and I recognise some of the artists. I am currently stood back admiring a stunning landscape.

'It's fabulous isn't it,' I startle slightly; I thought I was on my own. I look round to see Rita. She like me is dressed in jeans and a shirt her pale hair in plait down her back. Her hands are clasped behind her back. I haven't seen her since I have been out of bed. The pleasure I feel at seeing her is... unexpected.

'Yes, it is,' I answer as she moves closer.

'Do you like paintings?' She asks smiling as her blue eyes study me.

'Yes,' I answer. Her familiar scent calms me, and I relax giving her a slow smile. She stares at me for a moment. Her cheeks pinken and I can't help the smirk. She looks away.

'The best ones are in the east wing; in grandma's apartments would you like to see them. She has a Monet you might like.' She blinks slowly her hand slipping into mine waiting for my answer. For a moment I am lost as our eyes connect.

'I would like that,' her blush deepens as she smiles at me.

'You don't say much do you,' I burst out laughing and she stops walking and laughs as well. 'I talk to much don't I.'

'Um yes a bit, but it's nice,' I smile as she leads me along the corridors. I have no idea which part of the château I am in now and I am glad Rita is with me.

'I read you didn't have a conventional upbringing. Not in a home with other boys,' she gazes at me.

'Yes, I was in a home once. You have read my file?'

'Yes, when I was told you were my match,'

'Anything of interest?' I raise a brow.

'Only that you are a rare twin. Do you miss him?'

'Yes,' I say quietly.

'Oh, sorry have I upset you,' she bites her lip her gaze somewhere on a spot on the floor.

'No, really its fine,' I reassure giving her arm a squeeze. 'We were being hunted even back then it was safer to separate us. The home I was in was attacked. I can't say if they were after me or just Adams in general,'

'Is that when you met that girl?'

'Janey, yes she saved my life,'

'That is why you are so valuable. You are proven,' I wince at this. It sort of annoys me.

'Yes,' I smile as I think about Edward.

'Your brother is with my sister. She was distraught when he got shot,'

'Is she nice your sister?'

'Sophie... she isn't like us a bit feral grandma says. The youngest so no one bothered with her much you know. She ran away after our father died. They were very close. I should have listened. Been there for her, but I wasn't,' she turns to me. 'I regret that,' she looks away and we walk in silence.

'Mum sent her to a community. I haven't seen her for a while as I was away at school. Then mum sent her to meet your brother, but he ran before they met. She tracked him and caught him. Dad taught her to hunt. Not boys though,' Rita giggles at this and I can't help but chuckle this is all fascinating.

'I bet he wasn't impressed at being caught.'

'No, he wasn't. He gave her such a hard time. Sophie was quite put out,' she giggles at this. 'I should have run away,' her voice quiet. 'Gone with Sophie,' her posture seems to slump, crumble almost. I search for something to say.

'Ah but then you wouldn't have met me,' I tease. 'You might have fallen for my brother instead,' I pretend to be shocked, and she giggles.

'We will never know,' she giggles again as we start walking again. 'Although he looks just like you, I believe,'

'Yes, identical twins. People say he is delicate not robust like me,'

She doesn't talk after that, and she doesn't look at me. She looks so sad now and I feel bad. She reminds me of Adam a bit. She doesn't belong here in this system like he didn't. To mentally delicate my Mother had once said about Adam and Rita she is the same, I think.

'Here we are,' Rita knocks on a green door and then pushes it open and walks in. It is much lighter in here and the décor isn't as heavy not so much chintz it's plainer. Rita leads me into a little sitting room and shows me the Monet, it is stunning, I have only seen paintings like this in books and to see it for real is awesome. I stand and gaze at it smiling. 'Do you like it?'

'Oh yes it's amazing,' I breathe completely captivated by it.

'I think it's a bit…. splodges, he went blind didn't he,' Rita cocks her head to one side as she gazes at it.

'Splodges? It's brilliant,' I answer still transfixed by the painting.

'Yeah, do you want to see the dungeons?' Rita turns to look at me. I can see she doesn't find the painting as interesting as I do.

'Yeah, why not,' I reply as she pulls me away from the painting and toward another door. We descend a set of stone steps. I feel the temperature drop as we go lower. I briefly worry I won't be able to get back up them. Rita leads me into a large stone room it is cold and damp and smells all earthy. I gaze around taking in the cobbled floor and the vaulted stone ceiling. The walls are lined with row upon row of wine bottles, all dusty.

'This is awesome,' I mutter as I slowly turn, my mouth slightly open, it is just like how I imagined a dungeon to be, apart from the wine.

'Oh, this isn't the best bit, come on,' Rita takes my hand and drags me further in. We enter another large room but this one has metal bars splitting it into a series of small prison cells. I walk up to a metal door and run my hands over it. I give it a shake like they do in books. It makes a satisfying metal clanging noise and I grin.

'Amazing,' I mutter, walking around imagining prisoners in here. I run my hand over the rough stone walls. I wonder how many other people have touched these walls. As my fingers run along the rusted rings attached to the walls and I imagine what it must have been like to be chained to these walls.

'You are so funny,' Rita giggles. 'No one was ever imprisoned in here it was built just for show and to store the estate wine,' Rita explains sort of ruining the illusion, but I don't honestly care they are still awesome.

'What, no I'm not, this is awesome. I have only read about dungeons in books, and this is real,' I beam at her as I walk around stopping next to her. 'Thank you for showing this to me,' we gaze at each other the tension palpable between us. I lick my lips. She moves nearer. Reaching up her lips over mine.

I kiss her back. My hands on her hips her hands around my waist. I nibble her lip and she parts them with a little moan as I deepen the kiss. She isn't like Gilly all dominating always fighting me. Rita is soft and compliant. I can feel her vulnerability just in this kiss. This kiss is nothing like we have shared before. Before I held back frightened of the bond but now, I let it do its thing.

Pulling back, she gazes at me. We are both breathing hard from the reaction of the kiss. I want to do that again but already I can see her closing off. A blush on her cheeks and she can't look at me.

'They will be looking for you,' Rita takes my hand and pulls me back to the stone stairs. Oh hell, I had forgotten about them. To be honest that kiss is pretty much all I can think about.

I start to climb them slowly, I let go of Rita's hand as she charges forward. I get halfway and have to stop, holding my chest, wheezing. I bend over trying to catch my breath my vision has dots dancing as my brain is pounding in my skull.

'Aaron, are you okay?' Rita asks, a worried frown on her face. I can't speak and just put my hand up indicating I need a minute, I try to take a deep breath, my chest really hurts, and I gasp in short breaths. This is the sort of pain that truly focuses the mind, I start the climb again. The pain in my chest is awesome and I feel lightheaded as sweat breaks out on my forehead. I will myself not to pass out, as falling down these stairs would make the pain in my chest the least of my problems.

'It's not far now Aaron,' Rita puts her arm around my waist as I trudge slowly upward. I get to the top and sink on to the carpet Rita sits next to me and peers into my face as I take deep breaths, I manage to nod and finally manage a smile. Before the darkness closes in as I can't breathe. I have no idea how long I lay there until I feel strong arms lift me up and a voice I recognise as Andrea, she is telling Rita off as she carries me back to my room.

'Sorry Naomi I didn't mean to hurt him,' Rita sobs she holds my hand.

'Rita, we told you he was fragile,' Naomi replies, her voice sounds annoyed.

'He liked the dungeon. I forgot about the steps. I didn't realise he wouldn't be able to get up them again, I am really sorry. Will he be alright?'

'Yes, he just needs oxygen again,' Naomi sighs as Andrea kicks the bedroom door open and strides to the bed, she lays me down and puts the oxygen mask over my face, I open my eyes and smile before drifting to sleep.

'Aaron, I brought you some dinner,' I open my eyes to see Rita holding a tray. I scoot up the bed and push the oxygen mask down my face.

'Thanks,' I smile at Rita, and she beams back visibly relaxing.

'I brought mine as well, I hope you don't mind,' she puts the tray on my legs and shuffles next to me. 'You have been asleep for ages; I got a right telling off. Andrea was very annoyed, she guarded the door and wouldn't let anyone in while you slept, I think she likes you,' she giggles.

'Of course, she likes me she is my bodyguard,' I chuckle and roll my eyes.

'Oh, I lost mine,' as she takes the covers off the plates, its pork chop and sausage and mashed potato with gravy. My stomach growls and I glance at Rita as we eat in silence. I can guess she means dead when she says *lost*. As I could so easily lose Andrea.

'Thanks for taking me,' I manage lifting the mask from my face. I had replaced it after dinner feeling breathless again. Rita is sat on my bed holding my hand. Her brow furrowed with concern.

'Aaron?'

'Hmm,' I look up in time for Rita's soft lips to touch mine as she kisses me tentatively. I am a bit startled, and then kiss her back. She pushes me back into the pillows as her tongue skims my lower lip asking for entry. I allow her and there is no stopping my groan of approval as her small hands fist my hair tugging on it. Eventually she pulls back breathing hard her cheeks flushed a shy smile on her lips which are pink. For my part I am enjoying all this kissing.

'Do you want to see the horse's tomorrow?' She gazes at me expectantly and I can see she is trying to make up for earlier.

'Yes please, I would like that, as long as there aren't any stairs,'

'No, no stairs and Gillian had your horse brought here so we could go riding when you are better,' she gushes all excited at that prospect. 'Gillian said you like horse riding that you are good at it,' she beams. 'Something we have in common that's good Naomi says,'

I lean forward and kiss her to show her I'm not cross with her because I have to stay in bed the rest of the day. She collects the trays and I lay down just resting. My mind thinking about kissing Rita.

I chuckle when Andrea enters my room scowling. I haven't seen Rita today and she didn't sleep with me last night.

'Naomi sent me to watch you, it would seem as soon as I take my eyes off you, you get into trouble,' she grumbles while pulling a couple of packs of cards from her pocket. 'Poker?' she looks at me while shuffling one of the packs and I nod grinning. She taught me when I was lonely. Missing Gillian when she was away.

'Andrea, at the beach…I could have lost you?' I gaze at her as I lose yet again, glad we aren't playing for money or even worse Vodka shots.

'No lamb can't get rid of me so easily. Certainly not from scum like them,' she grumbles.

'Who were they?'

'They were the Dread riders,' Andrea snorts derisively. 'A rambling horde; they are led by a Lady Ariella. She is a very astute woman and spends a lot of her time trading Adams and information. Gen-Corp have a treaty with her and monitor her Adams, as does the United Human Federation.'

'I don't think I like the sound of them,' I mutter sorting my cards.

'They have been after your brother almost caught him not long ago. Gillian had to intervene to keep him safe.' Andrea picks up a card while regarding me.

'You could have given me to them, named your price, you know what I am?' I glance up at her.

'That would not be beneficial to me or my reputation.' She answers as she beats me again. 'You will return to Tribe with Rita when your training is complete,'

'Taking Rita was a big risk for them,'

'Yes, an audacious move. It is dangerous for people like you and Rita,' She answers dealing the cards.

'What about my brother?' I glance at her as she studies her cards.

'There has been a problem that Gillian is sorting out. Don't worry he is safe,' she glances at me.

I am allowed up after lunch. I put my favourite black jeans on, and a warm jumper, the château is cold.

Rita appears and I stand up from the bed, smiling at seeing her, she grabs my hand and drags me out the room making me laugh.

'Rita, what's the rush,' I gasp following her.

'Slow down,' I manage, and she stops turning to me her eyes wide with worry.

'Oh, sorry I forgot again. I am so sorry, gosh I am so rubbish aren't I,' she puts her hand over her mouth.

'No, it's fine,' I chuckle pulling her in for a kiss.

'Andrea might say no,' Rita giggles. As she drags me across a cobbled yard to an elaborate building where the horses are. I want to admire the architecture, but Rita isn't having any of it as she pushes me inside. The stable resembles a mini stately home with just as much attention to detail as the château.

'This is amazing,' I turn in a circle admiring it until I hear Milton. I rush to his stable. Rita and kissing temporarily forgotten.

CHAPTER 16

I push the cream painted doors of the library open and step inside it is dark, so I flick the lights on and look around it is deserted. I hear a noise from the far end. I look at the note from Rita to meet her here.

'Rita is that you why are you hiding?' I ask loudly frowning as I walk further into the library. All the hairs on my neck stand on end and I shiver.

The rows of shelving containing the books seem intimidating. The room is cold the large fireplaces devoid of comforting warmth. I am used to this room and have spent many hours curled in one of the overstuffed chairs reading. Now though it is cold and empty. Outside the rain beats against the tall windows casting intricate shadows on the floor. An involuntary shiver skitters through my body.

Moving further in I glance up the metal winding staircase to the upper level that is shrouded in darkness. Turning as I hear footsteps on the wooden floor as a lamp flickers off. Bathing the area in darkness. Instinctively I wrap my arms around my body and start back toward the doors.

'Rita this isn't funny, you will get me in trouble with

Naomi,' I call again still nothing, but I catch a glimpse of someone behind a shelf, I take half a step forward, I hear Andrea shouting my name. I turn as the doors burst open and Andrea rushes in as a hand clamps over my face holding a piece of cloth over my nose and mouth. I struggle for a bit until my eyelids start to close and I am slowly lowered to the floor. The last thing I hear is Andrea's voice shouting and popping noises, as I sink into darkness, and someone pushes my sleeve up on the arm that has my number tattooed on it.

I wake in my bed, alone. It is dark and the curtains are closed. I climb out of bed and wobble to my door. It is locked. Frowning I shuffle back to bed. The room is cold. The fire that is normally lit is out.

Wriggling back under the covers. Only to startle awake when my door opens and Naomi bustles in. Followed by one of the maids who goes about sorting the fire.

'What's going on?' Pushing up as she sits on the bed. She takes her pen light thing and shines it in my eyes.

'We were attacked,'

'Who by? Is Rita, okay?'

'Rita is fine. Get some sleep and in the morning, you start your training,'

'Sure,' snuggling down as Andrea enters my room. They have a whispered conversation that I can't hear and then both leave. The maid has the fire going and comes over pulling the bedcovers straight she gives me a shy smile. Turning she leaves. Alone I hear the distinctive sound of my door being locked. Scrambling out of bed I stumble to the door and try it. It doesn't budge. Firmly locked. Why have they locked me in? Climbing back into bed I snuggle down closing my eyes. I will sort all this in the morning.

I wake to sunlight streaming in. Sitting up the maid from last night bustles in opening the curtains and disappearing into the bathroom. The sound of running water has me climbing out of bed.

'I can do that,' she startles and then blushes.

'Madam Naomi instructed me sir,'

'I am sure she did, but I don't need any help thank you,' I smile, and she blushes again. She is very young sixteen at most.

'This is my job,' she stutters out. 'I will get into trouble,' Well this is awkward.

'Okay, how about you go into the other room while I bathe and if I need you, I will call,' she nods, as I expel a breath with relief.

Walking down to the dining area I notice the place is deserted. The dining room is laid out for breakfast, so I make my tea and butter some toast. Moving to the window with my mug cradled in my hands. The clatter of horse's hooves draws my attention. A group of people enter the yard. They look resplendent in their scarlet cloaks with a royal crest emblazoned on it.

'Aaron,' turning to my name I am pleased to see Toby.

'What's going on?' I ask.

'Nice to see you as well,'

'Sorry. It is nice to see you,' Toby chuckles as he pours a coffee. He is dressed like the people outside. Jodhpurs and riding boots. Shirt and blazer under the cloak that he has discarded over a chair. He runs his finger through his hair while waiting for his coffee.

'Having to increase your security after yesterday,'

'How come you are here?'

'They thought it better if I train with you. Easier to guard us together. Had a few close calls myself,' he shrugs reaching for the jam to put on his toast. 'Sorry about Heath,'

'Thanks,' I don't know what else to say so sip my tea. A welcomed distraction of the door opening and a woman bustles in. Her hands laden with books. She looks at the two of us and smiles.

'Madame Spencer,' she introduces. 'I am here to start your political training. You will also have self-defence and of course the pleasure of sex,' She smiles and plonks the books down on a table. 'I want you both to read these,' she indicates the pile of books on the royal houses of Europe, fighting techniques and the Karma sutra. She hands us another on the great leaders of Europe. 'You have until Friday,' she smiles again and leaves the room.

'Well, this looks suitably dull and weird all at once,' Toby chuckles.

'No kidding,'

'Who are you matched too?' I glance at Toby. A smile pulls at his features giving him a wistful look.

'Princess Maria, captain of the imperial guard. She is amazing,' he manages a stupid grin on his face. 'She is descended from the British royal family. You know they all went into hiding together. The Spanish and Norwegian kings they devised a plan. They knew they were doomed if they didn't act got all the royal houses together and cooperating. As each country fell a coded message was set out to the people over the internet. Giving map co-ordinates. It was brilliant in its simplicity. I suppose that's how they have survived so long,'

'We have some reading to do,' I state as it occurs to me I am behind on my history.

'Library it is then,'

'So, Maria is she Tribe?'

'Tribe is the collective name. It is then split into houses or principalities. Then there is a queen who presides over it all. Keeping it unified. Maria is from one of those territories,' He explains as we walk.

Saturday and I don't have any lessons. It was as I drank

my second cup of tea that I realised I hadn't seen Rita since the attack and the royal guard arriving. Pushing to my feet I make my way up the sweeping staircase. Admiring the frescoes on the walls. I realised I didn't know where Rita's room was.

Walking along the hall admiring the artwork along the way I stop outside a door. Listening I can hear the sobs and instinct tells me it is Rita. Placing my hand on the handle I turn it and push open the door. Slipping inside the dark room I close the door. The large four poster bed dominates the room. Painted furniture in cream matches the pink and grey décor. Making my way to the bed dodging the clothes and books that litter the floor.

'Rita,' my voice quiet so as not to startle her.

'Go away,' her muffled reply.

'Why? I haven't seen you all week and I have missed you,' Sitting on the edge of the bed far enough away not to crowd her.

'Because this is a bad idea and you got hurt and that will keep happening because of me,'

'No Rita that wasn't your fault,' I plead.

'Of course, it was,' her head appears from under the quilt her features painted with anger. 'They will keep hunting us to use like farm animals we aren't people to them. And you don't deserve that,' she shouts at me her face blotched with red showing her rage.

'So, you are letting them win. You don't want me. Well fine if that is how you feel but please have the decency to tell me not make up some rubbish to justify your behaviour,' Pushing to my feet I glance at her in disgust.

'I am not letting them win they have won,' she leaps from the bed and blocks the door. 'I do want you,' tears glisten in her eyes.

'Then fight for me. Show them they haven't won. Please,' reaching out tucking her pale hair behind her ear.

'Why? Why should I bother to fight? So, they can breed us like animals?' She is shouting at me as I step back startled at her emotion. 'That's what all this is about,' she waves her hand around the room. 'Breeding babies that's all my life will be. Trapped in a gilded cage,' she bursts into tears again.

'Because I love you,' I shout back annoyed and angry. 'Because I have spent years training to be with you. Gave up my brother and the boy I loved to be with you. He gave his life so I could be with you,' I pull her close and crush my lips to hers. The bond snaps into place as we scramble to remove each other's clothes. I hoist her up against the door her legs wrap around my waist as my hips surge forward. Her hiss of pain makes me pause as I hold her gaze.

'No don't stop,' she gasps as she kisses me her hands in my hair as our frenzied movements bang against the door. With a cry I sink to the floor with Rita in my lap her head resting on my shoulder. Pushing up I stagger to the bed. Rita still wrapped around me. I need her again my thoughts only for her. I kiss her gently and we spend time exploring each other.

'I am sorry,' she whispers as she peppers my face with kisses. 'I thought I was trapping you with me and it made me so angry,' her voice is quiet now as she looks at me and I think it is the first time she sees me as a person.

'Being with you isn't trapping me. I want to be with you,' I answer slumping against the headboard exhausted from all that activity.

'You love me?' She looks at me. 'How do you know that. How do you know it isn't just our circumstance?'

'Because... because I have loved before,' I admit. Her hands are touching, stroking I reach down and capture them in mine if she doesn't stop, I will take her again. She lifts her head as she studies me.

'Tell me,' she straddles my waist joining us intimately. I suck in a breath.

'You want me to tell you about Heath,' she nods her eyebrows raise but she doesn't speak. 'I was lonely and missing Gilly and my brother. I was also scared they were teaching me all this stuff for you, and they wanted to study me, and I was scared they would hurt me and then he appeared. Well, he sort of ambushed me. Suddenly I wasn't alone,' I shrug. 'I don't know if that is love but it felt special,'

'Sorry Aaron,'

'It's alright, it was a long time ago,' I glance at her and start to move as she leans down and kisses me.

'Do you really love me?' she whispers slumped on my chest.

'Yes,' I get comfortable pulling her into me. 'I am exhausted, felt agitated and out of sorts for days now. Do you mind if I have a nap,' I mumble holding her tight.

'Sorry, that's the bond. I shouldn't have avoided you all week,'

'Ah yes the Echo thingy,' I mumble before closing my eyes. I wake feeling refreshed Rita is curled into me her head under my chin.

'Don't know about you but I am starving,' I announce kissing the top of her head as my tummy makes a loud grumble. Rita giggles.

'I think you should shower and get dressed.

'Everyone will wonder what we have been doing in here all day,'

'Rita, they are hoping we bonded...repeatedly,' I chuckle as she looks at me in shock. Sitting up she glares down at me. Brushing her hair from her face her eyes wide.

'No ... really,'

'Yeah really,'

'I can't leave this room, the shame,' she looks at me and I burst out laughing. 'Shut up Aaron,' she hits me with a pillow.

'No, stop, please,' I beg between chuckles. Kneeling up I pry the pillow from her grasp. 'Come on shower time,' dragging her from the bed. I show her how much fun showering together can be. The banana thing, big fat lie.

'Aaron?' Rita drifts into the library. I am curled in a chair by the fire reading another book on economics and democracy. Not sure I want to run a country it seems like a lot of paperwork. Toby had laughed at me and promised he would help me. When I had voiced that out loud. Rita bends and kisses me as I close my book.

'I have this,' she presents a small red velvet covered box. Opening it two gold bands nestle inside. My gaze finds hers as I bite my bottom lip. 'I claim you,' she whispers and slips the ring on my finger. She then pulls an envelope from behind her back. 'Your papers have come. We can go home,' she smiles as I slip the other ring onto her finger. 'Happy birthday,'

'So, I am officially yours,'

'Yes,' she scrambles into my lap pushing the book onto the floor. Her lips crash against mine.

'Do you love me?' her eyes search mine.

'Yes, very much.'

'Truly?' she frowns until I chuckle.

'Yes truly. When do we leave?'

'End of the week Andrea is making arrangements as we won't be able to do it in one go,'

CHAPTER 17

astening the saddlebag to Milton I am all packed to go. Around me the bustle of the group accompanying us. Six guard as well as Toby. Andrea and Naomi and of course me and Rita. I am a little excited to be going to Tribe at last.

It is going to take a couple of days and Andrea has already located safe places for us to spend the night.

'Ready,' Rita leads her horse next to mine her eyes shining with excitement.

'Absolutely,' leaning over for a kiss.

'Get a room you two,' Toby calls from behind us. With a chuckle I pull away. Placing my foot in the stirrup I bounce twice and swing my leg over Milton's back. Settling in the saddle as my other foot slips into the stirrup. Following the guard out the yard.

We make good progress through the morning. The scenery amazing with the abandoned villages crumbling as the land reclaims. We don't see any other people this part is sparsely populated according to all the reading I have done recently.

'Race you,' Rita trots up to me as we crest a hill. The view over lakes and farmland with it patch work of fields stitched together by woodland is amazing. I glance at her and that is all the encouragement she needs as we both career down the hill laughing and cheering as we go the guard joins us and Toby is soon catching me up. We come to a stop at the bottom laughing as we catch our breath. Our spirits are high as we turn toward the small town and our first overnight stop.

Entering what was left of the town turned the mood sombre. The guard somehow moved so Rita ,Toby and I were in the middle with them surrounding us.

'Toby, Aaron, put your hoods up and wrap your cloaks around you please,' Andrea instructed. I glanced at Toby as we moved along the remains of the street. Either side crumbling buildings overgrown with shrubs. A shiver skittered down my spine as we moved further in.

Ahead I could see Andrea talking to the captain of the guard. She glanced back at Toby and I her expression one of concern. Out the corner of my eye I would catch glimpses of people scuttling down streets and alleyways. All giving us a wide berth. I can't help feeling we are being watched and our progress monitored.

We arrive at what is the most intact building we have seen so far. Intact is possibly a slight exaggeration. It has four walls and a roof. Andrea dismounts and we all do the same. I stand with Toby and Rita. Rita brushes my hand and I grasp hers. I don't like this it feels wrong.

'Aaron you are with Rita and Bonnie and Lynda are your guards you do not go anywhere without them understood,' We both nod as two guards flank us. I look for Toby and see he is stood with Maria and another guard I don't know. The remaining two are in discussion with Andrea. They nod and take the horses. Lynda turns to me.

'May I,' her voice is surprisingly soft.

'Um, yes,' I am not sure what it is she is asking permission for until her hands pull my cloak, so it shrouds my body hiding the fact I am male. She then reaches up and pulls my hood, so it conceals my face.

'I suggest you do not speak,' she smiles, and I feel Rita tighten her grip on my hand. I notice Toby is shrouded in his cloak now.

Entering the building the smell of unwashed bodies mixed with tobacco and alcohol assault my nostrils. The room is murky with wall lights flickering through the haze. The conversations stop for a moment as all eyes are on us. Rita moves closer to my side.

'I have three rooms booked,' Andrea instructs the bar tender. She looks us over.

'Sign here,' she pushes a book toward Andrea. 'Traveling to Tribe?' She asks while drying a glass. The question sounds casual but at least three pairs of eyes are watching us and paying close attention.

'Yes, we are returning to the capitol, Stockholm,' Andrea answers.

'Haven't seen this many guards,' the bar tender appraises us. I am thankful we are all dressed the same. 'Do you have males with you?'

'What's it to you?' Andrea narrows her eyes at the bar girl.

'I could make the night one of profit,' she looks Andrea in the eye.

'No, and if I had we are royal guard so that is off limits you know the rules,'

'Just asking,' the girl huffs and grabs some keys passing them to Andrea.

'We are tired could you send up refreshments,' Andrea passes a pile of notes across the bar.

'Certainly,' the bar girl smiles, and I shiver at her expression.

Bonnie enters the room first she stalks around it and then ushers us inside. Lynda has gone to talk to Andrea. I sit on the bed with Rita trying to ignore the musty mouldy smell. Lynda walks in and looks around.

'Stay covered,' she instructs, and we both pull our hoods up again and wrap our cloaks around us. A knock on the door has Lynda pulling her gun as she opens it. A girl stands with a tray. 'Thank you,' Lynda takes the tray as the girl tries to come inside. Shutting the door, she places the tray on a chest of drawers that have seen better days.

'Eat,' Lynda instructs. 'I suggest we sleep in our clothes in case we must leave in a hurry. Rita pours me a drink which I accept gratefully. The food looks inauspicious, but I am hungry so take a pie of some sort and tentatively eat it.

'You two take the bed,' I curl up with Rita using our cloaks as a blanket. I wake a little while later and run to the sink throwing up, crumpling to the floor as our door opens and Andrea rushes in, she takes one look at me and hurries over scooping me up. Lynda has Rita shivering in her arms.

'Drugged the food to see if we had Echo's,' Andrea growls. Taking me down the stairs and out a back door I hadn't noticed earlier.

Outside is chaos. I notice Maria peering around a wall behind her one of the guards has Toby he is leaning over and being sick in the gutter. Two women dressed in long black coats make a grab for him. From my hiding spot I can see the fight break out. These women don't look like the ones from the tavern. These are well dressed. Another of the guards' rushes to their aid shooting a shabby looking woman as an exchange of fire breaks out.

More Gun fire drowning out the shouting. Toby goes to run, after a brief exchange with Maria. Another shot and

Toby stumbles. I go to get up as Andrea grabs me forcing me back. When I look over Maria has scooped up Toby while shooting at another group of women. I feel relief as Maria has Toby limp in her arms as the two guards that were dealing with the horses are shielding them. All have their guns drawn.

'I can walk Andrea,' I mumble.

'Not safe,' Andrea has us concealed behind the building using it as cover. Attention is on Tobies group, so we creep toward the stables. The click of a loading gun has us stop in our tracks.

'Well, what do we have here?' A woman steps from the shadows as three more move to surround us. Already Andrea, Lynda and Bonnie have their weapons ready. I am pushed from behind and in doing so my hood slips down. 'Well would you look at that,' They converge on us as Andrea grabs me and knocks me to the ground as guns go off.

Arms wrap around my middle, and I am hauled to my feet. Stumbling forward it is then I notice the bodies littering the ground.

'Move now,' Lynda has hold of me as Bonnie drags Rita toward the horses. Light splashes through the dark as we near the stable and I can see the limp form of Toby being passed up to Maria.

'We will go east to the safe house you take him northeast there is a camp. Tell Florence the situation,'

'He will get sick out here,' Maria replies concern in her voice.

'You need to get Prince Toby safe now. Aaron is tougher than he looks. We will only be a day behind,' Maria nods in agreement and then clatters away from the Inn urging her horse into a gallop followed by the remaining guards.

The constant drizzle of rain is draining my energy reserves as I shiver from cold. I look around to see where we are, but everything is grey and muddy. We are still in open countryside, and I can't see any houses anywhere not even farm buildings. Part of me is relieved, people are just trouble.

Gun fire had followed us as they chased us. We were on superior horses and soon our pursuers give up. Lynda has Rita while Bonnie is behind us leading the horses laden with supplies. Now I am leaning against Andrea concealed beneath my cloak as she holds me tight.

'Soon be safe Aaron,' her voice sincere as if I would ever doubt her.

'Toby where is he?' I ask.

'Safe with Maria safer to split up,'

'Was he hurt?'

'Nothing serious a bullet grazed him that's all. He will wake with a headache,' Andrea reassures.

'But he is an Echo,' I worry about my friend.

'Maria will get him safe. That's why we sent them ahead,'

We finally slow as we near a small village and I am so grateful. I really need to stretch my legs. Andrea signals to Lynda as she leads the way to a cottage. Strong arms lift me down and I follow to where there is a small barn for the horses. I sit on a bale with Rita. Andrea looks us both over as we shiver still suffering the effects of the drug in the food. While Lynda and Bonnie unload the horses and brush them down before feeding them. I stroke Milton while I wait, nobody talks, the trauma of the last few days has drained us of anything to say.

'I will get the generator going,' Bonnie mutters disappearing around the side of the house.

We trudge to the house and Andrea feels for the key on the lintel above the door. Unlocking, Andrea puts a code into a keypad. She pushes the door open and we all troop inside, as she switches on the lights. A cold damp permeates through the house, showing it has been empty a while. I shiver and wrap my arms around myself as I glance around. We are standing in a kitchen if the sink and stove are anything to go by. A fire is laid out in the hearth and Andrea soon gets it going as Rita changes from her soiled clothing. Handing me clean clothes I do the same. The dry clothes are amazing, and I feel better already. Rita gathers them up and loads the washer. She has a thing for clean clothes.

'How does it work?' I ask indicating the house.

'A generator in the shed behind. This is a safe house. We have a few scattered along the route. Someone checks them every few months. Keeps them stocked. Checks, they are clean. That they haven't been broken into. Somewhere safe when traveling,' Bonnie replies as she comes in the door, removing her cloak.

Rita has the washer going and is now looking through the cupboards. I can hear Andrea in the other room checking it is secure. I smile at Rita and fill the kettle at the sink and switch it on. Andrea's fire soon warms the place up as Rita finds some tins of soup and heats it up while making cheese on toast to go with it.

'All secure upstairs,' Bonnie says walking in.

'All secure down here as well,' Andrea replies.

We sit in silence and eat the toast and soup which although is just plain tomato is delicious. I help Rita wash up then we climb the stairs both still feeling the effect of the drug.

'Can I sleep with you,' she bites her lip as she holds my gaze.

'Sure, I thought you were anyway,'

'You did?' she says as she follows me into the room.

'Course,' I am too tired for this conversation. She is so insecure, and I don't understand why? Pulling my jumper and shirt over my head. Dropping my trousers, I climb into the bed. Closing my eyes, I hear the rustle of clothes then the bed dips and she snuggles down around me. I just lay there worrying about Toby. Until I hear voices. Concentrating I listen.

'Andrea, we have to get him somewhere safe before he gets sick,'

'I know Lynda but where is safe. All of us together is just attracting to much attention,'

'Can't Rita get him to Sara. They can over winter there and then we collect them in the spring when all this nonsense has died down with his twin. Besides they bonded if she is pregnant, we need her somewhere safe,'

'Okay, you two go on tell Sara to expect them. I will stay here another day and then get them to the ferry,'

'So, you won't cross with them?'

'No, I need to go back. Madame Ramsbottom needs help with the twin.'

'Okay, stay safe,'

'And you, we will see you in the spring,' I hear the door open and close as the house goes quiet.

'Aaron,' Rita's breathy voice distracts he as her lips find mine. I pull her against me.

I am awake early. Leaving Rita to sleep I go and sort out the horses. Andrea appears just as I finish doing the hay nets.

'Feeling better,' she is still watching me as I sweep up. Putting away the wheelbarrow and broom I lean against Milton's stall.

'Andrea is Rita strong enough. I worry that now I have completed the bond it could kill her, She is so delicate, and I don't just mean physically,' I couldn't sleep after we had made love and worried about this last night. 'If anything happens to her, I don't want to be passed around like some new toy.'

'Rita is complicated,' Andrea pauses. 'We failed her, and she got taken. They had her for months before they caught you. They messed with her, mentally. She needs you. Just give her time,'

'She is more valuable than me if she is pregnant. I don't think she is yet as I still feel the pull around her, but it is only a matter of time.'

'The pair of you together that is a temptation many would risk their life for and that is a worry,'

'Why not move us separately?'

'Rita needs you. Without you we may lose her anyway.'

'She would do that?'

'Some of the Adams do. Your brother was a worry before he ran. Emma failed him almost completely. If it wasn't for his watcher, it might have been a different outcome,'

'I see Rita claimed you that is good will keep you safe,' the anxiety slowly melting away. We stand like that for what seems like ages before Andrea speaks again.

'Can I ask you something and I need an honest answer,'

'Sure,' my curiosity peaked.

'What do you know about the poison, Aaron?' This catches me off guard not the question I was expecting. Not sure what I was expecting but this isn't it.

'That out here I will get sick as my body tries to purge it. But as I am exposed to more of it, I will suffer a kind of anaphylactic shock and my bodies reaction to that could kill me,' I look at Andrea and bite my lip unsure. 'Most the population is affected by it even the Adams now. I read a report that Gillian was now testing the girls. Finding the clean ones and using them as matches instead of surrogates. My brother he was intimate with a girl before Sophie. Ellie, I believe her name is. She had a son. Adams son, and he is robust like a natural and has a natural immunity. No sickness. When I was fourteen the home, I was in was attacked my mother murdered. A girl saved my life, and she has a son, my son and he is strong and robust he also has a natural immunity.'

'Your brother does he know?'

'No, we are worried he might run again,'

'When you say we you mean Gillian?'

'And Celina,' I shrug.

'You are very well informed. That about sums it up but it's the bit about you I was interested in,' Andrea shrugs.

'Are you worried about how I will react?'

'Everyone reacts different. But yes, I am worried. I want you safe to give you the best chance. Your brother was very sick and at one point they thought he might die,'

'Will I die?'

'I hope not?'

'Well, that wasn't very reassuring,' I smile and Andrea chuckles. 'I have, bonded with Rita so it might not be such a disaster. For you as opposed to me who will be dead,' I joke. Not that it is funny.

'You won't die, but good to know,' Andrea smirks making me smile.

'If I do, promise you will look after her,' she must have seen all those conflicting emotions on my face. I release my lip which I am currently worrying with my teeth and attempt to smile at her.

'It will be fine Aaron,'

'If it isn't promise me, you will look after her,' I hold Andrea's gaze.

'If it is within my power, I will do everything to keep her safe. You won't die,'

'Thank you,'

Andrea smiles at me and she squeezes my shoulder in a reassuring gesture, but I don't feel very reassured. Scare me, well they have succeeded I am scared, as all sorts of stupid ideas run through my head. Andrea was lying, that thought is at the front. Everyone lies to me at some point, Gilly, Rita, even Toby did and now Andrea. I sigh and wipe my eyes I really have got to stop crying it makes me weak. Rita is sick today and just stays in bed. She is an Echo but unlike me she has more immunity to the contaminant. I take her a cup of tea.

'Hi how are you feeling?' she turns over and gives me a wobbly smile. Her face pale and purple marks under her eyes.

'Better,' wriggling up she takes the tea. 'Thank you,' she sips it. I bend and kiss her cheek.

'No Aaron I'm all sweaty and disgusting,' she complains.

'I like you all sweaty,' I flirt back, and she giggles I drift back downstairs.

Andreas phone rings and she takes it from her pocket walking out the room as she answers it, I can't hear what she is saying. I find a music channel and just listen to it not paying any attention until Rita comes in with a hot chocolate for me, she smiles gently at me, and I know she is worried, probably waiting for all my questions to start but I don't. I need to think, sort out everything that is in my head. I sit and drink the chocolate it is soothing and nice. She has been different around me since we left the château. I catch her looking at me as if she is waiting for me to break or something.

Andrea makes us some supper and after I drift back upstairs to bed. I have a restless night dreaming of burning houses and bodies and me melting, whatever that's about. Sitting up I let my eyes adjust to the dark before climbing out of bed to go to the bathroom. Rita stays in her room as she still feels sick. I told her I loved her and now I doubt everything.

Shuffling along the hall on my way back to bed. Only to stop at the sound of crying. Pausing to listen trying to decide where it is coming from. Downstairs I can hear Andrea talking on her phone in rapid Russian. I creep along a bit more and pause outside the other bedroom. Quiet sniffles have me pushing the door open.

'Rita are you okay?' stepping inside my hand on the door handle.

'N…no,' her voice trembles. This has me rushing across the room.

'What's the matter?' she throws the duvet to one side, and I climb in. She immediately snuggles into me.

'I don't like the dark,' she mumbles into my chest. 'But I can't sleep with a light on,'

'Well, aren't you conflicted,' I chuckle.

'Don't you make fun of me tuber,' her mumbled indignation is a delight.

'Wow that was rude,' closing my eyes getting comfortable.

'I heard you talking to Andrea. I heard what you said,' she sniffles again.

'I am just worried that's all,' I reassure.

'Don't be. I will take care of you,' her sleepy voice mumbles.

'Yeah, but who takes care of you,' I sigh as I settle to sleep.

'Aaron,' Rita is saying my name, and I can feel her touching my face. I could open my eyes, but I am just so comfy and tired.

'You are so beautiful,' she whispers.

'Rita, go to sleep,'

'I can't, can I kiss you?'

'Then you will sleep?'

'Yes promise,' her voice is eager, and I smile. The bed shifts as she moves about. Finally, I feel her lips on mine, soft and hesitant.

'Rita, keep still,' I place my hands on her hips.

'Why it feels really nice,' she wiggles against me again as her lips move against mine.

'Yes, I know it does, but we are meant to be sleeping' She wriggles about a bit more and I groan.

'Aaron, I need this I need you,' she whispers in my ear before kissing my neck. This might not be a bad idea. If I get her pregnant, then if I don't survive this the objective has been achieved.

'Rita, I love you if this is what you need that's okay by me,'

'Really,' she is sitting up looking at me.

'Yes really,' I chuckle.

'Naomi said you have been trained in this,' I groan and curse Naomi.

'Yes, you know that' I say as patiently as possible.

'I want a baby Aaron,' she looks down at me.

'I want you to have my baby,' my thumb strokes her cheek as I cradle her face.

'I love you as well,' she whispers her hands push my pyjama bottoms down. 'I had lessons as well let me do this for you,' Brushing away her hair to see her face. Her smile is radiant as her eyes twinkle. A flush on her cheeks she is so beautiful.

'Okay,' I let her take charge.

* * *

Standing in the stable the smell of horse and hay is comforting. Resting against Milton our heads touching his soft breath mingled with mine. I pull back, his velvet soft nose against my hand snuffling for more carrot.

My thoughts are on Rita and what we did. She kept me

busy most of the night exploring, kissing, and of course joining.

Do I really want her to be pregnant? Yes, I do but I want to be with her every step. I certainly don't want to be dead. With a sigh I lean my head against Milton inhaling his scent.

Gillian bought him for me and taught me to ride. I chuckle at that pun. I miss her, didn't have this conflict with her it was all straightforward, and the consequence wasn't such a burden.

I enjoyed our time together. They were fun and Gilly was fun to be with. I understand now she was preparing me for this. For my match. For Rita. I remember something being said when I was sick when they thought I was asleep. I miss Gilly and our time together.

I brush Milton, it sooths me until Rita appears in the doorway.

'Aaron are you coming in for breakfast,' her voice is timid and she can't look me in the eye.

'Yes, let me finish here,' I make a point of smiling at her. She looks up at me a blush staining her cheeks.

'Oh...um okay,' she turns to leave.

'Rita, if you wait a minute we can walk across together,' I call to her. Rita walks back in and settles on to a bale to watch me. She doesn't speak and honestly it is making me nervous. Putting the brush back in the bucket I walk over and sit next to her.

'Rita what's the matter?' I take her hand in mine revelling at its smallness.

'Do you still like me?' She looks up at me and then glances back down her chin has a small wobble as she bites her lip.

'Of course, I do. What's brought this on?' Keeping my voice level my tone gentle.

'You weren't there when I woke up and I kind of forced you last night and I shouldn't have done that and I am sorry,' she takes a shuddering breath. 'I used you knowing you couldn't deny me because you are an Adam,' she blurts out. Her head down so as not to make eye contact.

'Rita, honey you didn't force me. That's just ridiculous. Besides you know I am not really an Adam. I haven't had that sort of training. I was never milked only occasionally for the doctors,' I run my hand through my hair in frustration. 'I… I like you okay,' heat floods my cheeks.

'I… we don't have to make a baby, we can wait,' she looks at me with an earnest expression. I laugh and her expression turns to indignation.

'I think that is a moot point,' I chuckle and kiss her.

'Oh, so you don't mind, and you aren't avoiding me,'

'No, I am not avoiding you. I had to see to the horses this morning and I didn't want to disturb you as you looked so peaceful,' wrapping my arms around her I pull her to me. 'Last night was great,' tipping her head up with my finger under her chin I place a soft kiss on her lips. 'Come on, I am starving,' pulling away I take her hands and pull her up. Keeping hold of her hand as I lead her back to the house. 'Time to say goodbye to Andrea,'

'You will miss her?'

'Yes, we have been together a while,'

'You are lucky people just love you,' she observes. I have never really thought about it.

'Yes, I suppose,' pushing the door open to be greeted by the smell of bacon.

CHAPTER 18

*T*ipping my head back I enjoy the warm sun on my face. Milton's gentle trot sooths me and my mind empties. Around the rolling countryside is beautiful in its abandonment. Just the sound of bird song and Milton's steady clop.

My attention is snapped back when Rita is beside me her hand on my reins bringing us to a stop.

'Aaron there is a check point ahead,' Rita gazes at me a worried frown etched into her brow.

'You have my movement papers, it will be fine,' I reassure.

'Aaron, thank you,'

'What for?'

'You trust me, believe in me,' she smiles.

'Of course I do I love you,' reaching across I kiss her with a passion that takes us both by surprise.

Staying back, I dismount Milton and watch Rita as she talks to the security. They aren't Gen-Corp. Two are but the others are dressed similar to me. Whereas my tunic is black with the royal crest on the pocket, there's are red. The cloaks that wrap around them have gold braid around the edge the same as mine. I take comfort in their familiarity. A line of gold up the side of their trousers which are tucked into black riding boots. A lot fancier than my plain black trousers. They certainly look impressive and a little intimidating. I recognise them as Guard.

They talk for a while, and I can see Rita is relaxed. I watch as they bow their heads to her, and it makes me smile. Enjoying seeing her in her role, a princess of Tribe. It is then I notice the two Gen-Corp security are walking toward me. I keep my posture submissive. My head bowed with my arms behind my back in the posture of an Adam.

'Arm,' one commands as they stop a few steps in front of me. Pushing up my sleeve I reveal the number tattoo on my lower arm above my wrist. They scan it and then look at me.

'Thank you, sir,' they nod at me and then saunter back to the security hut. My shoulders relax with relief.

'Your highness,' they acknowledge Rita as they walk past her. Following Rita are the other guards.

'Aaron this is Lisa and Lou, and they will accompany us for this next leg of the journey,' Rita introduces.

'Hello, Aaron, aren't you lovely,' Lisa smiles at me as she looks me over.

'Right time is of the essence so shall we get a shuffle on,' Lou glances at me a smile on her lips. It is all I can do not to laugh when she winks at me.

'All these princelings should shake up the dynamic in the principality,' Lisa remarks before mounting her horse.

* * *

THIS FEELS like flying as we gallop across the countryside. Horse riding is something I excel at and thoroughly enjoy. The wind in my hair blowing in my face. The feeling of this magnificent animal beneath me. I feel free for the first time in a long time, and it is a heady exhilaration.

I have no idea where we are going but I trust Lisa and Lou to keep us safe. We finally slow and Rita comes alongside me. Her chest heaving as she gets her breath back.

'Village up ahead it is mostly abandoned but we can overnight there and rest the horses okay,' her pale eyes rake over me as a smile twitches her lips.

'Where are we going?'

'To find the Romany,' she grins at the look on my face, I guess. As it must be registering the shock her words filled me with.

'Why are we finding the Romany? I thought we were going to a safe house?' Don't get me wrong I am utterly fascinated with the Romany having only read about them in books.

They weren't as affected by the contraceptive and kept their men safe. Eventually they succumbed but not as quickly as other areas. They also kept valuable trade links open. I read a report on how they kept their girls clean and breeding. That they often move Adams around when they are sold. Sometimes buying them for their girls.

'The safe house is to over winter in. We need the Romany for the spring. It is far too dangerous to travel alone through this part of Scandinavia.' Lisa answers as she comes up on my other side. Lou is behind always watching.

'Um will I have been sick by then?'

'Yes, but what was Norway is very contaminated due to its geography. That is the safest crossing from here.'

'Here is what was Denmark?'

'Yes,' I digest all this.

'We all get sick there. You are more vulnerable than us,' Lou answers.

'They will keep you safe and if you do get sick, they will

know how to care for you. Tribe is where you should be and I promise you I will get you there,' Rita's voice is so sincere I smile.

'Which part of Tribe are you from?'

'What was Sweden. That's where we will head too in the spring.'

'Rita, I trust you and we will get there together,' her beaming smile is reward enough. I do trust her, and I reckon between the two of us we could get to this place called Tribe. Reaching across I kiss Rita making her blush.

'Oh, aren't you two cute,' Lisa giggles as she moves ahead of us. Entering the village, a shiver runs down my spine. It is ghostly in the half light. Nature has taken over and the houses are all in various states of collapse. An owl hoots as a fox barks and it just adds to the eery atmosphere. Lisa is stopped outside a house that for the most part is intact. I jump down as she pushes the door open and disappears inside. A few minutes later she gestures to us that it is safe. Lou takes the horses. I turn to see her lead them to a ramshackle barn.

Sniffing the air my nose wrinkles at the musty smell. Mould is growing up the walls that can no longer keep the damp weather out. Following Rita up the stairs she has organised a room we can sleep in. She has a fire going in the grate and now it is warm it doesn't seem so bad. Lou and Lisa are downstairs keeping watch.

'Here,' Rita hands me a sandwich as I sit cross legged next to her. Rummaging in my bag I pass her a bottle of water.

'Do you know where they are?'

'Yes roughly,'

'Roughly!' Oh, so not sure about this.

'A day's ride if we don't run into any trouble,'

'Trouble what sort of trouble?'

'The desperate kind of trouble you are very valuable,'

'Oh,' swigging my water. 'Is that why Lisa and Lou are with us?'

'Yes, but they won't stop a determined group should we come across any. Most live in the city and a lot of the original population has died. But there are a few,'

'Oh,' I think all that over.

'Right, I want an early start, so I suggest we sleep now and start again at dawn,' Rita has already unpacked our bedding looking at it I realise we will be sleeping together again.

'Your horsemanship is excellent,' Rita murmurs as we lay snuggled up to each other.

'Gillian thought it would be useful and I like horses and animals in general,' Rita is snuggled into my front. 'Rita, when you were sick was that the contaminant?'

'Yes, it doesn't affect me as severely as it will you, I am a girl it doesn't affect us the same way. Besides I grew up out here so have a certain immunity,' she turns I can see the light reflected from her eyes. Reaching up she brushes my hair from my eyes. 'You are so beautiful,' I snort.

'Yeah, even though I look like a girl,'

'No, you don't,' she mutters her lips brush mine so soft I close my eyes to savour the sensation. 'Sometimes I can't believe you are mine,' she whispers.

'Ditto,' leaning forward I plant a kiss on her lips. My eyes widen as she kisses me back pushing her tongue into my mouth making a small growl in her throat as she pulls me closer her leg hooking around mine. My hands drift under her top feeling her ribs and the indentation of her waist. My belly seems to coil in anticipation as she rubs against my groin. 'Rita, not sure this is the place' I manage to gasp.

'Hush Aaron and enjoy,' she answers. Despite my better judgement I am soon lost in her. We lay a sweaty mess some-time later.

'Amazing' her voice soft as she tucks her body into mine.

'Yes, amazing,' I hear her chuckle.

'Did you love her?'

'Who?'

'Gilly,'

'No…I don't think so. We were both lonely I suppose. She was fun, clever and she was a little like you,'

'How,' I smile at the indignation wrapped around that one word.

'She had no expectations. All she required was my company when she was home,' I shrug finding it hard to explain.

'Rita, Aaron are you awake?' Lous voice quiet but urgent.

'Yes,'

'Get dressed,' I yank my trousers up and do them up. Rita tucks her shirt in having dragged her trousers on. She smooths her hair as if that will disguise what we were doing.

'What's going on?' Rita whispers.

'Mumbles,' Lou whispers her gun in her hand. It is then I hear it. The shuffle of feet and a manic chatter. Lou puts her finger to her lips. I tie my boots quickly. Lisa signals from the bottom of the stairs and we creep down. Something wipes across the window. Followed by more manic chattering. The door handle rattles. I glance at Rita her eyes wide in her face. My arm wraps around her as I pull her close into my side.

'We get to the horses,' Lou whispers. I nod in agreement. Rita trembles next to me.

'Rita, sweetheart it will be alright,' I reassure. We creep out the back door and move along the wall. My hand holds Rita's tight. Stopping I peer around the corner of the house. Before pushing Rita forward. Putting my finger to my lips in a shushing motion. Hunching down we run across the over-grown garden using the shrubs as cover.

Lisa already has the horses ready. She is waiting in the remains of the lane that ran through this village. I gaze around as we lead the horses away checking the overgrown trees and bushes, listening for any sign we have been followed. Once it is safe, I help Rita into her saddle and then slip my foot into the stirrup with a last glance around I bounce up into my saddle and follow the girls to open countryside where we kick the horses into a gallop. The darkness shrouding our departure.

CHAPTER 19

*R*ita hugs Lou and Lisa in turn. They hug me as well and it is a bit awkward. The salt air swirls around me filling my lungs. I can't take in the sights and sounds fast enough. I have never been anywhere as busy as this. Throngs of people going about their business. Taking little interest in us. Stalls selling fish and everything else as people talk and bustle about. I am amazed to see a few Adams.

'See you both in the city,' Lisa mounts her horse.

'Yes, when will you both return?'

'Couple of months once we meet up with Florence. She is sorting the Sophie mess,' Lou pulls up next to us.

'Sara is expecting you both.' Lisa moves her horse forward and they both wave at us. Turning we walk the horses to the jetty as the boat comes into view. Standing on the jetty I watch the boat chugs closer. We walk the horses on and are stopped by security I stand quietly as Rita shows our papers. I push my sleeve up and they run the scanner over the number tattoo on my wrist. I hold my breath, but they appear satisfied, and we board the boat.

'Did you show my papers?'

'Yes, your number shows you are matched to me,' Rita explains.

'Did that happen on my birthday?' I am curious about this as I am not sure how it works.

'Well sort of. Once I was registered as your match, they issued them. Naomi applied for them when we decided to move you. Because you are only just of age, we had to have valid reason for the move,' she looks across at me. 'You were already with me as your match. Moving us together is a risk so that had to be for a good reason and a special licence had to be applied for,' she explains.

'Is that in case I am stolen?'

'Yes, why?'

'No reason just wanted to know,' I shrug.

'Aaron, I will protect you,'

'I know, I just want to know how all this works,' I shrug. 'It is interesting,' Rita smiles at me and I can see she finds that amusing.

'Oh yeah fascinating. Showing the world how we are controlled,' Rita mutters out and sometimes I think she thinks this is a game of defiance. In a way it is the question is who will win. She would have got on ever so well with Adam I decide as I follow behind her. He is still causing trouble I note. If Lou's remark was anything to go by. This makes me smile. My attention now taken by the horses stabling. It is busy with people and I move closer to Rita as we stand in line.

'What's Sophie like?'

'Why?'

'She is with my brother. Gilly said he loves her,'

'Well, she looks a bit like me I suppose but she isn't like us. A bit wild, you know. Always outside with the animals or hunting with the guard. She is an excellent shot with a bow and arrow even on horseback. Dad adored her, the boy he never had. Mum despaired she never wore dresses or shoes coming to that, dressed like a boy mostly. Hated being a Princess. Rita pauses handing over the horses boarding passes.

A girl smiles shyly at me as she takes Milton's reins. I smile back until Rita nudges me sharply in the ribs.

'Ouch Rita what was that for,' I grumble rubbing my side.

'Concentrate we aren't safe here,' she snaps back. We walk up from the deck the horses are kept on for this crossing. 'Right lets collect our cabin key,'

'Sure, what happened to Sophie?' I am still fascinated by this wild girl related to Rita.

'Mum sort of gave up since she is the youngest so never likely to sit on the throne it didn't matter so much. She ran away when she was fourteen just after dad died, she took it very badly they were close. Mum was furious, but honestly it was for the best. She belongs to some sort of farming commune, I think. Mum keeps tabs on her is friendly with the commune leader. She was meant to meet your brother to see if they would make a good match,' Rita pauses. 'Honestly, I was surprised mum considered matching Sophie I thought they would let her go her own way. Can't waste a good Echo girl I suppose,'

'But he ran,'

'Yeah,'

'Do you miss her?'

'A bit, we didn't spend much time together as I was queen training,' she looks over at me. 'Do you miss your brother?'

'Sometimes, I saw him not long ago and I will see him again soon,'

'Sorry about your dad,'

'Yeah, he was an old Adam they can't cope with the toxin, and it kills them eventually. I think the newer ones are more resilient,' I blanch at her answer and stop walking. She said that as if Adams are just a commodity and frankly it was shocking. To her I suppose they are even me.

We line up to collect our cabin key. The crossing is going to take a couple of days. We are crossing from what was Denmark to what was once Norway but from what Rita says it all belongs to Tribe. That makes sense it would have been easy to shut off here. The border that connects Denmark to Europe would have been easy to close especially as Germany is sparsely populated hit hard by the contaminant. I watch Rita as she argues with the woman in the kiosk.

'Oh, aren't you cute,' a woman walks over to me her eyes sliding over my body. Turning my attention to her I smile as I take in her smart dress and perfect make up, she looks a bit like a Mother.

'Hello young man aren't you lovely,' she smiles back and pulls me forward lifting my arms she runs her hands over me as I stand, terrified.

'Please don't touch me,' I garble out stepping back from her. She ignores me as she contemplates me. Her eyes travel my body and then rest on my face. The heat of her gaze causes me to blush.

'A bit small but a lovely specimen. My daughter would adore you,' she smiles as she stands back one arm crossed as her hand supports her chin as if in thought. Rita comes over and frowns at the woman.

'I… I am matched,' I stutter out.

'I will give you fifteen thousand for him,' the woman says turning to Rita. Who has finished getting our cabin key.

'Sorry he isn't for sale,' Rita answers her voice showing her annoyance.

'Of course he is, name your price,' the woman looks Rita over. I swallow as I realise, she wants to buy me like a horse. This realisation makes me feel sick to the stomach.

'Do you have his papers may I see them,'

'No, you may not he isn't for sale,' Would Rita sell me? I glance at her as I chew the inside of my cheek. How has this never occurred to me before. I never considered I would be sold. I had always assumed I would be euthanised. I remember the women in the bar and the conversation they had. Making it sound like they are acquiring a pet. Rita has claimed me that must mean something.

'Is he good? Has he been proven?' She asks, and I take a minute before I realise what she means, and nothing stops my blush.

'Oh, look isn't he cute,' she gushes. 'I will give you twenty-five thousand if you can prove he is clean and fertile,' she says, and I open my mouth to object, but Rita catches my eye and shakes her head, so I close it.

'Look I am sorry, but he really isn't for sale,' Rita explains patiently although I get the impression, she is anything but patient. She pulls out some paperwork and a small wallet that she opens and shows the woman. Then takes my hand with the ring on, holding it up.

'Oh, what a shame you know they don't make them as good as this anymore,' the woman says with one last glance at me. Rita takes my arm and steers me away from the office.

'You know they charged me extra for the horses when I booked, they said it was included in the price this cabin better be good,' she looks at me waiting for a comment I suppose but, in all honesty, I didn't hear a word.

'Sorry,' I manage.

'Are you okay Aaron. Oh, don't mind her she was just pushing her luck she knew you weren't really for sale,' Rita peers at me with a smile.

'What did you show her?' I ask instead.

'What oh those are your movement papers and owner-ship papers no big deal really,' Ria answers and it all feels a bit flippant like she is trying to distract me from something important. 'You know I showed them to you on your birthday remember,'

'She was serious about buying me,' I stammer out still in total shock from the events a moment ago and Rita is bothered about stabling fees.

'What?' Rita stops and looks at me.

'You own me? You have my ownership papers,' I say slowly looking her in the eye so she can see my displeasure. 'You own me, you can sell me or euthanise me?' I bark out. 'Whenever you want. This means nothing,' I yank the ring off. 'And…. And I can't stop you. I have no say,' no longer shouting. My voice is quiet now. I can feel tears behind my eyes and I force them back.

'Yes, I do and yes, I could do those things, but I love you. You are mine as I am yours,' she says taking my hand. I want to pull away, but I don't.

'But you are not mine. I don't own you. I just love you and hope you love me enough to keep me,' Holding her gaze it is all I can do not to cry. Why is this so devastating I knew how it works but I thought … I didn't think it was Rita that actually owned me I thought it was Tribe.

'Those papers are your movement papers. I need them just to move you around,' she is annoyed I can tell by her posture she has let go of my arm and her hands are shoved in her pockets. 'Yes, I also have your ownership papers. I own you and yes that is barbaric but that is how it is. Me and you we aren't equal. You have no rights and I own you okay,' her voice is very quiet, and I can tell she is only just holding it together. 'I can't change the world.' She hangs her head, so I can't see her expression.

Turning she starts walking again. I stand for a moment as I slip the ring back on my finger before catching up with her. She stops again and slides a card into the handle of a door and pushes it open. Stepping in she reaches for me and pulls me in slamming the door. She is angry now. Her body trembles.

'What do you want me to say you are male you are an Echo those two facts make you valuable and very desirable and my property,' she glares at me while holding me quite forcefully against the wall. 'You are mine and I am yours we are Echo's. What else do you want me to say. Just because I can't be sold doesn't make my life any better than yours, I am still manipulated. Expected to fulfil my duty. Have a baby with you whether I want that or not okay,' her voice is shrill not quite shouting, but I can see she is on the verge of tears. 'I don't just belong to Tribe. I am owned by it same as you.'

'I am sorry Rita… she, she frightened me,' We sink to the floor tears on our faces. She wipes her face on her sleeve. 'I didn't understand, I thought Tribe owned me not you personally,'

'Oh, and that makes a difference,' she snaps back, and I realise I didn't explain that so well.

'Yes, of course it does,' I run a frustrated hand through my hair. She takes them and holds them in hers. Finally her gaze lifts to mine.

'When I turned Sixteen, I was given my matching papers. Nothing romantic just a folder with your details and photograph, Here,' she pulls out her wallet and shows me a picture, I immediately burst out laughing as it isn't me but my brother.

'What's so funny,' she snaps still cross.

'That's Adam,' I explain. 'Look here he has a small mole that I don't have. That's how our Mother could tell us apart, See,' I tilt my head so she can see.

'Oh, she giggles.

'Sorry Rita I shouldn't have shouted,'

'I should have been more considerate of your feelings. As

I know how you feel. I felt the same when that folder was given to me. My choices removed. I could no longer meet someone and fall in love. I could no longer choose if I wanted to breed. Something that could cost me my life if it went wrong. So yes, you may not own me but as soon as those results came through linking me to you my life as it had been. Was over,' a sob escapes her throat. She hangs her head, and her hair falls like a curtain closing on her grief.

'Does this mean anything?' I hold up my left hand with the gold band on my finger. My other hand brushes her hair behind her ear.

'Yes, I love you,' she takes my hand in hers locking our fingers together. 'I did fall in love. With a gentle brave boy,' she brushes my hair away from my face her hand still wrapped around mine. 'And I wouldn't change it for the world,'

'Somehow I fell in love with a sad beautiful girl,' I mutter before kissing her. Before I know it, the kissing escalates.

'Why is being together so dangerous,' Rita is draped over me on the bed as I let strands of her hair trickle through my fingers.

Lifting her head, she gazes at me. 'Together we can breed and make boys, naturally. I believe they are stronger. Better than Tubers,' her hand is lazily drifting south, and my body is more than happy to oblige. Rita giggles and raises a brow. 'You are already proven that alone makes you very valuable,'

'Hey this is all I am trained to do,' smirking at her.

'Yeah, your training in this is outstanding,' she giggles.

'Do you think I will die?' I say quietly and yeah, the dying thing is still bothering me, obviously.

'There is a risk when you get sick. As an Echo we work a bit differently and the toxin affects us differently. I need somewhere safe for you to be when that happens. Because it will happen. You must trust me Aaron,' her mouth is on mine, and it isn't long before I forget what was bothering me so much.

'There will be more women like that, and you need to let me handle it. Play at being an *Adam*,' Rita says much later, and it takes a while for my sluggish brain to process the words.

'Why, she was just rude she didn't hurt me,' my sleepy mumbled answer.

'Today it was civilised next time and there will be a next time. It might not be, and I will be dead, and you will be taken and abused in the most awful ways okay. Or we will be kept like animals, forced to breed. Our babies taken away. That is the world I am trying to protect you from,' she didn't shout she said it all matter of fact and it made it even more chilling. 'Being a princess of Tribe won't protect us. It just puts the bounty on us higher,' she whispers snuggled into my side.

'I just want you to tell me these things. Knowledge is power,' my answer makes me chuckle. 'I sound like Adam.'

'Just be as clever as him,' she mutters.

'Sorry about earlier it's just that isn't the first time that has happened. When I was caught two women in a bar had a similar discussion how we are bought and sold. I don't want to be sold I want to be with you,' I try to smile.

'You will I promise I won't sell you. No one will you are a member of Tribe now.'

'Yeah, but what if that isn't your decision to make,'

'Aaron, you belong to Tribe. They want back. I couldn't sell you if I wanted to. Which I don't. Please understand.'

'I am trying. The more information you give me the better. I can't protect myself if I don't know the danger,'

Okay so what else do you want to know what else is worrying you?' She kneels up and looks at me.

'I don't understand this sickness?' I take in a breath and compose my thoughts. 'I don't understand why I will get sick when I have been sick already. Why will it happen now and not before when I was sick and weak?'

'Well mostly because when you were injured at the castle Naomi was screening your food. Giving you medicine to counteract the toxin. I can't do that out here. You won't be properly safe until I get you to my home.'

'We won't get there before winter though,' I bite my lip with worry. 'What if you are pregnant already,'

'Aaron, I have it all organised,' she takes my face in her hands and leans down to kiss me. 'We are going to my friends after this and then the Romany will escort us to the city and my home in the spring,' She looks at her knotted fingers in her lap. 'Please I am doing my best,' she whispers out.

'I know you are,' my hands pry hers loose as I reach over and kiss her softly. 'Now let me sleep,' I say with a smirk.

'I thought you were created to pleasure me not sleep,'

'Honey, I am,' pinning her beneath me kissing her as she giggles. She snuggles into me, and I wrap my arms around her my chin resting on the top of her head.

CHAPTER 20

The boat is amazing although it isn't really a boat it is a ferry. It has three decks. The lower deck is where the horses are along with cargo. I am going there now to see Milton. I have an apple for him. Rita said I had to be careful after the incident yesterday with the woman that wanted to buy me. I figured this early no one would be about. Stepping inside I stop as the stable girl looks at me.

'Hello,' I smile taking in her appearance. Her black hair is in a ponytail, and she has a grubby set of riding clothes on. Her boots are scuffed and need a clean. I walk to where Milton is and give him the apple. Stroking his nose, I talk to him softly.

'You an Echo?'

'Err, yes,' I look at her closely. 'You have met others like me?'

'Only girls, you all have certain distinctions and similarities,'

'Oh,' I wait for her to elaborate, but she doesn't.

'That your horse?'

'Yes, his name is Milton, you know because of his colour,' I answer with a smile.

'You shouldn't be wandering about on your own. Where is your Mother?'

'I don't have one. I have a match,' I hold my hand up with the ring. 'She is in our cabin. I just came to check my horse,' She walks toward me her brush still in her hand.

'I have never met an Echo boy before, never met an Adam either to be honest,' she is stood before me looking me over. 'You are very beautiful, where are you being taken?'

'Erm Tribe,' I answer a bit unnerved by her.

'Yes, I know that where in Tribe?'

'The city, Rita calls it the Capital,' I explain.

'Of course, a beautiful specimen like you must belong to Princess Rita,' She smiles at me.

'What do you know about Tribe?' Specimen what the hell, bit rude I think deciding after yesterday not to voice my disgust.

'Not much but more than you,' she smiles and steps back. Oh, a challenge. Well, I accept a grin on my face.

'I can help you with the horses if you tell me,' She gazes at me while thinking over my proposition.

'You are very different to how I expected,' she says at last. 'Okay grab that wheelbarrow and spade. I do as she asks. Removing my cloak, I hang it up.

'Aaron,' I say.

'Hetty,' she answers with a smile. 'What do you want to know?'

'Will I be safe there?'

'Well, yes, in that Gen-Corp have no control they do have treaties and stuff, but you won't be sold or anything like that,' she shovels up a pile of dung and dumps it into the wheelbarrow. Well, that cleared up that worry.

'So, they don't sell Adams then?'

'Oh yes, they do but you aren't an Adam you are an Echo, and they don't sell those. They are used for breeding,' Her spade scrapes the deck while I digest that.

'You will be in the city only the true population are allowed to breed as they are clean the rest of the population is contaminated.'

'How are they clean?'

'When the disaster occurred, they didn't take part. It was easy to cut off from the rest of the continent because of the geography. Sweden already had an established royal family and at the time a very political King. Denmark and some other royal families took control. They shut their borders and limited imports. As the male population decreased, they started breeding selectively. Tested all their remaining males. No men now though. The royal family are all female ruled by Queen Lydia. Rumour has it that Queen Lydia had a son, He was sickly at birth, so no one has seen the prince. So, I don't know if that is true. They then stopped people entering or leaving,' we finish cleaning out and start on the hay racks.

'How do you know this?'

'Oh, when I got the job and saw where it was, I did research. The information is all there if you look hard enough,' she shrugs.

'What happened after that, they must have done something else?' I question fascinated by this information.

'I can't tell you no one knows they closed the borders. As the populations fell everywhere it didn't really matter and they were sort of forgotten. They didn't join with Gen-Corp or have any communication with the rest of the world for about Fifty years,' she shrugs.

'So what changed?'

'Heard gossip that the borders opened because Queen

Lydia's consort died and that he was natural,' she says this last bit in a whisper looking around as if frightened someone might hear us. How intriguing. Adam would love this he adores mysteries to solve.

'Do you live there?'

'No not really I live in the fishing port where this ferry docks, and I don't originate from there,'

'Oh, so how did you know to come here?' This is fascinating, and I will be quizzing Rita later. She has been holding out on me or I just haven't been asking the right questions.

'About ten years ago they emerged opened their borders and sent diplomats out contacted Gen-Corp and The United Human Federation but wanted no part in the Adam program or anything else. They wanted people, workers. My prospects were limited where I was very few jobs for the likes of me,' she smiled. 'So here I am.'

'What do you mean you are lovely,' a frown mars my brow as I don't understand.

'Oh, you are sweet. I am dirty, infertile,' she shrugs. They just want the likes of me to die and to be fair in another fifty years they get there wish,' she shrugs.

'That is awful,'

'But true,'

'Who are they?'

'Gen-Corp, Tribe, the United human federation take your pick,'

'Will I be tested?' She laughs, and I step back a little bit offended.

'All I do know is it is very controlled they test anyone coming in from outside and rumour has it the only place you will see men and children is in the cities. To be fair children are rarer than men these days,' she shrugs as we tidy up having finished our tasks.

'Thank you for helping,' she holds her hand out to me I take it shaking.

'Thank you for answering my questions,'

'Stay safe Aaron, I will see you tomorrow when we dock,' I walk back up to the cabin deciding to spend the rest of the day just reading maybe look at some maps. Pushing the door open I am confronted by Rita.

'Aaron, where have you been all morning?' Rita is cross. 'You stink. Shower now and then we need another talk,' she stands with her hands on her hips, and I don't know, why but she looks adorable. With a smile, I bend and kiss her. 'Ugh Aaron, you stink of horse,' she complains, but I see the smile on her lips.

Walking out the bathroom, I rub my hair dry with the towel. I sit next to her, taking her hand in mine, marvelling at how small it is.

'I went to see Milton and then I got talking to Hetty the stable girl she had never seen a boy before. So, I helped her with her jobs, and she told me about Tribe,'

'Aaron, you should have told me where you were going. I was anxious,' Rita chastises me.

'I know but I wanted time to myself,'

'You weren't though, you were with this Hetty person,' if I'm not mistaken Rita sounds jealous. 'I can answer your questions,' she says her voice betraying her hurt.

'Rita, sorry if I worried you,' I decide to apologise as I don't want Rita upset. 'I have lots of question for you don't worry about that,' I chuckle at her surprised expression.

'Well in that case why don't I order us some food. I assume you are hungry?' She asks so she must be happy with my apology.

'Yeah, I am,' I grin as she gets up.

'Right, well, I will fetch us some lunch,' she smiles. 'You

can put your pyjamas on, and we can watch films and stuff,' she stops at the door and turns to look at me. 'Aaron, you can ask me anything you know that don't you?'

'I know Rita,' satisfied with my answer she leaves the room.

CHAPTER 21

*W*e have a good day's ride before our next stop. I feel a bit off today not sure why. The morning ride is amazing the scenery spectacular. Vast forests and sweeping plains with large lakes their shores lapping at the tree line. The sunlight sparkling off the water.

I lay back with my hands behind my head my eyes closed.

'Aaron, do you want another sandwich?' I open one eye to peer at Rita.

'No, I am good,'

'Are you alright?'

'Yeah why?'

'You haven't eaten much,' Rita replies. I don't open my eyes I can hear her packing away.

'Headache,' my answer.

'Oh, we are nearly there,' she answers, and I can hear the worry in her voice.

'Rita it's just a headache,' I smile hoping to reassure her. Sitting up I climb to my feet and help pack away the last bits. Then we are moving again, Rita wants to arrive before dark.

The vast forest is amazing as we slowly navigate through it coming out in pasture. A few houses spread out.

Sliding down I am exhausted, the headache I have been trying to ignore is building behind my eyes. I walk slowly behind Rita to the house. A young girl comes out to meet us. Her smiling open honest face is deceptive as it gives her an innocent look. I don't miss her sharp eyes surveying me taking in every detail. She hugs Rita and I watch as Rita seems to melt into her as if they have known each other a long time. They are quite the contrast Rita so fair and this girl so dark.

'Why don't you two go and wash up while I sort out supper,' her voice is soft with an accent that I can't place. It adds to the innocent persona that I am sure is just a front. Rita leads me through the house. It gives me the impression of warmth and safety. Soft light from lamps giving it a warm glow as heat radiates out from a wood burner set in the chimney that dominates the centre of the room. A delicious aroma wraps around us from the kitchen.

I lay on the bed while Rita showers. Closing my eyes just for a moment.

I feel a cold soft cloth wipe the sweat from my body as my head is lifted and cool water runs down my throat. Careful hands lay me back down as a soft voice talks to me.

'Sorry Adam I should have stayed...stayed with you,' I mumble delirious.

'Shh, you are safe,' soft hands sooth me.

'Mother... where are you?' opening my eyes I can't focus the light hurts and I try to throw my arms over my face.

'Calm down, sleep,' voices murmur around me.

'Such delicate creatures it's a wonder any of them survive out here,'

'Please Sara you have to save him. Isn't there something you can give him,'

'No honey you know that. Just keep him cool and wait for the fever to break,'

'Sara, thank you,'

'We do our best for him that's all we can do,' the door shuts, and I can't hear the rest of the muffled conversation.

'Will he survive?' Rita's voice full of worry.

'Yes, he is stronger than he looks,' the soft accent strangely soothing. I feel cold on my head and drops of water in my mouth as a wet cloth is placed to moisten my lips. Drifting back to sleep with no idea of the time.

'Please don't die,' I feel the bed dip, and Rita holds my hand. 'I love you so much that sometimes it hurts. I watched you cry when you thought you were alone after Heath. I know everything you do is for me. You gave up so much and all you got in return is a broken girl who doesn't deserve you,' a cool cloth is wiping my dry feverish skin. It feels so nice as a few drops of water trickle into my mouth and my lips are dampened again.

'You don't trust me though do you. You prove that when you run from me. Seeking others rather than talk to me. Frightened I will break even more,' she sighs. 'Mother wants you for Florence. She said you don't have enough political training and I should match to someone like Thomas. Thomas is matched to Gillian so that won't work. I told her I wanted you. That I won't be queen for ages yet,' I hear a sigh. 'Toby likes you says he can work with you. So that's something. Mother listens to Toby. Toby should be king not me. He is like dad and much better at it all than me. Stupid line of succession,'

'Rita, you must eat you need to be strong for him,'

'I know Sara,'

'You like him, don't you? Oh, Rita never thought you would fall for one,'

'Why Sara you knew as well as did I would be matched,' Rita's voice lacking any gentleness from earlier.

'I know but I didn't think you would love him. You used to hate being around the *Adams,*'

'He is different they didn't mess with him. He is kind and sweet. He doesn't have any expectations you know,' Rita's voice soft and caring. 'When he looks at me and blinks those big blue eyes, I just melt a little,' she sighs again. 'He is my match, but he isn't submissive like the *Adams.* He challenges me,'

'Well, he isn't out of the woods yet not until that fever breaks, he has a fifty-fifty chance don't you forget that I don't want you broken when he dies,'

'I won't break,' Rita whispers as the door opens and closes. 'Not completely,' she lays next to me brushing my hair off my face. I drift back to the heat and fever and sleep.

Waking I am alone pushing up I notice I have pyjamas on, certainly not mine they are pink with large yellow flowers. Reaching across I pick up the glass of water and drink it in one go. I sit for a while listening to the quiet of the house. I feel weak drifting back to sleep waking as she climbs in next to me. She snuggles down her arm going over my waist as she curls around me.

'Aaron are you awake?' Her quiet voice in the dark.

'Yes,'

'How are you?' Concern fills the room.

'Fine I think,'

'Good, Sara thought you would die,'

'Is Sara the girl?'

'Yes, my friend this is her house,' I smile and relax.

'I am not going to die. Well not yet anyway,' I mumble.

'That's good then,'

'Yeah, fabulous,' she giggles as she snuggles into me.

'Night Aaron,' I listen as her breathing settles as she sleeps.

I WAKE TOO hot and can't move I look down, wrapped around me is Rita, her head tucked into my chest, and her hair is tickling my chin; her lips are slightly open as she breathes, deeply asleep.

I lay still, not sure what to do. I don't want to wake her as she looks so peaceful. It gives me chance to study her. It amazes me that I haven't really studied her features before now. Usually thier is something distracting me. I chuckle at this thought.

I gaze at her face. It's quite a nice face, straight delicate nose, high cheek bones, and that mouth with its slightly full bottom lip, so she looks like she is pouting. I move my gaze back up to her hair, and notice she is awake watching me. She blushes and moves away from me.

'You are beautiful. Also you look like me,' I say.

'And you are delirious,'

'I am not,' my voice full of indignation.

'Need to get you well before Florence arrives. She appears to have sorted Sophie out and wants to visit,'

'Who is Florence? She was at the castle.' Scrunching up my face while I try to get my sluggish brain to work. Rita is watching me. She looks worried.

'My sister. She is Guard,'

'Who is Toby, I mean I know who he is but who is he to you?' Finally, it clicks, and it blurts out. 'He is your brother the sickly prince,'

'Yes,' is all she says but I can see worry on her face. Why is she worried about me knowing that?

'Why don't you want me to know that?' I scramble up not

caring I have pink pyjamas on. 'You're the crown princess. The heir aren't you,'

'Yes,'

'Why have you concealed that?'

'I haven't, you know I am a princess of Tribe,' she glares at me pushing up, so she is lent against the headboard.

'You aren't just a princess though are you. Is that why they took you is that why this is so dangerous?'

'Yes... don't you want me?' Her voice small.

'Too late for that. I love you. Besides I have spent the last two years learning to run a country,' realisation hits. 'Your country,' I blurt. 'Rita, you don't need to hide anything from me I love you. Nothing will change that,'

'I thought... I don't know what I thought,' she looks up at me. 'Love you as well,'

'Good to know, in this together remember,' I take in a shuddering breath. 'Who hurt you?' I say at last and her whole body relaxes.

'No one not really but... it was different for me I had extra lessons and stuff and I never really knew if they were my friends because of who I was or if they genuinely liked me,' she shrugs. As I get a glimpse of the root to her insecurities.

'Well when I first met you, I had a need to rescue you and protect you. We can assume I like you for you.' I smile, and she gives me a wobbly smile back. 'I had extra lessons with Toby. I will be having words with him,' I grumble and Rita giggles.

'He likes you.'

'I like him,' I smile.

How do you feel?' Her voice tentative.

'A bit yucky would like a shower but I don't have the strength,'

'I can help you,' her eagerness is endearing.

Rita climbs out of bed and walks to the bathroom. Damn she is wearing some sort of silky top and shorts set and to be honest she might as well be naked. How did I miss that?

'I think a bath would be better,' she strolls back in and gazes at me a slow smile pulls at her lips. 'What's the matter Aaron? Do you feel ill again,' she asks her voice full of concern? Trying to ignore her as I climb out of bed staggering in my weakened state. Her arm is around my waist. Then her eyes widen? 'Oh my?' She moves away from me. 'Should it do that?' She giggles. I raise a brow at her making her giggle again. 'Would you like me to milk you,' she is trying not to laugh.

'No,' I frown as I grumble. Rita giggles again and her eyes keep straying down there. 'Yeah, thanks for that,' I mutter dryly.

'You are well trained,' she sniggers.

'Yeah, well my body is making promises it has no chance of honouring,' I chuckle.

I manage the bath, but it totally exhausts me but that is more Rita's fault than the bath. She just can't keep her hands to herself. I stagger back to bed noticing I have clean sheets that's nice my last coherent thought.

'Aaron, I brought you some soup,' Rita pushes the door open.

'Yeah,' I mutter pushing up. It is dark again another day lost to sleep.

'Are you okay?' She puts the tray on my legs and bites her lip.

'Yeah, just tired the bath took a lot out of me,' smiling I sit up. 'Feel so weak,'

'Yeah, well you have been so ill Sara thought you might die at one point.' She sits down and gazes at me. 'Glad you didn't,' she smiles shyly.

'Not as glad as I am,' I chuckle breaking the tension.

'Well eat this then tomorrow you can sit outside for a bit get some air hmm,'

'Yeah, that sounds like a plan,' I eat the soup, chicken and its delicious. 'Rita thank you,' I gaze up at her.

'You are very welcome,' she leans over and kisses me as she picks up the tray.

I amble downstairs taking in the house it is impressive. All open plan in wood, glass and Steele. I find Rita in the kitchen with its cream enamel appliances on pale marble work surfaces and shaker style cabinets. The living area is a riot of colour with knitted throws and cushions on the sumptuous sofas. One wall is floor to ceiling glass giving an uninterrupted view of the fjord and mountains.

'Tea,' she asks.

'Yes please,' sinking onto one of the sofas tired already.

'Here you go, oh goodness you look very pale are you alright,' Rita fusses around me organising cushions and pulling a throw over my legs. Sipping my tea, I just smile. May be go outside tomorrow I think as exhaustion over-whelms me.

CHAPTER 22

I wake early and slip out of bed without waking Rita. The need to stretch my legs and get my body moving is overwhelming. I decide to go and visit Milton. I take my clothes and get dressed in the bathroom before going downstairs. The kitchen is deserted but someone is about the fire is lit and I make tea. Pulling my boots on I take my tea out to the stables. Milton greets me softly and I rub his nose. Sinking onto a bale I drink my tea. I feed and water the horses and then muck them out the activity getting my muscles working again.

I am so engrossed in my task the cough behind me startles me making the person laugh.

'You have done my job, thank you,' she says walking toward me. Twinkling brown eyes smile at me as she holds her hand out.

'Sara,' she says. I take her hand and shake. 'I don't think we have been properly introduced,'

'Aaron,' her small frame seems to fill the space. I remember her studying me. Assessing me I also remember she thought I would die.

'Are you up to this sort of activity?'

'Yes, I feel much better, sorry if I have caused any inconvenience,' I answer unsure and intimidated all at once.

'No trouble, Lou briefed me that you would get sick. It was just a waiting game. Do you want to come and check the sheep with me?'

'Yeah sure,' we saddle up the horses. I take my cloak from the hook. I love it as it wraps me in warmth. Leading Milton outside I mount him getting comfortable adjusting his bridle before following Sara up on to the pasture.

The flock is scattered over a large area. We slowly make our way around them. Sara's keen eyes checking them. She stops and jumps down. I frown as I can't see what it is, she has found. Standing she has a small lamb in her arms.

'A bit cold this one, here put it in your cloak,' she passes it to me, I do as instructed slipping it into my cloak. It is cold but its eyes are trained on my face. Sara strides away and tackles a sheep to the ground checking her over I then see two more lambs. Righting the ewe, Sara calls her lambs, and we watch as they suckle. Sara takes a spray can from her coat pocket and marks the Ewe and lambs with a number. Once Sara is satisfied, she walks back to her horse. She pulls a bottle from one of her saddle bags.

'Here you stay here and feed that one while I check the rest,' I nod and take the bottle pushing it against the lambs mouth it soon latches on and sucks greedily while nestled in my cloak.

I watch as Sara checks the rest of the sheep, now I know what to look for I can see more lambs. Smiling at their antics it all lifts my mood.

'Alright Aaron?' Sara is back beside me.

'Yeah, here you go he has finished the milk,' I pass back the bottle.

'Sorry about the things I said. I just worry about Rita,' she says putting the bottle away.

'Sorry that you thought I was going to die or sorry that I heard,' okay so I am being rude, but I don't want pity or apologies.

'So, you are Rita's match?' She says taking me by surprise.

'How do you know Rita isn't my Mother,' I raise a brow as she laughs.

'Rita isn't your Mother,'

'How do you know that?'

'Because she looks at you like she wants to eat you,' she chuckles. 'No Mother should look at her charge like that,' Oh didn't expect that answer and it makes me smile. 'I have known Rita for many years, and she is not your Mother.'

'No, she is my match,' I chuckle.

'Yes, she is,' Sara nods.

'You thought I was going to die?' blunt I know. 'Do you still think that?'

'Hard to say, you are small but the way you handle that horse I suspect you have a hidden strength,'

'Thanks, I think,'

'Rita knows how to care for you, just enjoy the here and now that's my advice,' she urges her horse into a trot.

'Sara, thank you,'

'What for?' she frowns,

'For being nice to me and honest,' I blush.

'Come on let's get back I don't know about you, but I am hungry,'

'What about the lamb?'

'I have a pen for orphans in the barn we can put him in there,' I follow Sara.

'Right breakfast,' she announces turning her gaze on me. 'Did you know Rita is an amazing cook,'

'No, I didn't,' I say with a smile.

'She will soon put some meat on you,' Sara chuckles as she saunters to the door.

'You go ahead I will sort the horses,' I volunteer, not quite ready to go in yet.

'Okay if you are sure,' she answers as she leaves the barn. Walking slowly to the stable the horses follow behind. Removing the horses tack I then fill their hay racks. Sinking on to a bale I lay back closing my eyes still exhausted from the sickness.

'Aaron?' Her voice pulls me from my doze. Sitting up I plaster a smile on my face. 'I brought you a bacon sandwich and some tea,' I see her hesitation as she watches me before she sits next to me.

'Thanks,' I take the sandwich and tuck into it.

'Are you okay,' she is nervous unsure.

'I am fine,' putting my mug down I pull her in for a kiss. 'Still tired that's all.'

* * *

As I slowly recovered, I started to help Sara more on the farm it is only small but enough to feed us and sell spare for things we don't have. Sara explained there a lot of these small family farms across the country. We are staying here for the winter the weather too bad to even attempt travel. Our escort delayed.

Rita, it turned out is a demon in the kitchen and enjoys cooking she has been feeding me up with healthy food and every day my health improves. In the evenings both the girls knit making me jumpers and throws for the beds or sofas. I am content to just read books on how to care for the animals. I like it here and deep-down dread the day we must leave. My mind wonders to Adam. Is this what he was doing with Rita's sister? He will be with Gilly now. Did he find peace in that community?

Today it is snowing quite hard. I silently rejoice because the more snow the longer we stay. Sara and I have milked the cows and fed the other animals then come back in. Sara only has six cows, so it never takes long to milk them. They are lovely brown and white and quite friendly. Rita uses it to make butter and cheese. For a princess she is very domesticated.

I feed the pigs we only have three of those, but one sow is due to farrow this week and I am quite excited about that. While I do that Sara collects the eggs.

I am completely engrossed in my vegetable book until my attention is pulled to the conversation in the kitchen.

'Sophie has re-emerged, and she has a baby. Confronted your mother demanding she gets her boy back from Gen-Corp.'

'Yes, he is Aaron's brother I believe.'

'He has a brother?'

'Yes, twins. Gillian has the brother because Lady Arellia wants him. He got shot or something.'

'Bloody hell. We need to get Aaron to the capital and the Queen before this all gets nasty.'

'My thoughts exactly especially as those bikers have been spotted this side of the border.'

'Gillian will protect him.' Rita's voice full of conviction.

'Why is Gillian involved?'

'She was his companion. They are friends she adores him.' Rita walks into the room carrying the bowl of popcorn. 'But she knows he is with me she knows he is my match so why make all this fuss?'

'I have no idea,' Sara answers. Frowning I stuff some popcorn into my mouth.

'You have a brother?' Sara looks at me.

'Yes, he is with Gilly,' I explain.

'Doing what?' She gazes at me intently.

'Adam he is different to other males, he is smart. His education was different to a normal Adam and Gilly she wanted his help with something.' I hold her gaze. 'He ran away when he was seventeen. Met up with the United Human Federation and then ran away from them and met someone called Sophie. Gilly has tried to protect him, but he is being hunted,' I explain.

'You are Echo's, and we should be careful you aren't seen together. In fact, get to the Capital where you can both be protected. Rita, you know you are as valuable as him,'

'Yes, Sara I know but he isn't strong he needs more time. He won't survive out there in these temperatures,' Rita gives Sara a look before muttering. 'You know I can't now not in this condition,' I frown at them as Sara huffs. She makes no further comment.

We settle to watch the film, but my attention isn't on it as I think about everything I have heard.

'Sophie your sister?' I ask at last.

'Oh, yes, the one I told you about,' Rita explains.

We settle into bed Rita sleeps with me. I don't object I quite like it. Tonight, I am worried about Adam and where he is. Reaching for Rita, I cuddle her she turns and kisses me.

'Can we practice,' she mumbles making me smile.

'I know you are pregnant,' I answer.

'How do you know?' Rita straddles my waist.

'The bond. My need to be with you, to touch you vanished,'

'We can still practice?'

'Yes, we can still practice,' I comply to her request.

.   .   .

THE DAYS BLEND into weeks which soon become months. I have filled out and have a healthy colour to my skin my hair almost white from being outdoors. Sara taught me to run the farm to milk the cows and plough the fields with the horses. We have settled into a nice routine, and I am happy and content even thinking about my brother has become less.

I amble into the kitchen putting the milk in the fridge, the smell of dinner invades my nostrils grinning as my tummy rumbles. Moving to where Rita is at the sink, I wrap my arms around her feeling her melt into me. My hands cup her swollen belly as she leans back to kiss me. This is the reason we have stayed here so long.

It delighted me when Rita revealed she was pregnant. Although the amount of sex we are having it shouldn't have been much of a surprise, we are both Echo's perfectly matched. Now with just weeks to go, she is so excited about the birth and being a mother. She wants to call it Daisy, which is cute. Sara says it is a boy, not a girl. She used to work in the city as a scientist until she retired out here.

I think I love Rita. I know she loves me and now we will be family. Sara pretends not to like me but has warmed to me, I think. Equally as excited about the baby as Rita. The knitting has got phenetic as they make cute clothes and shawls.

'HUMPH,' I groan, Rita giggles at my reaction and I can't help but smile. As Sara throws bales at me to stack. I think she is trying to knock me off. After a bit we send Rita to lie down. We are getting ready for winter again.

The baby comes the next week in the middle of the night. I hold Rita as she delivers our son, and we all cry as we lay him in her arms. He is beautiful and strong, feeding from his mother moments after birth.

Sara goes to register his birth and the following week we get visitors. They arrive on horses their cloaks emblazoned with the royal coat of arms. I see Rita rush out and embrace one of them.

'Aaron, where are you?' Rita calls.

'He is asleep with the baby,' Sara's soft voice. The door opening wakes me, Charlie is asleep on my chest his favourite place as he can hear my heart. By my side his empty bottle. Rita expresses so Sara and I can feed him so she can sleep. The door opening rouses me from my slumber.

'Oh, Rita they are so cute,' the girl gushes as she surveys us.

'They are, aren't they?' Rita answers, her voice full of pride?

'Aaron, this is my sister Florence,' gently I sit up, adjusting Charlie, so he stays asleep, giving me a chance to gaze at the girl. She is fair like us and beautiful and I can see her resemblance to Rita. She is taller though, with an athletic build not as delicate as Rita.

'We have met before,' I hold out my hand and she shakes. Rita has turned to the others with Florence. 'You were at the castle,'

'Yes, you remember?' She cocks her head to study me.

'Jeremy, Anton, I have missed you,' Rita hugs them, and they laugh hugging her back I had completely missed they were men. Not as fair as me and much bigger but somehow the same.

CHAPTER 23

*C*harlie is sat on a bale at eighteen months he is a round happy baby. He is watching me intently as he chews his toy car dribble on his chin. Rita says he is getting his teeth. I smile at him as I repair the chicken pen. He has grown and thrived, and I have never loved anything so much. He enjoys being out here with me helping with the animals. He is sleepy now sat on the bale and I will take him inside for his nap when I have finished this. He smiles back at me his little pudgy legs kick in his boots. We should have left in the summer, but Rita is pregnant again and she is due soon, so we have decided to stay until after the baby.

She is so happy, and it makes me happy as well. Guard comes quite often to check on us Lisa and Lou were here last week.

'What's that noise?' I frown as I can hear a rumbling noise and it is getting nearer. Sara looks up in alarm and finishes what she is doing. She moves to the door and takes her shot gun from the doorway where it had been leaning. She peers out and swears moving back to me.

'Aaron, you must do exactly as I say and keep really quiet,'

She looks at me and I nod my head a tremor skitters down my spine and I can feel sweat on my neck. I pull baby Charlie into me putting my finger to my lips in a shushing motion. His chubby hand pats my face.

Sara takes my hand and leads me to the back of the stable to another much smaller door. Carefully Sara lifts the latch and squeezes through the door taking me with her.

She leads me around the back of the house so she can get a better look. In the yard there are a group of motor bikes and two people stood guard watching they are dressed in long black coats and black leather tight trousers their faces hidden behind black helmets but they each hold a shotgun in their hands. They are possibly the most frightening thing I have ever seen, and I know they are after me and Charlie.

I am hidden behind some dense shrubbery with Sara's body practically covering mine. We have a perfect view of the house and yard.

'Vigilantes, they are really bad news, this is a very bad development,' she whispers her breath in my hair tickling my ear.

'What do they want?' I ask even though I think I know the answer. Another black clad person comes out the house followed by Rita and two more people dressed like the others all holding shot guns I feel Sara stiffen against me.

'Food, the horses possibly, you or Charlie or all three of you,' Sara whispers a tremor in her voice. I cuddle Charlie tight he has his thumb in, his other hand in my shirt, I can see he is sleepy.

'Search the place, and find the other woman,' the lead person instructs the other three.

'Damn,' Sara mutters. As the first figure grabs Rita forcing her to kneel as the other two figures come back, the two by the bikes have not moved.

'We found the horses like she said, but no sign of anyone else. She could be telling the truth,'

'I am, telling you the truth my sister is in the furthest field she won't be back for hours. I am a princess of the royal house you do not want to do this,' Rita says tears on her face and a small trickle of blood in the corner of her mouth as if she has been backhanded.

'Aaron, I have to go out there,' Sara hisses in my ear her body tense her shot gun in her hand. 'You edge to the barn and hide okay,'

'No, no, I have to protect my family,' I beg terrified my hand on her arm keeping her with me.

'No Aaron you will make the situation worse you need to protect Charlie. I must prove I am here,' Sara gazes at me before kissing me. 'It will be fine Aaron, now go,' she gets to her feet, and I do the same. I grab her and stop her from going.

'Be careful,'

'Go,' she pushes me in the direction I must go.

I haven't run far when I hear a gun shot, Charlie whimpers as my body shakes from the noise as I continue running. The buzzing has grown into a deafening growl it almost drowns out the two bangs of Sara's gun as she places two shots in the front tire of the leading biker. The tire rips itself to pieces and the bike flips unseating the biker and hurling her through the air.

I make it to the barn and scramble up the bales crawling to a gap in the boarding I can see the house.

'Hey! Hey you! Girl! You wrecked my bike!' the injured biker yelled as she limped over to where Sara was stood.

Hey, I'm talking to you!' the injured biker snarled as she reached to place her hand on Sara's shoulder. This was a mistake. The second she touched her, Sara grabbed her wrist, twisting it and dislocating her elbow. A moment later the biker was once again on her back, groaning in pain.

The rest of the bikers laugh at this, 'I like your spirit girl.' One of the bikers, I assume their leader. 'Let her through,' immediately two of the bikers part to let her into the circle.

'Thank you, now what do you want?' Sara demands marching purposefully over and standing protectively by Rita's side. 'I am royal guard, and you are trespassing,'

'What do you think we want? The breeder, hand him over.'

'I don't know what you're talking about,' Sara bluffed suddenly cautious.

'Sure, you don't, now where is he,' the biker demanded.

'Look my charge is a princess of the royal house her match is currently in the capital. You know how sick they get. He will be annoyed if you harm her or the baby,' Sara lies quickly.

'Yeah, sure he is,' the lead biker replied, 'I'll tell you what, hand over the breeder and we won't shoot you in the face and leave you for the crows.'

'You could do that, or you could leave us and go about your business happily, like civilized human beings,' Sara replies with a grin.

'Yeah, no, that's not happening, last chance, hand him over,' The biker orders.

'He isn't here. I'm sure we can come to some sort of agreement,' Sara argues with a nervous smile.

'No, I'm afraid the time for negotiation is ended.' The lead biker replies with her own grin, before suddenly throwing her shotgun into a spin, grabbing the barrel and using it as a bat to hit Sara round the face with. Caught off guard, Sara had no chance to dodge and was quickly knocked down swinging the gun the biker shoots her.

'Sara,' Rita cries out fighting to get free, only to find herself staring down the barrel of the lead biker's shotgun.

'You are very valuable, do as you are told, and you won't be harmed, if you don't do as I say I won't be able to help you,' understand?' Rita nods her head.

I walk out holding Charlie. 'I am here please don't hurt her,'

Rita uses this distraction to punch the woman holding her grabbing the gun she shoots another woman. Shots ring out dropping Rita to the ground as I feel a burn in my side dropping me to one knee pain engulfing my side. The woman with the gun walks over to me. She pushes me to one side squatting down she looks at the blood blooming across my shirt.

'Damn, such a waste,' she mutters and then notices Charlie asleep tucked in my coat. 'Maybe not a waste of time after all,' she reaches in and pulls Charlie free and pops him into her jacket he hardly stirs as I try to stop her, she punches me down shock making me too weak to fight. 'You unfortunately won't survive the night,' She kicks me with the toe of her boot. 'What a waste,' The remaining vigilantes roar away but not before setting the house on fire.

'Aaron,' Rita's weak voice has me pulling all my remaining strength to crawl over to her. I pull Rita onto my lap blood is everywhere hers as well as mine. Her eyes open and she manages a weak smile. I can see I am too late.

'Aaron, save the baby,'

'How,'

'Cut it out, you know how, please do this for me,'

'I can't you will die,' I sob.

'I am dying you know that get some blankets,' Rita instructs as she puts my hand on her belly, I can feel the baby moving still alive. 'Please he is innocent try to save him she pleads,' Scrambling to my feet I put the paltry fire out and rush into the house. Going into the kitchen I grab a knife and some throws and cushions from the lounge. I find a first aid kit and bandage my side grabbing a glass of water I chug it down.

When I get back, I can see Rita has gone. Holding back the grief I place my things on the grass. Turning to Rita I rip her smock and with shaking hands I make the incision.

Blood is everywhere but I focus on my task pulling the baby free. He lets out a wail and I smile at his angry form. Wrapping him in a blanket to keep him warm as I tie off the cord. Taking him, I place him to Rita's breast hoping the milk is there. Just enough to sustain him tonight. He latches on and suckles. Her body still warm.

'Look at him Rita,' I whisper as tears fall down my face. With a shaky hand I close her eyes. Holding her in my lap. Eventually, I stagger to my feet the sleeping baby in my arms Rita cold and still.

* * *

THE THUD of the spade as it hits the soft earth. The rhythm soothes the rage that thrums through my body. Thoughts crash inside my head as I dig the graves in Sara and Rita's favourite spot in the meadow. Across from me my baby son sleeps in his basket. Murder is upmost on my mind. I want to kill them all for taking them away from me.

He stirs and I throw the spade down sitting cross legged I reach for him so small and fragile. He is growing weaker I want him to survive but he isn't robust like Charlie. He was born too early. I don't want to think about Charlie the pain too much.

I try to persuade him to suckle desperate for him to live. Losing him will break me but that is inevitable. I need a plan the wound in my side isn't healing and already I am starting to get sick. But he will die without me. I have to find Florence and her soldiers.

Winter is coming he won't survive the elements and I don't know where Florence is. It's all hopeless. He takes the bottle and I finish the graves. Picking up his basket my work here done if I die now, it will be okay as I know he won't last the night. The house is cold and silent as I limp up to the bedroom Rita and I shared. Her smell still on the pillow I crawl into bed with the baby.

CHAPTER 24

I had tried so hard to keep myself and him alive. I was losing that battle. The infection in my wound was inevitable as I couldn't get all the shot out. I am wracked with fever from the infection. I am running out of milk for baby not that it was the right milk.

'Sara,' someone is shouting is the only thought in my head. Sara is gone I want to shout back but I can't.

'Daisy what are you doing? We shouldn't be here you saw the graves they are dead,'

'Sukie you are wrong. Who dug the graves?' Her voice smug.

'Well, anyone and they certainly aren't here now,' the other voice grumbles.

I hear the voices and the footsteps as they come up the stairs. I listen as they open doors. It is sheer desperation that gets me trying to push upright. Panting from pain my legs tangle in the sheet and I topple to the floor as the door bursts open.

'I told you Sukie,' a girl rushes to my side. 'Hey, it's okay,' her voice soft and soothing as she drags me up. If she is appalled by the blood that covers me, she doesn't say.

'Daisy there is a baby?'

'See to it,' Daisy barks as she rolls me over and rips my shirt. 'Wow,' she mutters as her fingers probe the wound and I hiss with pain. 'Shush sweetie you are safe now,' she mutters as she rolls me back onto my back.

'Baby,' I whisper. My eyes open and I take in a round face framed by curly brown hair.

'Sukie, take the child to Betsy, she can feed it and get Kristian to come and take care of the animals,' Daisy orders.

'No... my son... don't take him,' I push up only to be pushed back down.

'Shush, he needs feeding and taking care of. No one is taking him,' she reassures me, and I relax. I listen as doors close.

'Right let's sort you out,' she pushes to her feet, and I watch her leave the room. The sound of feet running down the wooden stairs then I hear cupboards opening and closing. I close my eyes as she bursts back into the room.

'Okay ready,' she rolls me onto my side again and goes about laying a towel on the bed. She rolls me back and pours some of Sara's vodka into a glass. She wraps her arm around my shoulders and puts the glass to my lips. I gaze at her confused.

'For the pain, because this is going to hurt,' she explains frankly, and I gulp down the vodka letting it burn its way down. She moves me back onto my side so she can access the wound. I can't see her only hear her as she settles and then searing pain engulfs me and I cry out before passing out.

I wake to the smell of fresh air and cleanness if that is a smell. Baby is crying. I try to push up but the pain that streaks across my stomach has me laying back down, panting. I notice I am in clean pyjamas and the bed feels clean. The door opening has me trying to sit up again.

'Hey, calm down,' the girl smiles at me her curly hair seems to bounce with every step.

'Baby?' my voice is gruff.

'He is fine,' she giggles. 'I said he. Who would have thought,' she helps me sit up and passes me the mug that was in her hand when she came in. 'It's just tea,' she raises a brow. I sip it and grimace at the sweetness of it.

'Who are you,' I put the tea down and turn my attention to her.

'We live at the next farm. We heard the herd baying and came to investigate,'

'Who is we?' Rude I know but this is important.

'My sisters and I of course. Kristian is my elder sister Betsy match,' she smiles. Betsy has a baby so she can feed yours,' she bites her lip and I know what she wants to ask. Please don't, I think. Not sure I can talk about it yet.

'Thank you,' my fingers twist the sheet.

'What happened where is Sara?' She does anyway.

'They killed her,' I gaze up at her. 'They took my son and killed Rita,' I whisper.

'Who?'

'I don't know they were on bikes,'

'In that case I think it best we move you to our farm,'

'The animals?'

'Kristian will sort them,' she smiles as she climbs to her feet. 'You sleep and we will move tomorrow okay,' I nod and lay back down.

'Name, what's your name,' I mutter.

'Daisy,' she smiles from where she is stood by the door.

'Aaron, my name is Aaron,' Sucking in a breath I come to a decision. 'Daisy, I need to stay here the guard will come here soon,' I get it out seeing her eyes widen in surprise.

'It will be fine they will come to our farm when they see you aren't here,' she smiles brightly.' I can leave a message,' she says from the door looking back at me.

'Thank you,' I close my eyes and let sleep wrap around me. I don't really wake properly again as the fever takes me. My body desperately fighting the infection.

'No, Aaron come on don't die,' she pleads. Her hand strokes my hair as she wipes the sweat from my face.

'Save him. Keep him safe for Rita,' I mumble the strain of being shot taking its toll on my body.

'What's his name? Where did he come from?'

'He doesn't have one. I had to cut him from Rita's belly,' I manage before I sink into the dark painless sleep.

'Why shoot a heavily pregnant woman it makes no sense,'

'Is he dead? He looks dead?'

'No Sukie he has just passed out again,' Daisy sighs. 'He is very sick.'

'We need to get them to the Capital. They belong to the royal family,'

'He is stunning even in that state. I haven't seen one like this for a very long time,'

'What is he? Because I am sure he isn't an Adam,'

'No he isn't I believe he is an Echo child,'

'Wow. That makes no sense why shoot him?'

'He mentioned Rita do you think he meant the princess?'

'Possibly that would explain why he was at Sara's.'

'Let's get him back to ours that's the safest thing to do,'

'The snow is too heavy to get to the Capital' a male voice. Kristian, I guess.

'He said the guard would come,'

'I can stay with him,'

'No, we leave a note,' I feel arms lift me up as the blanket is wrapped around me.

'Daisy don't get attached he isn't for you,'

'I know that I'm not stupid,' Daisy snaps.

I wake a couple of times. Daisy seems to be my main care giver and I have no strength to object. She talks constantly.

'Kristian has sorted all the animals. Betsy has made cheese and butter she is very good at it. I don't have the patience. I want to be a doctor. I can't though I am clean and will be matched next year. It is my duty to reproduce. Your baby is very cute. Beautiful like you.' I feel her wipe my face with a cool cloth as I slip back to sleep.

Pushing out of the bed that isn't mine I stagger downstairs. This house isn't like mine it is full of clutter. Pictures of the family that live here. I push a door open and find myself in a large kitchen. A young woman is at the sink and by the picture window a crib is being rocked by a young teenager.

'Hey, you shouldn't be out of bed,' the woman rushes over to me and helps me sit. 'Tea?' she smiles at me she has the same curly brown hair and large brown eyes as Daisy, so I guess she is Betsy.

'Thank you. My baby?'

'He is adorable. Do you want a cuddle?'

'Yes please,' The teen gets up and reaches into the cradle bringing out a blanket wrapped bundle.

'Here you go,' she places it in my arms. He is awake large liquid blue eyes like mine study my face.

'Hello you,' I mutter. He looks like me and I feel bad that I am glad.

THE SOUND of horses clattering into the yard frightens me. I pick up baby and shuffle upstairs to the room I am using. Shutting the door annoyed that I can't lock it. Climbing into the bed. Baby is against my chest I curl around him. I know Betsy watched me and thinks I am weird but honestly, I don't care. The voice's downstairs drift toward me.

'Betsy, Daisy what happened?' A girl's voice full of authority fills the silent house.

'They were attacked we assume. After the boy,' They are interrupted by another voice.

'Florence, we found two graves freshly dug in the meadow,'

'No, please,' the first voice full of anguish.

'Florence, sit down let me make you tea,' Betsy reassures. Florence, I scramble from the bed making baby grumble. Dashing from the room I clatter down the stairs. Bursting into the room. There she is and Lisa and Lou are with her.

'Florence,' the feeling of relief is so overwhelming I burst into tears.

'Aaron what happened we got reports of vigilantes in the area came to warn you all.' Lou has me wrapped in her arms. While Lisa has the baby.

'They are dead they killed them and took Charlie, and I couldn't stop them,' I crumple. Aware of strong arms around me.

'Shush Aaron you are safe,' Lou sooths.

'Who did this?'

'Bikers,' the effort to speak about this is so much harder than I thought. I pull out a chair and sink onto it. Betsy takes baby and feeds him. Another guard walks in and I startle when I realise, they are male.

'Florence, we found some of the bikers that did this,'

'A child was there a child with them?'

'You don't understand the bikers they are all dead,'

'What do we do?'

'What MC do they belong too,'

'Dread riders,'

'Damn, okay inform my mother,'

'Yes, your majesty,'

Florence turns her attention to me. I can see she is holding back tears. She looks so much like Rita it hurts to look at her.

'I lost them Flo, I failed,' is all I say. She gathers me to her, and we cry together.

CHAPTER 25

The morning light filters across the room. I remember waking to find Florence feeding the baby in the early hours. Turning my head, I find the baby asleep. Curled into my chest, hesitantly I let my finger brush lightly through his soft hair. His little lips pucker as he snuggles tighter to me. Naomi had explained he needed my smell to thrive, go figure.

We are in the palace in the city. How ironic it was only another week's ride. The city is amazing. Beautiful architecture nestled against modern buildings. The streets clean and bustling with people. People who aren't starving. Even with Gilly I didn't see anything like this.

The wound in my side is healing, leaving a peppering of small scars. A constant reminder of what a failure I am. With a tired sigh I pull the quilt up and close my eyes. Sleep is the only way to forget to block it all out.

Crying wakes, me, that and his gentle wriggling as he demands to be fed again. Pushing up I hold him to me as he snuffles into my neck looking for food. I reach for the bottle that always appears when I sleep like magic. I smile at the absurd thought as I test the bottle before pushing it against his mouth.

Once he is changed and settled in his crib, I lay on the bed. I don't want to leave this room. A tray is sat on the bedside table I peer at it and then pick at the food on the plate not hungry. I startle as the door opens and Florence walks in. Her eyes travel the room and then stop on me.

A frown creases her brow as she studies me her arms crossed. My heart stutters as she is beautiful and the image of Rita. Stood now in jeans and a shirt out of uniform. The only difference she oozes confidence and authority.

'Right, you, that's enough wallowing time you learnt how to defend yourself,'

'Get lost I don't want any part of your stupid plan,' I snarl she has been harassing me for days now.

'Unlucky,' with that she pulls away the blanket I am hiding under.

'What the hell,' jumping to my feet I lunge at her.

'There it is,' she dances out my way.

'There what is,' I shout angry beyond rational thought.

'The fire,' she laughs, bloody laughs and I charge at her again pushing her on to the bed pinning her down with my body. With ease she flips us pinning my hands above my head. I wriggle to get free unfortunately that causes another reaction one I certainly don't want. 'Oh, Aaron aren't you full of surprises,' she chuckles and rubs me some more.

'Stop, please just stop,' I burst into tears. She leaps off me like a scolded cat and then gathers me to her.

'Sorry, I am so sorry,' she soothes as I sob all the grief pouring out. Pushing away I stagger to my feet stepping away from her. Wiping my eyes with my hand. I walk to the door pulling it open.

'Can you go please,' I say my voice strong considering I have humiliated myself without even trying.

'Why are you doing this,' she looks at me and I see with a clarity I haven't had for weeks. She doesn't understand.

'Leave me alone, I don't need your missed placed sympathy thank you,'

'Aaron, you need to leave this room care for your baby son properly,' her eyes rest on me her face full of sympathy. 'He needs a father who is strong,'

'No, he doesn't, and I don't want him. I don't want to see him in fact every time I hear him cry, I die a little more inside. I had to cut him from her dead body, mutilate the person I loved more than life itself and I will never get that image out of my head ever. Now leave me alone...please and take him with you,' my voice cold as I turn away from her waiting for the door to close indicating she has gone.

'No Aaron I can't do that,'

'Yes, you can. Don't you get it I want to die. Every day I hope no I pray I won't wake up ever,' I am shouting now as the tears roll down my face. 'I didn't want this, but she made me love her and I suddenly had a future I thought I would never have. Now she is gone, and I don't know what to do with all this emotion inside me,' I sink to the floor exhausted as I bury my head in my hands.

'Oh, Aaron no,' she holds me tight as I rock with the black hole of grief that is consuming me. 'He needs you and you and I both know if Rita were here, she would slap you for turning your back on him. Her last breath was to beg you to save him. You are betraying her last wish,' with that she climbs to her feet. I didn't even get up as the door banged shut.

My life changed after that. No bottle or food came I had to go and fetch it myself. Oddly I never came across anyone. It is like they hear him cry and leave the building. Deep down I am so grateful. I don't want to have to observe the social niceties.

Baby is the image of me not like Charlie at all as he was all Rita. Small and delicate already I can see he will be pretty like me. A blessing in one way but not in another as he gets sick, and Doctor Naomi has to monitor him frequently. The bond that had always been there reinforced to the extent I became anxious when he was away from me for long periods.

* * *

'I HAVE MEETINGS ALL MORNING,' Florence smiles at me and I scowl back. I am in her royal suite of rooms. She thinks I am going to break and watches me constantly. Maybe I will just give her the satisfaction of being right. She thinks I am weak to delicate for the role I was trained for now Rita is gone. I don't care I have given them what they wanted an heir.

I sit on the bed; I am nervous Florence is leaving me and I am not sure I like the idea. I know she said I was safe here, but I still don't know anyone, and I am certainly not used to all these people. I really don't want her to leave me on my own. Baby is with Naomi, and it is giving me the jitters as I worry about him. He is sick because he is like me. His little body unable to cope with the contaminant. Naomi thinks it's because he was born early.

'Can't I come?' I grumble as Florence brushes her hair and generally tidies herself up.

'No, you aren't ready. I won't be long you will be fine I will send someone to look after you,' she turns and smiles at me I scowl back.

'I am not a baby, I don't need a babysitter,' I growl glaring at her.

'If that's the case, why are you behaving like one,' she glares back at me her mouth in a thin line. I have really annoyed her.

'Can I see baby?'

'Yes, that would be good he needs your scent,'

'I will be fine I s'pose,' I mutter, looking away from her.

'Good,' she leaves the rooms and I sit and brood for a bit before getting babies things and go to collect him.

I wander along the hallway, admiring the paintings and tapestries. No one takes any notice of me which is good I suppose. I had noticed a small walled garden when I left the rooms we had been allotted and I am making my way there. I am going to sit and read to baby, until someone comes to find me. I don't want some stupid babysitter I'm not a baby. I huff and stuff my hands in my pockets as I brood. Baby in his sling against my chest so he can hear my heartbeat. He is sleeping but it is fitful, and I stroke his soft hair to sooth him. I can't lose him now; it would destroy me.

The garden is lovely with raised beds full of vegetables and soft fruit. I have never gardened, and this is beautiful. The grass walkways between each rectangle shaped bed. Insects buzz around the flowers that I recognise from inside. It never occurred to me this was where they came from. I pluck a couple of strawberries and bite into them relishing the juice and flavour as it floods my mouth. It reminds me of Rita and the pleasure she got from growing things. I can think about the happy times concerning her now.

I choose a large apple tree to sit under. I gaze upward at the soaring trunks around me that seem to be teaming with life. There branches are so carefully pruned to allow the burgeoning fruit to ripen.

This isn't what Florence wanted me to do, she wants me to make friends talk to people, but I don't know how to do that. If I tell her she will laugh at me. I am getting tired of being laughed at because I don't understand this world. A world I am having to be part of. Don't get me wrong I want to learn about it. What little I have seen and been told about it is fascinating, but I feel I need help adjusting not leaving to cope on my own. I sigh and rub my face with my hands and start to read. Baby is asleep his little hand inside my shirt. I have undone a couple of buttons, so he has skin contact.

I am momentarily distracted from my book when a girl walks over to me. Well walking isn't quite right she sort of glides, well that is how it looks. The long colourful skirt she is wearing swishes around her legs concealing her feet. She sits down beside me and peers at baby flicking her long black hair over her shoulder. She smells like vanilla ice cream and earth as she sits to close to me. I would move but the tree root is stopping me.

'Oh, he is just so cute,' she looks up at me and I stare into a pair of luminous green eyes. Her pink lips turn up in a smile and reveals a pair of dimples on her cheeks she is beautiful, and I blush.

'Thanks,' I mumble feeling embarrassed and look away from her.

'You are so lovely, Florence said you were pretty. My names Marina, um Florence thought you might like to come shopping with me and get something to eat. It is market day and as it is such a lovely day we could walk. You can bring baby it's not far from here a group of us are going. You could get some bits for baby,' her gaze slides over me as if she is taking in every detail before she eats me or something. She has that hungry look in her eyes. I swallow she makes me edgy; do I want to spend time with her?

'Oh, um yeah is it safe for me, I don't want to get anyone in trouble,' I mumble, this girl makes me nervous and self-conscious, I blush again.

'Yeah, it's safe with us, besides you are so pretty you would never guess you're a boy. Not compared to some of the girls here, very masculine some of them,' She giggles at the look of shock on my face at her statement. I think I should be offended by that remark definitely took a hit to my masculinity.

'We have lots of Adam's here it isn't like the rest of the world you know,' she smiles and no I don't know.

She climbs to her feet and holds out her hand, I take it and she pulls me up, I stand awkwardly she is far too close to me, her eyes slide down and study my lips as if she is contemplating whether or not to kiss me. Please don't I silently pray as I realise the damn tree is trapping me again and I can't step back.

'I just need to take baby back get his coat and stuff,' I mumble, she hasn't let go of my hand yet, or moved away from me. I can feel her heat and I don't want to pull away as that might seem rude. Or is that just an excuse and I just don't want to pull away, break the contact. She holds my hand firmly I like that.

She finally lets go of my hand and steps away from me allowing me space to collect up babies' things and put them in his bag, more importantly a chance to get a grip and restore my composure.

'May I hold him?'

'Erm of course,' I untie his sling and carefully pass him to her.

'Oh, he is so small and pretty like you,' her gaze slides over me again.

'Yeah, he looks like me,' I answer and yeah, I know I sounded feeble.

'I love the city it is so vibrant. You will love it,' she chatters away as we walk.

'There are other males?' I am intrigued by this.

'Oh yes. I am getting an Adam as I am clean and fertile isn't that exciting,' her eyes shine.

'You are matched then?' I am surprised by this.

She snorts. 'Oh no, the council will select some that are for sale,' I stop walking in shock.

'You will just buy them?'

'Well yes, how else will we acquire them,' we start walking again as I mull that over. 'You are upset about that aren't you?'

'I...um well sort of. I mean I know we are bought and sold if we don't match,' I stutter out. 'The way you said it was more shocking. Like you were buying your lunch or a new pair of shoes not an actual person,' my explanation isn't very good I appreciate that.

'So, you would prefer they are just euthanised the spare ones,'

'No, no of course not,' she is cross I can tell.

'They have a good life with us,' she huffs. 'You know I have no choice either,' she sighs. 'I was tested when I became a woman and I am clean of the contaminate and fertile, so it is my duty to breed with the Adam chosen for me. You know how babies are made obviously,' her gaze drifts to baby asleep in her arms. 'I will have to do that with a stranger. Not only that he will be scared, and it takes time to break through the indoctrination of his previous life. I would prefer to fall in love, but that choice has been taken from me as I have to do my duty,' she huffs.

'Sorry, I didn't mean to offend. I just.... I mean I know we are sold. Rita and Andrea had to fend off prospective offers for me,' I smile. 'I sorry. Rita said something similar once she um didn't want or like the arrangement,' I shrug.

'I don't not like the idea it just isn't ideal. I view it as,' she pauses. 'I am saving his life,' she shrugs. We are at the door that leads to the suite of rooms I share with Florence.

I understand they want me to bond to her and I find it weird if a little incestuous. Marina follows me inside. Her gaze taking in every detail.

'I haven't been in the royal suite in ages,' she says sitting on the bed. 'It hasn't changed much,' gazing around as I change baby and put his coat on. I find my cloak.

'Sorry Marina…for earlier,' I sit next to her.

'That's okay,' she takes my hand and examines it. 'Did you love her. Princess Rita?' her gaze travels to my face.

'Yes, very much,'

'You were friends you know before,'

'Yes, we were friends. She was like you not happy she had a match,' I smile remembering. 'There was an incident and I almost died. That's how we met. Neither of us knew the other was our match. That came later,' pushing to my feet moving away sucking in air.

'Sorry she died, Princess Rita was lovely,'

'You knew her?' I turn to her my eyes wide with surprise.

'Yes, we were friends,'

'Yes, she was lovely,' my surprise turns to melancholy.

I find a note and a shopping list and some money from Florence. *Have some fun Aaron,* is all the note says I smile as I shove them in my pocket. I remove my bag and go through its contents removing my change of clothes and reading book, plus my laptop. I don't need them to go shopping.

'Can we be friends?' She is beside me.

'I thought we already were,' giving her a lopsided smile. She takes my hand as we saunter out the rooms.

I look up as a boy crashes into us. I grab his shoulders to steady him. He looks just like me with pale blond hair and startling blue eyes an Echo child. He is just smaller than me which is amusing. He lives here as well. I quite like him and his general childlike ways. Always in a state of enthusiasm. Florence finds it funny the way he follows me everywhere. He stands for a moment getting his breath back.

'You coming into town Aaron?' He gasps out. Excitement all over his face.

'Yes Robert, if only to keep you out of trouble,' with a chuckle I glance at Marinna. I can see from her face she is trying to hold in a giggle.

'Oh, hello Marina,' he smiles and blushes. 'Gotta go some girl said I could touch her breasts, amazing,' he darts out the door and is gone. I stand and stare at the space he was in and then laugh.

'Sorry he is a bit excitable,' I explain to Marina trying to fill the awkward silence left by his statement and departure.

'Oh, don't worry I am used to Robert,' she replies guiding me along the hall. She brushes against me, and I know it was deliberate her hand grazes my backside and I almost jump at this obvious intrusion.

'You sleep with Florence?' She raises a brow and I blush. Damn it what is wrong with me, I really need to man up.

'Yeah, sort of, she is very protective,' I say it with as much nonchalance as I possibly can. I know she is smirking at me. 'They, um want us to bond.'

'Eww that is wrong,' she blurts out.

'Yeah, I know but they can't waste a good Echo boy can they,' I shrug and look away.

* * *

SHE LEADS me over to where a group of teens are waiting and she is right some of the girls don't look anything like girls, they are way more masculine than me, I relax a bit this might be fun. They eye me up and I try to look like I don't care.

'Oh, ain't he pretty,' one of the girls says as she walks up to me and goes to touch me I step back.

'Please don't touch me,' I say making a point of not looking her in the eye, so it isn't a challenge. The girl stands back and looks me over.

'Oh, and why can't I touch you little boy, how you going

to stop me?' She smirks at me and steps closer I swallow and look at her entire massive bulk, damn.

'It's cool Paula, he doesn't like being touched, Florence told me, he ain't being disrespectful. He was Rita's boy,' Marina steps in as I ball my hands into fists waiting for the fight, not that I am going to stand much chance against Paula she is huge and as Florence enjoys pointing out I am weedy. Marina reaches down and takes my hand uncurling my fingers.

'We are protecting him. You know the rules around Adams. Besides he's just an innocent and he belongs to Florence,' Marina steps forward sort of aggressively in a non-threatening way if you know what I mean. Paula backs off and the group lose interest and move off. I let out the breath I was holding and follow Marina still holding her hand I notice some of the others pair off holding hands.

The walk into the town is lovely. We meander down the narrow streets that bustle with people. Many greet Marina and pay me little attention as they stop to fuss over baby. Marina has him and he is quite happy with her.

I gaze into shop windows. This is so new as I have never been shopping before. Marina finds it funny that I have to look at everything and we soon fall behind the group.

We eat sticky buns from a bakery. It took me ages to make up my mind and I had to look at everything. The baker gave me samples to try. It was amazing. There was even a shop for babies and children. I have seen a few running about while their mother's gossip.

Marina finds a stall with street food, and we sit in a park on a bench eating. We get lots of admiring glances as Marina feeds baby. We are the perfect contrast her all dark. Dark hair, skin and eyes and me so pale. Almost white hair and translucent skin. I don't feel threatened here with all the people around us. It just feels nice.

Once we finish eating and sorting baby, Marina leads me over to a van, car thing. It is long, and sort of lozenge shaped and painted two colours pale blue on the bottom and white on top with a row of windows. I know it is a Volks wagon camper van from the car books I have read but it's far more modern.

A huge grin covers my face as I gaze at it; I run my hand over it feeling the cold metal beneath my fingers. A voice breaks my rapture and I jump slightly.

'You like it then?'

'Oh, yeah it's amazing,' I reply without thinking. 'How does it work what fuel do you use,' I hear a deep chuckle next to me.

'If you pop the hood, you'll find a sealed metal box with a micro hydrogen fusion cell in it. That bad boy generates enough electricity to power this things motor for about the next half a million years.'

'How does that work?' I ask in wonder.

'Not a clue I'm afraid. It fuses hydrogen atoms to generate energy, don't ask how because I don't know. It then stores the energy given off in a set of really powerful capacitors. They are in turn attached to a modulator that supplies the correct amount of electricity to power the motor. Paula over there she knows exactly how this works. If you climb aboard, you get a ride in it,' the voice chuckles and I look up into a pair of blue eyes nearly as blue as mine, framed by light brown hair set in a perfect face, an Adam. He laughs at the shock on my face. As I take in his guard uniform.

'Ed,' he smiles holding out his hand.

'Hello,' I stutter gazing at him. I am completely floored how can this be? He is much older than me, well past retirement age he has lines around his eyes and mouth indicating he laughs a lot.

'Aaron,' I manage shaking his hand.

'Yes, I know my wife never stops telling me about you and your gorgeous baby,' he chuckles.

'Oh...um sorry,'

'Is Florence your match?'

'No...she died, my match, having my son. She was Florence's sister,' that wasn't exactly the truth, and I don't know why I said all that. I look into his blue eyes and shrug. I don't really understand all this matching stuff. He frowns at me and shakes his head as if puzzled by me.

'Ah Rita's boy. I am so sorry for your loss Rita was delightful,' he answers.

'Yes , yes she was,' I manage.

'Right well better get going, who is looking after you today?' I can tell he is embarrassed by my answer. Who wouldn't be. Don't know why I said all that?

'Um Marina,' I answer still in a state of shock as I try to process everything. I look up alarmed I can hear motor bikes. Ed grabs hold of me and puts me in the bus.

'Aaron, go sit down and stay with the other kids okay,' I nod my head at Ed as I do as he says sitting next to Robert, I put my arm around him and hold him tight.

'Aaron, do you think they will take us like they did Princess Rita?' He looks at me his eyes swimming with tears. 'And Sophie and she never came back, and I miss her,' he snivels.

'No one will take us, Ed will look after us,' I tell him trying to reassure him. As Ed climbs on the bus just as a shot rings out Robert jumps and the tears that were threatening to fall run down his cheeks as he buries his head in my chest clinging to me.

'I want to go home,' he whimpers, and I know exactly what he means as I hold him tight. The bus rumbles to life and I look up meeting Marina's eyes. She looks as if she is going to speak and then changes her mind. She tucks baby into her coat concealing him. Ed drives away. Heading back to the palace. I can hear bikes roaring.

'What's going on Ed?' One of the girls asks as we speed away two bikes either side of the van.

'Well girls these two little Prince's we have amongst us are no ordinary males and lots of people want them.'

'Cool, we will protect them won't we girls,' another girl shouts and a hell yeah is cheered throughout the van. I can't help it and a grin twitches my lips, even Robert lifts his head and wipes his face with the back of his hand and manages a watery smile.

The bikes push aggressively against the van causing Ed to swear about his paint work. Ed pulls his pistol out and opens the window and shoots the offending bikes front tyre out sending it flipping into the pavement as people jump out the way.

'Circle round Ed head to the lower entrance if they drive us off the road here, we will stand no chance,' Paula instructs, and Ed throws the van into a tight turn causing another bike to crash off the road and slide on its side across the grass verge. The girls give a collective cheer it doesn't last as deafening bang crashes around the van as a window is shot out, a couple of girls scream as glass showers them.

I push Robert to the floor and cover him with my body picking glass out of his hair as he whimpers. 'It's fine Robert, you are fine,' I whisper in his ear and feel him relax a little.

On the floor I can't see anything and all I can hear is a gun going off and Ed using some very colourful swear words. My point of gravity shifting drastically takes my brain by surprise. It was a full five minutes until I realise, we have crashed.

I am showered with yet more glass and the screech of twisting metal, intermingled with the screams of the girls is all I can hear, I hold tightly to Robert as we are thrown about like clothes in a washing machine. As I try to locate Marina and baby. I can hear him crying.

The van finally comes to a stop and the silence is deafening until the sobs of the girls starts and Ed slowly crawls toward me half his face covered in blood. I gingerly lift my weight off of Robert and peer down at him. He too has blood trickling down his face, but he manages a smile to show me he is okay.

I glance around and it is carnage. Somehow Robert and I were shielded by the seat but the girls on the side that hit the ground were not nearly as lucky. Ed reaches my side and looks me over placing his hands on my shoulders and pulling me up onto my knees.

'Are you hurt?' He asks concern and fright on his face.

'No, we are fine,' I manage pulling Robert out from under the seat. 'Where is Marina?'

'Her and the baby are safe. We need to get out, come on,' He turns, and crawls back the way he came. I grab Robert and push him in front of me. By the time we climb out some of the girls are out now and huddled around Ed who is bloodied. Our group are battered but amazingly no one died, and we all seem to just have cuts and bruises. A group are huddled around Marina protecting her. She sits crossed legged feeding baby.

The sound of shotguns loading makes us all freeze and stop what we are doing the girls push Robert and I behind them and then close around us hiding us from sight as the three leather clad women walk up to our group their guns pointing at Ed.

'Well look what we have here. Ain't you pretty,' she seems to be the leader as the other two follow her. They all have guns. Stopping in front of Ed she takes his chin in her hand inspecting his face. Ed puts his hand up and pushes her away with a growl.

'Don't you disrespect me,' in a blink of an eye she hits Ed with her gun sending him crashing to the floor and fresh blood pouring down his face. Marina gasps and sinks to her knees next to him her hand going to his neck to feel for a pulse.

'You idiot you could have killed him, in fact you morons nearly killed us all,' Marina hisses cradling Ed's head in her lap. 'This is my man, how dare you touch him,' She glares at them venom in her voice. As Paula steps forward her mouth in a thin line as she towers over the woman.

'We are guard you have no business attacking us woman,' She growls and the woman steps back slightly.

'You have two of our Adams and we have come to reclaim them,' the woman glares at Paula.

'There are no Adams in this group. Even if there were you cannot have them as they have sanctuary. You know that, or do you want to break the treaty and cause all-out war?'

'I like war?' The gun going off is such a shock that everything seems to stop and then Paula crumples to the ground. I grab Robert and slowly back away as the girls get over the shock Marina takes Eds pistol and shoots the woman that shot Paula as the girl's snarl and converge on the remaining two women who start shooting randomly.

The clatter of hooves and booted feet are the first indication more guard have arrived on the scene. I pull Robert away and start to run as fast as I can ducking into a doorway as the shots ring out. I feel Robert stumble but pull him up slipping into an alleyway. I end up in a park away from the streets. There is a small stream running through it and a lot of reeds that are easily taller than me. I scramble down the bank and sit hidden, letting the angry tears flow. Robert crouches next to me his face buried in my shoulder as his body trembles from shock.

'Ed,' he stutters. 'Aaron, I hurt,' he glances up at me as his

219

face pales and I look down at him his shirt blooming with blood.

'Damn Robert, where?' I pull his shirt up and I see the mess some pellets have peppered his side. I remove my shirt and tear it into strips and use it as padding and bandages putting pressure on it, but I know it is futile.

'I am so tired; I will just sleep for a bit,' Robert looks at me and then slowly closes his eyes.

'No Robert stay awake, stay with me, please don't leave me?' I beg holding him in my arms rocking as tears drip onto him from my chin. I hadn't even noticed I was crying.

'Not leaving you, just gonna have a nap,' Robert whispers a small smile on his lips. 'You have a right phobia about being left.'

'Yeah, I do so stay please,' I beg.

'Not going anywhere just gonna have a nap,'

I know the minute she is next to me.

'Aaron sweetie,'

'I hate it here. I want to be dead. I want to be with Rita,' I answer wiping my face with the back of my hand.

'No sweetheart don't ever say that,' she pulls me into her.

'You should leave me, give me back to Gen-Corp before I get you killed,' I gaze up at her so like my Rita.

'No that is not happening any of it,' her hands grasp my face as she looks deep into my eyes. 'I love you. You idiot,'

'You shouldn't, I can't love you back,' I let my gaze drop.

'I know and I am sorry,' she reaches across, and her lips touch mine. Distracting me as Robert is lifted away.

'Come on Baby needs his daddy to calm him,' She pulls me to my feet. 'Besides I have justice to deliver for my brother,' she snarls anger grating in her words. I never considered Robert was a prince. Why? My mind needing a puzzle to stop it from snapping.

CHAPTER 26

The palace is quiet as I sit and feed baby. I had dismissed his nurse I don't want them fussing around me. Looking up as the door bursts open and Naomi rushes in. I place baby against my shoulder rubbing his back. Watching Florence as she stalks about the apartment on her phone.

'Are you hurt, let me see,' Naomi fusses around me.

Naomi it isn't my blood, I just need a shower and a change of clothes,' I sigh as she runs her hands over me. 'How is Ed?'

'He is still unconscious, but he should wake up soon.'

'No one else died then?"

'What, no, no one died. Robert had a lucky escape it was a graze,'

'He, I thought,' I burst into tears. Florence drops her phone and has me wrapped in her arms as I tremble with my sobs.

'Florence, sorry?' I just lay down exhausted.

'Aaron, you didn't lose him it wasn't your fault. You both should have had more protection,' she says over her shoulder as I undress. 'I am going to finish your training as Rita would have done to keep you safe,' her voice is muffled by the running water. She emerges from the bathroom. Her gaze sweeps my body checking for damage I suppose. 'Have your bath and a sleep I will care for baby tonight,' she smiles. I can see the sympathy and worry she thinks I will break again.

I lay in the bath relieved she isn't in here with me. I scrub my skin and wash my hair. What am I doing here? Is my main thought. Rita is dead so in theory I don't belong here now. I don't have a match she is dead. So, what is my position? Honestly, I don't know. Climbing out the tub I think all this through. One thing I am sure about wherever I go I can't take my son. Strolling into my room I gaze at all the people. I am exhausted with this.

'Can you all just leave please,' all eyes turn to me. 'Please, just go. All of you,'

'Aaron,' Florence watches me her posture wary.

'I am tired I want to sleep. Can we talk about this tomorrow please,' I check baby he appears to be clean and fed. Asleep with a bit of milky dribble on his chin. Hardly feeling the scratch on my arm. 'What was that' I slur wiping away the tears. I hadn't noticed I was crying.

'Just a sedative you should have a sleep, recover, we can't afford for you to get sick,' Florence turns the bed back. She helps me in and tucks the blankets around me.

'Stay... please,' I slur my eyes closed already. I feel her take my hand.

I wake alone, I don't care, or wonder where everyone is, not even baby. I stumble out of bed and head to the door the only thing in my head is I want a drink and I don't mean a cup of tea. I pull the door open and gaze around eventually I spot Marina. She is sat reading a book dressed in another flamboyant outfit as she rocks baby in his cradle. The carpet feels soft as I feel it tickle my bare feet as I make my way toward her.

'Aaron what are you doing out of bed? She surveys me and smirks. 'Did you forget something?' I frown and then realise I only have my boxers and a t-shirt on. Damn who took my clothes; I look at Marina and then start to laugh.

'Aaron you idiot,' Climbing to her feet she walks toward me.

'Yeah, I know but I need something,' I growl frustrated.

'Do you really I thought you would never ask,' she winks at me suggestively and wraps her arm around me.

'No, no, not that, I need a drink, alcohol,' I manage and then gaze at her with expectation.

'Oh, do you now well I might just know where we can get you some hmm,' I nod with enthusiasm and follow her down the back stairs to the kitchens and servant quarters.

'If I do this, what do I get in return?' Marina asks all innocent and I know exactly what she wants.

'I will mate with you,' I answer hoping I have injected enough nonchalance, so she thinks I don't care about what I am offering.

'Deal,' she grins and bangs on a blue door its paint peeling. It opens and a very cross old woman glares at us both.

'What you want Marina?'

'Whiskey.'

'Got money.'

'Yes,' Marina pulls some folded up notes from her jean pocket and hands them to the old woman, who examines them for a minute and then goes inside slamming the door in our faces. We stand for a few minutes hearing what I assume is the woman looking for the whiskey. Eventually as I am losing my nerve the door swings open again and an arm and hand reach out with a bottle of what I assume is whiskey'.

'Thanks,' Marina says as she grabs the bottle and then

pulls me away and back toward some stairs and a long passageway, we are deep beneath the palace now. I shiver as it isn't very warm down here. She pushes open another door its hinges squeak in protest, I can hear music. A small smile settles on my lips, its time I decide to act my age. As we get nearer, I see people sat around tables smoking and talking they look up at us as Marina leads me to the door.

'What you doing with him?' One asks as in my undressed state I can't be mistaken for a girl.

'He wants to play,' Marina retorts and they smile.

'Does he now,' one says, she looks me up and down. 'Here boy try this,' she passes me the thing she is smoking I take a drag and then cough, a lot, my eyes watering, I take another drag and let the smoke fill my lungs, I feel all relaxed and I can't honestly remember why I was so anxious.

'Thanks,' I mutter as they go back to their conversation and smoking.

Marina leads me inside. There are more people drinking and smoking and the music is louder. As Marina leads me through the crowd some smirk at me and I feel a couple of hands touch me I really don't care.

'Is the back room free?' Marina demands and a voice belonging to a girl with hair that I can only describe as lilac although it could be pink, but she is surrounded by so much smoke it is hard to distinguish the colour exactly.

'Yeah, it's free, is he legal?' She laughs and ruffles my hair. I scowl at her and she laughs at me.

'Let's hope so,' Marina counters back and the place erupts into laughter.

I enter the room taking in the bed and tatty furniture. Marina pushes me down, so I am sat on the bed, she hands me the bottle and I open it and take a swig as she locks the door, I frown at this.

'We don't want Naomi or Florence barging in now do

we?' she says as she moves to the bed and climbs up beside me. I pass her the bottle and she takes a large mouthful. To be honest, I would be surprised if they know this place exists.

'Better,' she asks.

'Yes much,' I reach over and kiss her, she doesn't need much encouragement and removes the bottle from my hands she places it on the floor. She then returns her attention to me removing my t-shirt and her top she places my hands on her large breasts as she kisses me, her body covering mine. I push my hips into her suggestively. I hear her moan softly and that's all the encouragement I need.

We lay later drinking the whiskey, I would say I feel better but in truth I just feel numb and now very drunk.

'What happened to you? What happened to Rita?' Marina takes my hand linking our fingers.

'Dead, she is dead, and I had to cut baby from her body,' I answer as I draw circles with my finger on her flat belly dipping it into her belly button now and again. 'I miss her so much. She died because of me she warned me of the dangers and I ... I got her pregnant again when we should have been here and safe,'

'Aaron no she loved you so much. None of it was your fault.'

'Yeah, yeah, so everyone says,' I say as my hand travels lower. Her smooth dark skin is so beautiful as I absently wonder what a baby from our union would look like. She moans as my fingers find their quarry. Her hands in my hair. I lose myself in pleasuring her again while chasing my release. We lay a sweaty mess as the euphoria blocks out my miserable circumstance. A commotion outside drawers our attention as the music stops and I hear the unmistakable voice of Florence.

'Where is he? You had better not have harmed him in any way?'

'Course we ain't. He just wanted some fun. Who are we to deny him that?' Someone answers and I hear Florence snarl back a reply as I pull my clothes on what little I have, anyway. I take the bottle and drink some more whiskey as Florence barges in. She stands momentarily as she takes in the scene before her, me drunk and Marina naked next to me.

'Damn Aaron what the hell,' she strides to the bed and grabs hold of me yanking me to my feet, I sway and grin at her offering her some whiskey. 'Marina what have you done to him?' Florence glares at Marina. 'You are supposed to watch him. Keep him out of trouble,'

'Nothing he didn't want to do,' Marina glares back, her eyes flash with anger, and I giggle as her breasts wobble as she moves, glaring at Florence. 'Maybe if you saw him as a person he wouldn't be so messed up,'

'Leave me alone Florence, I am having a good time,' I pick the bottle up and take an exaggerated swig and grin at her.

'Aaron honey come on this isn't like you.' She goes to take the bottle, but I dance out of her way giggling.

'Mine don't want to share.' I giggle and drink some more. 'What do you know about me...nothing. You don't love me like she did. Hell, you don't even like me,' I slur, taking another mouthful of the whiskey.

'See leave him alone if he wants to party that's up to him, get lost Florence,' Marina squares up to Florence. I pass her the bottle and she drinks some.

'Oh, put some bloody clothes on and I am taking him with me.' Florence growls unimpressed.

'Get lost Flo, maybe if you let him have some fun, he wouldn't be such a mental wreck. After all he has done his duty. Provided an heir,' she shouts back, she thinks I'm a mental wreck, yeah, she is right I am. I giggle again and stagger about. I really can't walk and now I feel sick. I rush to the bathroom just in time to throw up. I groan and sink to the floor, my body deciding to purge the alcohol like it would a poison.

'Oh, great and now he is ill, do you know this could kill him?' Florence snarls as she strides over to me, scooping me up into her arms.

'Well better that than what you have planned for him, does he know? No of course he doesn't, or he would have run by now,' Marina growls back and then laughs mirthlessly, I wonder what she means but I really don't care anymore. I rest my head against Florence's chest. 'Life isn't all about duty,'

'What would you know,' Florence snarls back.

'Plenty she was my best friend and I saw every day how it crushed her. Going to do that to him now,' Marina snarls and Florence finches.

'That is not your concern,' Florence answers as she kicks the door shut and glares at everyone in the room.

'Florence, do you love me?' I slur, I am so drunk.

'Yes, Aaron I do,' her voice quiet and I can hear the hurt in it.

'I killed them both,' I hiccup. 'Careful I don't get you killed,' I hiccup again.

'No you didn't you are brave, and sweet and I am sorry,' she kisses the top of my head.

'You can put me down now.'

'Can you walk?'

'No, probably not,' I giggle, and Florence rolls her eyes.

'You are a ridiculous drunk...why are you drunk, what's going on Aaron?'

'Everyone I love is dead?' I snivel, I am a pathetic drunk.

'Oh Aaron, is this what this is about?' I nod as I feel her hold me tighter, I shut my eyes and pass out.

* * *

'AARON, YOU AWAKE?'

'Hmm,' I moan I feel horrible, and Naomi was in earlier giving me some lecture on getting a grip and stuff. How alcohol isn't the answer. I pulled the pillow over my head and ignored her as best I could.

'I brought you something to eat, you must be hungry you have been in here for hours now.' Marina coaxes me and I reluctantly sit up as the aroma of burger wafts around me. She passes me a paper bag and I fish the burger box out and open it. Inside is the most fabulous thing I have seen in ages. I grin at Marina and eat it as she eats hers. She passes me a large cardboard cup with a lid and a straw. I place my lips around the straw and suck up the drink glad when my mouth floods with something sweet and fizzy.

I finish my burger and lay back with my drink and leisurely eat my fries, letting out a loud burp making Marina grin as she does the same, we both giggle and I feel so much better.

Marina tidies up the food wrappers and shoves them in the large paper bag they came in and then comes and sits on the bed with me.

'You alright Aaron?' Marina pulls her legs up and shuffles about getting comfortable.

'Yeah, feel much better,' I smile as we lapse into silence again.

'I got a right telling off from Naomi,' she giggles.

'Yeah, Naomi gave me a lecture on getting a grip,' I chuckle.

'That's better, that's the Aaron I know and love. They have you on suicide watch,' Her face is serious as she looks me in the eye.

'I won't do that, maybe a couple of weeks ago but not

now. Rita would be disappointed in me if I did,' I try a smile but my lip wobbles. 'I miss her so much,'

'I know you do. I told Florence to give you time to grieve,'

'She doesn't understand,' I suck up more of my drink it is icy cold and feels great in my mouth.

'Rita died in front of me and…and I lost little Charlie. They took him and I couldn't stop them,' I look away. 'I'm a pathetic excuse of a man, how can I be normal, be around Florence and baby, when I can't protect them,' I look at Marina searching her face for the look of disgust at what I have done.

'Oh Aaron, you aren't pathetic you silly boy, you are brave and strong and loyal to your friends, and from what Naomi and Florence have said you were put in a horrible position and through it all you have protected your baby son,' she takes my hands kneeling in front of me.

'How do you handle all that, you get drunk that is very normal, we all love you, you idiot?' Marina pulls me to her in a hug as tears stream down her face and mine. I pull back slightly and crush my lips to hers tasting the salt of our tears as our mouths join. It's not enough, I want to feel her skin against mine as I pull her clothes out of my way, she doesn't stop me as her hands touch me. I need the release physical and mentally.

'You know this is becoming a habit,' I chuckle as I lay curled around Marina.

'A nice habit,' she laughs back as she turns facing me.

'Yeah, a nice habit,' I lean in and kiss her.

'You gonna get out of bed then and stop wallowing in self-pity.'

'Self-pity, I was properly depressed, how rude,' I splutter. 'Yeah, baby has had me up already with his demands, who put him in here anyway?'

'Oh, that was Florence, she thought it might help,' Marina

climbs off the bed and collects her clothes. I watch her as she puts them on, she smirks at me.

'In what universe does a crying baby help!' I raise a brow as she giggles. I watch her get dressed.

'Like what you see?' She teases and wriggles her bottom at me as she bends over the crib and gazing with what I can only describe as longing at baby. 'He is just adorable can I hold him?' She looks at me waiting for my permission.

'Yes, go ahead I need a shower anyway,' I climb out of bed and walk around the room to where she is holding baby. 'Maybe you have one in your belly now,' I kiss her cheek.

'I doubt it I am not your genetic match, but nice thought,' she cuddles baby, and he snuffles her chest making me smile as I amble to the door that leads to the bathroom, smiling as I listen to Marina coo at the baby.

'You are an echo though, aren't you?' I gaze at her as that realisation slams into me.

'Of course, why else would I be in the palace,' she winks at me with a giggle.

I stand under the shower and lean against the tiles and let the hot water run over me. I find clothes in the drawers. I finish doing up the buttons on the blue shirt I had finally settled on, to go with the light brown chinos I had on, I turn to Marina.

'Do I look respectable now?' I ask my eyes twinkling with mischief.

'Now you have shaved you do.' She giggles, come on people want to talk to you and I think this little fella needs Heidi as she has a working set of boobs,' Marina holds her hand out to me, in her other arm nestles baby.

CHAPTER 27

*F*lorence kept her word and left me alone mostly eventually turning up with a gun. 'Time you learnt to shoot,' standing in the doorway her gaze on me.

'Okay,' Our relationship slowly developed spending so much time together it was bound too. I am sure they have sent Marina away as I haven't seen her in ages. Florence isn't like Rita. To look at, yes, but that is where the similarities end. She is direct and argumentative. I have yet to find her soft side.

I struggled after Robert. All the grief I felt at the loss of Rita flooding back. Florence left me for a bit but now she is on my case again. I don't see Marina so much after our drunken afternoon. I think Naomi is doing that on purpose. Hoping I will bond with Florence instead. Fat chance of that. Florence doesn't even like me and I am not all that keen on her.

We stand in the shooting range deep beneath the castle. Other soldiers are down here practising. They bow their heads in respect when they see us. This I find weird. Florence places ear defenders on me and then positions me.

My handshakes with the gun in it. Taking a steadying breath, I fire.

'Not like that,' she barks, and I flinch hearing her huff behind me she kicks my legs apart, so I soften my knees. Her hands wrap around mine. I pull the trigger the gun goes off and I crumple to the ground with a whimper. Memories crowding in.

'Oh, for goodness' sake what is the point,' she stomps off and I drag myself up and stumble to my room and bed. I hear Naomi shouting at Florence.

'He isn't ready for that do you want to break him completely,' Naomi berates Florence.

'He is broken this is never going to work,'

'It has to work you just need to change tack,'

'We are running out of time if we want to get the other one back,' Florence huffs.

'I don't care Florence you can't do this to him,' Naomi argues back. 'They aren't meant for this. Those men have gone, are extinct,'

'Oh, really how do you explain Thomas?'

'He is a natural. Aaron is engineered you know that'

'I don't care, I need him strong. Rita is gone. I must step up and he will step up with me or I will kill him myself,' I hear the door slam. A silence falls and I am frightened I realise, of her.

'Aaron, get out here now,' she is banging on my locked door.

'No go away I don't want to see you,'

'Oh, grow up you ridiculous idiot. What would Rita say,'

'Who the hell knows she is dead, you heartless cow,' I shout back. Having thrown myself on the bed my pillow over my head blocking out her noise.

Close combat today and I am rubbish at it as she pins me to the ground yet again.

'I have had enough,' I whimper from my position on the ground. With Florence pinning me down my arms twisted behind my back.

'No get up and go again,'

'No, I have had enough,' I scramble to my feet and glare at her.

'I say when we are finished,' she scowls at me.

'Yeah, well you are delusional then,' I stomp away.

'Better than being pathetic,' she shouts at my retreating back.

'Aaron open this door…now,' she bangs on the door as I bury my face in my pillows.

'No go away,' I shout.

I stayed in my room for two days. Only sneaking out when she had gone. Waking to a voice I turn to find her feeding baby. Damn it I forgot to lock the door.

'Here,' she passes me a mug of tea and then carries on fussing over baby. I feel a new line of attack is about to take place. One that is going to use my baby son against me.

'What do you want,' I ask suspicion evident by my tone. Sipping the tea.

'Nothing,' she says loftily. Climbing to her feet she leaves the room. I glance at baby who gurgles back waving his arms in the air chuckling at his fingers. I take baby to my garden. Well, it isn't mine, but no one goes there but me and the gardener.

'Aaron,' I glance up to see Toby walking toward me. 'The staff said you were here,' he sits next to me.

'Toby, where have you been?'

'Well getting shot delayed me a bit,' he chuckles as I roll my eyes.

'Yeah, imagine,' the sarcasm evident.

'What else oh I became a dad that delayed us again,'

'Congratulations,' I say automatically.

'I see you have… Aaron sorry that was a nasty business,'

'Please don't,' I say automatically.

'Okay, but later if you want to talk,'

'Thanks,' I try to smile but, in the end, I turn my attention to baby in his pram. 'Glad you're back,'

'So, you are matched to Florence,' he pauses. 'A bit heartless but can't waste a good Echo boy,' his tone is angry. 'Sorry Aaron,'

'It's okay,' it's not as realisation slams into me. How have I been so stupid?

The following night I wake to her in my room. In her arms baby sucks his bottle. She is in her night dress. I ignore her and turn over, going back to sleep too tired to fight. Startling when I feel her climb into bed with me. With a sigh, I close my eyes.

I didn't see Florence for a couple of days. She left me alone. No more combat training, no guns. Part of me was so relieved it was ridiculous, but another part of me knew it was a trap. I suspect it is Toby, he always looks out for me. Of course, it didn't last.

Florence sort of moved in with me. I felt it was sort of by stealth rather than permission, but I had to admire her persistence. She even helped with baby, which was good as I got more sleep for a while.

The door banging wakes me enough to witness Florence drift in with baby. She puts him in his crib, fussing over him. It is still dark outside, and the palace is quiet.

'What are you doing in my room?' I growl at her.

'Naomi says you need more rest, so it makes sense for me to sleep here and look after the baby,' she smiles at me.

'No…I…oh for goodness' sake. Turn the light off,' I grumble, annoyed that I can't come up with a counterargument. Which isn't normal, as I have argued with pretty much everything, she has suggested so far. Secretly, I enjoy arguing with her. Getting enjoyment from the way she tests me constantly. Yeah, weird but fun. I still miss Rita so much, but it is getting easier.

'Aaron, why did you run to Marina? You can talk to me.' turning over, I lay on my back.

'No, I couldn't. You are Rita's sister,' I sigh. 'Marina, she is like Rita was…she has no expectations of me. You want me to be someone I am not? You look at me with disappointment as you try to see why your sister loved me.'

'I…sorry,'

'It's alright. I don't mind. I know I am not what you want.'

'Truce!'

'Friends would be better.' her hand moves to mine. I don't pull away.

Our days merge into weeks and then months. I can fire a gun with a certain amount of accuracy, and I can hold my own in close combat. I have a flair for knives. Accurately throwing them. Of course, the thought of actually throwing one at a person horrifies me. Florence knows that as well and I think she despises me for my weakness as she views it.

I sort of like her now. Don't get me wrong, I still argue at every opportunity. We have a relationship now rather than a tolerance for each other.

'Florence, are you okay?' I sit on the bed, feeding Jack the baby. Yeah, I have finally given him a name. Now I know he will not die. He is five months now. He looks just like me. Sometimes he smiles, and I see Rita in him. He can sit up now and has two bottom teeth and a mop of blond curls. The palace staff can't resist him and often ask to watch him. He seems to adore them all, gurgling and chuckling.

I hear the shower turn off, and then Florence throws up. She does this most mornings but won't tell me what is wrong. Even Doctor Naomi won't talk to me, quoting patient confidentiality or some such.

'What's wrong with you?' I ask, changing Jack's nappy. She sits next to me and takes my hand.

'I am pregnant,' she says and my universe crumbles.

'How?'

'Well, at a guess, all the sex,' she answers in her most sarcastic voice.

'I know that but... I...thought,' what did I think, how stupid am I? Yeah, she smashed through that last barrier in that way she has familiarity and stealth her principal weapons. Getting under my skin and slowly putting the pieces of my heart back together. This little family unit she has built to make me feel secure again. The bond snapping into place. So familiar I hardly notice.

Standing up, I walk to the cot and put Jack down for a sleep. Then I leave the room. How could she? To say I am devastated is an understatement. Milton is in his stall, brought here from the farm. Something else Florence did for me. That thought isn't enough to make me stay as I saddle him up and leave. I didn't see the hurt on her face or the tears as they pooled in her eyes. There was no consideration of her feelings as I left. As the black emotions caused by Rita's death consume me again.

Kneeling as I gaze at the grave. Someone has planted daisies on it, her favourite flower. Not me, probably Florence, and I know I have let them both down. I am a poor excuse of a man, and it should be me in the cold ground. The tears fall down my face. I don't wipe them away.

'I lost him, Rita, and I don't know what to do without you,' I know when she is behind me.

'Boy, why are you crying?' Startled, I turn around, and it wasn't Florence behind me.

'My name is Aaron,' I answer, wiping my face on my sleeve.

'Yes, you have his face,' I frown as I survey the girl before me. She is fair and similar to look at as Florence and Rita. Not as lean, rounder and softer, but still beautiful. She is holding a baby that has my eyes.

'Who are you?' I manage eventually.

'Sophie, and you are going to get my boy back. She would want you to do that,' she nods.

'Who would?' I am so confused by this odd girl.

'Rita, my sister. You asked her what to do. She would want you to find my boy and maybe your baby they took.' she nods again as if we have decided. Turning, she walks away as I sit, slightly stunned. I watch her talk to Florence. They both look at me before turning away again.

'Come on you, Jack misses his daddy,' Florence says, wrapping her arms around me.

'Florence, I am sorry, and a baby will be lovely. All these princes, your mum will be pleased,' I smile as Florence snorts.

'We will find him, Aaron, I promise.'

'If he is still alive,' I answer, as I have had to face that reality.

'Of course, he is, if he is anything like his dad, far too stubborn to die,' she chuckles.

'Thank you, Florence,'

'It's alright Aaron, I know,' her hand links with mine and I feel a bit more whole again.

To be continued....